HEXES AND BONES

MAGIC AND MAYHEM
BOOK TWO

ALESHA ESCOBAR

Edited by
SAM GOODNO

CREATIVE
ALCHEMY

To Tanya Sotelo, my amazing patron.
Samantha Goodno (my bookish partner-in-crime), Priscilla Garcia,
Lana Turner, Athena, Ira Myriam, and all my amazing supporters and
readers.

CONTENTS

Chapter 1	1
Chapter 2	9
Chapter 3	18
Chapter 4	24
Chapter 5	30
Chapter 6	39
Chapter 7	46
Chapter 8	54
Chapter 9	61
Chapter 10	67
Chapter 11	76
Chapter 12	83
Chapter 13	92
Chapter 14	98
Chapter 15	104
Chapter 16	112
Chapter 17	117
Chapter 18	124
Chapter 19	133
Chapter 20	142
Chapter 21	150
Chapter 22	160
Chapter 23	168
Chapter 24	181
Chapter 25	186
Chapter 26	193
Chapter 27	198
Chapter 28	204
Chapter 29	211
Dear Reader	219
About Alesha Escobar	221
Also by Alesha Escobar	223

1

I narrow my eyes against the glare of the midday sun as I step out of my silver Corolla and shut the door. My ears perk up at the sound of footsteps approaching, crunching the gravel with a confident stride. But the additional patter of little hellish feet makes the hairs on the back of my neck raise, and I ball my fists. The familiar warmth of elemental fire fills my palms as I poise myself to incinerate whoever is foolish enough to sneak up on me with a couple of hellhounds in tow.

"These two are well-trained and won't show themselves unless I tell them to, Jack," the gruff voice of Samuel Mayhew assures me.

And when the head of a secret government organization pinky swears, they've *got* to be telling the truth, right?

I slowly turn and face the six-foot tall, bronze-skinned man who's standing ten feet across from me and wearing technomancer shades. His brown eyes meet mine through the lightly-tinted lenses. To the passerby, he's an elderly guy in a suit with expensive taste in eyewear. To me, he's a human playing around with forces that will come back to bite him in the ass—in this case, probably literally.

One of the invisible hellhounds snaps at me. The scent of

rotten flesh rolls off its tongue, and I gag. They say looking into the eyes of these creatures three times allows them to collect your soul. I'm not even gonna look once. I scan the parking lot to make sure we're alone, just in case I need to call forth fire and barbeque the infernal beasts.

"Listen," Samuel slips his hands into his pockets and, like any trained agent from the Department of Metaphysical Affairs, keeps his gaze on my fiery fists. "I've sent three men on separate occasions and tried to do this the polite way. You know why I'm here. I want to see him."

I roll my eyes and sigh, pretending not to be fazed by the menacing growl of the second hellhound. Although the creature is still invisible, I sense its hunger—for my spirit, my very essence. "Lucas doesn't belong to you or DMA," I tell Samuel. "If he doesn't want to go back, then it's not my fault."

Besides, if anyone has claim to the automaton, it's the master wizard Valerio Magnus—and he tasked me with keeping Lucas safe and out of DMA's hands. Talk about conflict of interests.

Samuel strokes his gray beard and takes a step forward. "Lucas doesn't *want* anything. He's a machine, a very well made one, but he sure as hell isn't a man. Don't let his ability to hold a conversation fool you. The robot belongs with us."

Well, I'll be damned. I'm actually offended on Lucas's behalf.

"I'm really getting tired of normal people prying to wizards' business," I gesture toward the technomancer shades, "stealing our artifacts, and acting like you're entitled to it all. You can go screw yourself."

Samuel's brown eyes catches me in a dark gaze. "Wrong answer."

Aw, hell. The black fur and blood-red eyes of the two hounds pop into view. I snap my eyes shut and stretch out my hands, palms forward, unleashing a burst of fire. The hounds snarl and bark, sending an unholy wind smashing into my stomach and blasting me backward into another parked car. I raise myself to my knees and keep my eyes closed, hands still

blazing with fire, ready for one or both hounds to launch at me
—but they don't.

Samuel sighs. "Danny Seyko, Brea Johnson...either of those
names mean anything to you?"

I quickly flex my fire-filled hands to my right when I feel a
shift in the air. One of the hounds yelps in response to the heat
and backs away.

"Uh, should I be familiar with those names?" Sweat trickles
down my face and my arms ache, but I know as soon as I let my
guard down, I'm dog food. Or worse, they steal my soul and
drag me to Hell.

"They were just normal kids, Jack, with no clue about what
really lurks in dark corners. I had to explain to their parents how
they were never coming home, and I lied to them about why.
Imagine if I had to tell them how Danny and Brea were killed by
a rogue wizard for being in the wrong place at the wrong time. A
'botched robbery' doesn't do them justice."

A sharp pang of air hits me in the gut and I double over.
Damn these hellhounds.

"Look, I'm sorry. I'm not that kind of wizard, and if I was
there, I would've helped them, okay?"

Samuel lets out a whistle, and the creatures back away and
fall silent. "You can open your eyes, Jack. I just wanted to make a
point."

I comply, slowly fluttering my eyelids open. "And your
point is?"

The older man frowns. "That there are bad wizards out there,
and it's humans like me and the DMA who are out there risking
our lives protecting people and cleaning up *your* messes. Lucas,
unfortunately, is a part of that. The agency confiscated him from
a dangerous wizard, so I would like him back. Now."

I catch the faint laughter of a young woman from somewhere
behind me, and I extinguish the fire in my hands. My gaze meets
Samuel's and we both pause, silently consenting to a temporary
truce. If there's one thing we can agree on, it's that an all-out

battle with human witnesses is a no-no. Within seconds, a gaggle of four girls with backpacks pass through the parking lot. Not uncommon, since some of the kids from the nearby high school like to take this route as a shortcut.

One of the girls, a brunette with glasses, eyes me with concern. "Hey, are you okay, sir?"

Samuel smoothly steps in closer to me, closing the gap between us. "Oh, I think this fella has had a little too much to drink." He pulls out his government badge and flashes it. "I'll take care of this, ladies."

The brunette nods, though she still has a worried expression. Her three friends whisper to her and pull her along, and they rush through the parking lot and down the adjoining alley.

I groan and stand, brushing off the dirt and loose gravel from my pants. "Where are your little demon spawn?"

Samuel smirks. "At my side. So, do I have your attention now?"

"Yeah, you could say that." How did this man even get a hold of hellhounds? He probably used those technomancer shades to find them.

He nods toward the brick building across from us. "Let's take this inside the shop, shall we?"

I shrug and head toward my place of employment, Willy's Whimsies, just across the alley. "You know the place is warded. Your dogs can't go in," I say over my shoulder, shuddering at the hounds' invisible eyes watching me.

Samuel follows me out of the parking lot and across the alley, finally slipping the technomancer shades into his suit pocket. "That's fine with me."

I shove my hand into my right pocket and pull out my keys, using the spare Willy gave me to unlock the back door. I let out a low breath as I hold the door open for him. "Come on in, if you dare."

He arches a gray eyebrow at me. "Really, I just want to talk."

I frown. "You have a weird way of showing it."

We head through the storage room and Samuel slows his steps as he scopes out Willy's collection of enchanted artifacts, ancient tomes, statues, and colorful gems. I reach out with my magical senses, feeling for the whereabouts of his hellhounds. The two little soul suckers have already circled around the store and are standing out front, awaiting their human master.

Samuel halts his steps and traces his finger along the carving in an African tribal blackwood mask. "I've got to hand it to Ms. Carter, she has quite an impressive stockpile."

I snort in response. "It's all legal and registered with the Cloaked Council, so don't even think about swiping our stash."

We step into the hallway and pass Willy's office. The hardwood floor creaks beneath our feet as we enter the shop, where New Age books and trinkets sit on shelves for gullible humans who think they're buying real magic. The stuff in the back we only sell to other wizards—and with good reason.

"Wilhelmina," Samuel says with a gracious smile as he approaches the sales counter. "How are you today?"

Willy's white, shoulder-length hair bounces as she turns to face him. "I'm doing well, considering your government goons put me in a coma a couple of weeks ago." She slips a cigarette into her mouth and lights it with a garish leopard print lighter.

Samuel digs into the bowl of assorted candies sitting on the countertop and pulls out a chocolate. "And for that, I'm sorry. And so is Agent Reid. I hope the monetary compensation the agency sent you is of some consolation."

The elderly woman takes a drag on her cigarette, letting the smoke swirl out on the exhale. "Yeah, it's not like I can sue your asses in court."

"I'm curious," Samuel glances around the shop and takes in the view of our dollar store ghost and jack-o'-lantern decorations. "Do you all do anything special during this time? I know Halloween's coming up in a few days."

My eyes narrow at him with suspicion. "Look, clearly Lucas isn't here at the shop, and if he were, I wouldn't let you take him from us. So, why are you loitering and being all chatty with us?"

He smirks and pops the chocolate into his mouth, relishing the sweet treat. "My wife made me quit sugar a few months back. She says it's more addictive than cocaine."

Willy puts out her cigarette in a nearby ash tray. She crosses her arms, the gold bangles on her wrist jingling with the movement. "You're stalling, Director Mayhew. What's going on?"

"I told you that I wanted the robot. I said he's dangerous, and I meant it. And you didn't listen." He pulls out a sleek, black hand-held radio. "So, I asked a team to raid your apartment, Jack, and bring Lucas back to the DMA office."

Samuel presses a button on the radio with his thumb and there's a sharp chirp.

Willy glares at him. "What do you think you're doing?"

The DMA director smirks. "Agent Bardwell," he says into the radio, "are your men in position?"

After a few seconds, Bardwell's voice responds. "Yes, sir. We're at his front door now, awaiting your orders."

Willy's seething, but I keep my cool—those agents have no clue what they're walking into.

"Do it," Samuel commands.

A crash echoes through the radio, probably Bardwell and his team knocking down my front door. A few different confused voices travel through the radio and then they turn into howls and shouts. Thunder, the crackle of electricity mixed with yelling, and a *boom* fill our ears. I smirk at Samuel just as his smug grin fades.

He hits the button again. "Bardwell! What's going on? Are you all right?"

Some of the men shouting and cursing, followed by a lion's roar, have me chuckling with satisfaction.

"Bardwell!" Samuel calls out again.

"Sir..." the agent responds, nearly out of breath. From the

sound of it, the guy is retreating and running down the hallway, away from my apartment door. "Director, our ward breakers didn't work. We can't get in, so we're falling back."

Samuel grits his teeth. "Any sign of the automaton?"

"No, sir," Bardwell answers.

"Okay, get the hell out of there. I'll see you at headquarters."

Samuel clicks off the radio and slips it back into his pocket. He flinches when he notices a sturdy bronze bowl hovering right above his head. He turns to Willy, knowing it's her telekinetic power at work.

"Stay away from Lucas," she says, "and stay away from my shop."

The bronze bowl quivers perilously in the air. It could easily smash his head.

"Uh, Willy," I say in a low voice. "You may want to rethink whacking him over the head like that."

Her cold gaze lands on Samuel. "Why shouldn't I? All he and the DMA have done is hurt us and our friends."

Samuel slowly holds his hands out, palms forward, to show he's not up to any tricks. "I'm sorry, Ms. Carter. I'm just doing my job—which, by the way, is known by the agency. They're expecting me to check in with the office in twenty minutes."

"Besides," I add, "he's got a couple of hellhounds outside. The moment we knock him out, they'll go crazy, maybe even break loose from whatever bond they have with him. It's not worth it, Willy."

Samuel, the smooth and calculating man that he is, already knows the outcome to this standoff. He straightens his posture and slips his hands in his pockets as if he's about to take a casual stroll. He's undoubtedly got a hand or two on a hidden weapon. That's what I would do if I were agitating wizards on their turf. Willy sticks her cigarette in her mouth and begrudgingly summons the bronze bowl, catching it in her hands and setting it on the countertop next to the cash register.

"Get out." Her voice is almost guttural and drips with disdain.

Samuel heads toward the front door. His invisible hounds whimper and scratch at the storefront window. The gray-haired man opens the door then glances over his shoulder. "I want that automaton by the end of the week, Jack. Or next time, I'll bring something far worse than hellhounds."

I reach for the cordless landline phone by the register. "And I'll call the Cloaked Council and let them know that you're breaking the truce. Do you really want the fury of the most powerful wizards raining down on you? On the people you say you're trying to protect?"

I brace myself for his anger, or at least a smart-ass remark. Instead, he lets out a low laugh and shakes his head. "I may have underestimated you."

"I would recommend that you *don't*. Goodbye, Samuel."

As soon as he exits the shop, Willy lets out an angry sigh before taking another drag and exhaling. "I can't believe DMA has the nerve...after everything..."

"I know, I know. I'll take care of it, Willy."

Exactly how? I'm not sure. Lucas can't evade the Department of Metaphysical Affairs forever. But one thing I do know, is that I'll step up to protect my friends, both human and non-human, from any threat.

2

"What if Samuel Mayhew just goes missing?" Willy asks with a devious, red-lipped grin. She hands me a hot cup of coffee from the pot that had been brewing in her office, and I gladly accept.

"Nah," I say, taking a sip of the bitter drink. "No one's going to believe the head of L.A.'s DMA office just mysteriously disappeared without pointing a finger at us. Besides, kidnapping's kind of illegal, right?"

She shrugs. "DMA has kidnapped *quite* a few wizards, let me tell you."

I believe her. The Department of Metaphysical Affairs has disappeared some unruly wizards who crossed their path and who made too much noise. The deal they forged with the Cloaked Council is that we keep our magic under wraps and not harm regular humans, and they leave us alone and even provide cover when magic goes awry.

In return, they get to learn about us, a dying breed of humans who make up a tiny population of the world yet could put up a formidable fight if we needed to. We usually police our own, through the Enforcers who work for the Cloaked Council, but as much as the DMA wants us to stay out of each other's business, they *love* getting into ours.

I shift in my stool at the countertop and face her. "Willy, when I was invited to the DMA office, they had this storage room called Pandora's Box."

Her eyebrows shoot up, then her expression settles as if something had been confirmed for her. "It's where they keep a lot of enchanted items, weapons, and artifacts, isn't it?"

I nod. "I think they only use the items on an as-needed basis, and the other stuff they probably use in experiments. Samuel had a pair of technomancer shades, and that's how he was able to find those hellhounds."

"Hmph," she says, twirling her cigarette and sitting up straight. "Combining magic and tech like that sounds like something Kenneth Cherish would do."

I sip more of my coffee. "Exactly. I don't believe a guy like Kenneth would just fall off the face of the earth."

Kenneth is the Theoretical Magic wizard who created Lucas, my automaton friend. Too bad Dr. Cherish hasn't been seen since 1988. Some say he's dead, others swear they saw him in London, Paris, or in Las Vegas, but I think DMA's got him stashed somewhere. Now all I have to do is find out where that is.

"And did they say anything about their wizard prison?" Willy asks, toying with her cigarette. "If they take enchanted items and throw them in a room, where do they toss wizards?"

I shrug. "Not sure, but that's what I'm going to find out."

Master Wizard Valerio Magnus made me an offer I just couldn't refuse—find Kenneth or get torn to shreds.

Willy gives me a pointed look. "Maybe you can ask your little girlfriend."

I chuckle, but inside I get a little squeamish. "Agent Reid isn't my girlfriend. We're friends. Barely."

Willy rolls her eyes. She's still pissed at Alanna for shooting her. At the time, Alanna mistakenly thought Willy was a dark wizard about to unleash the Apocalypse. Still, it's not a bad idea to poke around and see if she knows anything about DMA's secret prison, or Kenneth Cherish's whereabouts.

"Once I find Kenneth and hand him over to the Cloaked Council, Master Valerio will get off my back," I tell Willy. "Bonus, Lucas will be happy to see him again, plus everyone will know about how I found a living legend."

Not that I care what other wizards think of me. Still, it would be nice not to be treated like crap, especially since we're supposed to be sticking together.

"Just be careful, son." She slowly exhales a white swirl of smoke. "Headmaster Valerio may be on the Council, but at the end of the day he serves himself. That means he'll throw you under the bus if it benefits him."

I nod in agreement. Trust is hard to come by, and while I'll complete the task assigned to me by the master wizard, it doesn't mean I'll do it without question or without covering my ass.

The front door to the shop opens, and my tall, blond-haired automaton friend steps in. "Hey Lucas, you just missed Director Mayhew. I'm glad my landlord doesn't pursue me in the same way."

The automaton grins. "Thank you for helping me, Jack. I know sooner or later I'll have to face him."

He stands there holding the door open, presumably for another person approaching, and in steps Zara Wilson with her baby. My stomach tightens and I shoot her a sour look.

"What the hell are *you* doing here?" I ask, wondering why my wards didn't go off. It dawns on me that Lucas invited her in. I'll have to rethink allotting him certain privileges.

Zara brushes a wisp of dark hair out of her pale face and balances her squirmy baby on her hip. The little guy has dark curly hair and looks less than a year old. Kinda cute, but too bad he has a traitorous mother. A couple of weeks ago, Zara had agreed to lead me and Lucas to our friend Sal. She did, but not before entrapping us in a powerful binding circle and leaving us vulnerable to a dark wizard.

Lucas approaches the countertop, walking in step with Zara,

who's wearing a rather demure expression. "Jack," he says, "I understand your suspicion and fear—"

"I'm not afraid of her," I scoff, waving a dismissive hand at the petite young woman.

Zara clears her throat. "Listen, I'm sorry about leaving you in that chamber, okay? If I didn't get out of there when I did, Damon would've killed me and Charlie."

Willy hastily puts out her cigarette and coughs, waving away the dissipating smoke. "Oh...is that his name? What a little sweetheart!" She hops off her stool next to mine and goes around the countertop, holding her outstretched arms to the gurgling baby.

"I'm Zara," she says to Willy, gently handing her the child.

Willy cradles Charlie and chuckles with delight. I haven't seen her this happy since the delivery guy dropped his signature pad and bent over to retrieve it.

"Nice to meet you, Zara. I'm Wilhelmina Carter, owner of this establishment. Is there anything I can help you with?"

Lucas gestures to the baby. "Actually, there is."

Zara clasps her hands together. "Lucas told me you used to be a midwife for wizards back in the day."

Willy's gleeful expression falters and her breath stalls. "Oh... well, I'm kind of retired."

"You see," Zara reaches into her diaper bag and pulls out a slip of paper, "I've been writing down these symptoms and odd occurrences for the past few nights to keep track of them. I thought maybe it would help you get an idea of what's ailing him."

Willy takes the slip of paper and absentmindedly plants a kiss on top of Charlie's head. She's such a sucker for kids.

"Hmm...inconsolable during the day and seems to observe and hear things that aren't there, quiet at night, and...look at that —objects moved in and out of his crib by telekinesis."

Zara's eyes grow watery. "Last night he barely slept. One minute he'd run a fever and then the next minute turn freezing cold. I'm scared I'll lay him down one night and he won't wake up, and it's not like I can bring him to a normal pediatrician."

Willy hands her back the slip of paper and cradles Charlie, who coos and smiles at the older woman. "You're a blood wizard, are you not?"

Zara slowly nods. "But I don't think Charlie—"

"Your baby's psychic. Like me." Willy gives the child a sympathetic grin. "I can imprint him with a couple of sigils to protect his mind and dampen all the stimulation. Poor little guy must be experiencing sensory overload."

"Thank you!" Zara wipes a tear away with the back of her hand.

"I have a few potions in the back office that will help stabilize his temperature. It's part of the growing pains of a psychic. Come on." Willy hands her the baby and leads her to the hallway and down to her office.

As soon as they're out of earshot, I rest my arms on the countertop and lean forward. "So, Tin Man, you're hanging out with girls who like to trap us in fire circles in the middle of torture chambers?"

"Jack, she tracked me down and asked for my help. I had to—"

"Yeah, yeah," I say, gesturing for him to cease his explanation. "You were listening to this again, huh?" I lightly jab my index finger into the center of his metal chest. On the surface, Lucas looks like a walking Adonis, indistinguishable in appearance from human beings. Yet, beneath the surface, the automaton is metal and magic—and, he possesses a beating human heart.

The automaton's face breaks into a grin. "After spending time with you and Salvador, I've realized the importance of helping others and giving someone a second chance."

"Pfft! Not Zara Wilson. Now I've got to recalibrate my wards."

"Speaking of trust," he says with a hint of regret, "do you think Alanna would speak to me if I were to reach out to her?"

I shrug. "She's still convinced you know what happened that night her father died, but you don't want to fess up."

He nods in understanding. "I would if I could. I was there the night Martin killed himself—"

"*Allegedly...*"

"Allegedly. However, my programming's been altered in some way. I can't put all the pieces together."

"Then, get your noggin fixed." I finish off my coffee. Damn, would it kill Willy to add some cream and sugar?

Lucas raises a blond eyebrow. "In order to do that, I'll either have to find the man who created me or turn myself in to DMA and go to their laboratory."

Two very difficult options for different reasons.

"Listen, we'll figure it out, Tin Man. And Alanna's been around you since she was a kid, she still cares about you. She'll forgive you."

He leans his forearms on the countertop and looks me in the eye. "Human beings have pondered the question since the beginning of time, and I suppose it's my turn."

"And that is?" I prompt him.

"What is my purpose? Why did Kenneth make me?"

"He made a lot of things. But I wouldn't be surprised if you were his crowning achievement."

"What makes you say that?"

"Well, for one, that heart of yours. Both literally and figuratively. You've got heart, Tin Man, more than I've seen in some humans. You actually care about people. Plus...that thing inside you. Did Kenneth make an artificial heart and encage it in that gold wiring? Or, did the guy go serial killer and carve it out of someone and stick it inside you? No offense, buddy."

He sighs. "None taken."

I facetiously gasp. "What if...it's Kenneth's heart? What if he's inside you, or you're *him*?"

The automaton shakes his head and smirks. "I can always count on you for a brainstorming session. Either this heart has to belong to a murder victim or to my creator who's supposedly hiding inside me. Are you sure you're not drunk?"

"Well okay, Sherlock, I'm just floating a few ideas here. Maybe we can open you up and take another look. I mean, if it's cool and all."

Before Lucas can respond, there's a tap at the glass door of the shop's entrance. Our attention is drawn to the door, but neither of us see anything. There's another *Tap! Tap! Tap!* and Lucas chuckles. I squint my eyes, wondering what the automaton sees that I don't.

"What is it?" I ask. "I swear, if Samuel left those damn hellhounds right outside the shop, I'm gonna put DMA on blast and expose them to the world."

"Not at all." Lucas approaches the door and opens it.

"Lucas…"

A sphere of amethyst light zips into the shop and flits back and forth between one of the bookshelves and a display rack. As the ball of light rushes toward me, it feels like someone's holding a flame close to my face, and I duck behind the cash register.

"What did you just let in?" I ask, trying to follow the bouncing ball of energy. My skin tingles in response to its pure magic, and though I can tell it's not dark or malignant, I would rather it *not* knock over books and artifacts in this shop.

Lucas holds his hands out in a cupping position, uttering a few words in a language I don't understand. The amethyst sphere of power and light finally calms down and floats as if in water, landing in the automaton's hands.

"Jack," his eyes brighten, "it's a faerie."

"What?"

I jump up and slam my palms on the countertop. I stare at the miniature creature, who now stands still in Lucas's hands: slender feminine body, shimmering silver hair, and a semi-human face. I can make out eyes, nose, and mouth, but it's like

15

there's a filter over her face, making it blurry and even changing its appearance from second-to-second. A little creepy, if you ask me.

"Fascinating," Lucas says in awe.

"They don't usually venture into this realm," I say, ignoring the hiss the little monster gives me for speaking about her in third person. I finally stare her right in her shifting face. "What do you want?"

She crosses her arms and says something to Lucas in an indignant tone.

The automaton listens patiently then acts as interpreter. "She says her name is Olette, and she's a messenger faerie."

"Bullshit," I say. "All they do is roam forests in the wizard realms and make faerie dust."

Olette growls, and her face shifts into a huge mouth with razor-sharp teeth. She then pulls a tiny envelope from her pocket and hands it to Lucas.

"Oh my," he says, apparently pleased with the exchange. "Let's see what this is."

He takes the envelope, and it shudders with a breath of magic before growing to normal size.

"Okay, who sent you?" I ask the faerie.

Lucas opens the envelope. "It looks like you have an invoice for $2,000 from Baltazar Maune for…services rendered."

Baltazar Maune? *Services rendered*?

"Screw that guy, I'm not paying him a dime."

Olette rattles on about something to Lucas.

"Jack, she says her master will not send another invoice and he expects prompt payment."

I glare at the silver-haired creature. "I'm not going to pay the guy for something I never hired him to do!"

Baltazar Maune is a wizard known as "The Fixer." Just as there are fixers and clean-up guys in the human world, Baltazar is the go-to guy in the wizarding world. When the crap hits the fan and you don't want the Enforcers knocking at your door, or

DMA laying hands on you, you call Baltazar and have him wipe memories, scrub scenes clean of all traces of magic, or act as your alibi or PR man. I'll admit, the guy is good, and those with power and money utilize his services—but, that ain't me. I didn't hire him, and I'm not paying him.

"Jack, if you've received a bill from Mr. Maune, it's only fair to—"

"No way," I say, leaning in close to Olette to make my point. "Now get out of my shop. Maybe you can go roll around in a forest or something."

The faerie glares at me and makes another retort.

Lucas laughs. "Well, that's anatomically impossible, Olette."

"*Olette…*" I say her name with intent—with command. The goosebumps run down my arms in response to the drop in temperature. "*Exis nunc!*" I spew in Latin.

The faerie whines as she returns to her bright amethyst ball of light and zooms right out of the shop as if being plucked by an invisible hand.

That's True Name magic for you.

Know the Name of someone or something, then you can control it.

Lucas gives me a disappointed look. He hands me the invoice. "What are you going to do about this?"

Technically, I can pay it. I have the money. I've saved up over the years from working here at the shop, plus I have an inheritance stashed away. But, since I *didn't* hire Baltazar, he's not getting a penny.

I grab the invoice, crumple it, and toss it into the waste basket. "There. Easy-peasy. It's obviously some mistake. Besides, we've got more important things to do."

His gaze turns toward Zara and baby Charlie as they return with Willy in tow. "Indeed, my friend. More important things."

3

Baby Charlie's cheeks are rosy, and all is well with the world, I suppose. He seems calmer and happier, as does his mother. Zara's got a huge grin plastered across her face as she approaches, and she looks me dead in the eye.

"Thanks, Jack," she says with an amount of gratitude that makes me a little less antagonistic. "And really, I am sorry about what happened. I don't expect you to forgive me, but at least understand what I did was for my baby."

I shrug. "Eh, I get it. It's no big deal."

Willy chuckles. "Well, that's the closest you'll get to him accepting your apology, Zara. I'm glad I could help little Charlie."

"Speaking of…" Zara slides a hand into her jean pocket and offers a few folded bills to Willy. "This is for helping us."

Willy waves a hand through the air. "Your money is no good here." She adds with a smile, "Just take care of that little sweetie, and let me know if you need anything else."

I give Willy a side eye—*retired* from midwifery, huh?

Lucas gives me a critical look as if he's reading my thoughts. Hell, he probably can. Sometimes Tin Man is capable of some eerie stuff.

The automaton gestures toward the doorway. "Zara, allow me to escort you home."

My interest is piqued. "So, where are you staying, exactly?" I ask the petite young woman. "Not like I care, I just want to know you're nowhere near my neighborhood."

Zara rolls her eyes at my apparent disregard for our recent truce. "None of your business."

Lucas shakes his head. "I'll see you tonight at The Ruined Oak, Jack. And maybe then we can discuss how to deal with… you-know-what."

Yeah, the You-Know-What that has hellhounds and a shitload of weapons at their disposal, all aimed at me. Sure, we can strategize how to deal with them over tea and cookies.

"Bye, Lucas. Cute kid, Zara."

She sighs. "Bye, Jack, and thank you, Willy."

Willy grins and waves as they exit the shop, her expression finally falling when they're out of sight. I can tell something's bothering her.

"The baby's going to be okay, right? He won't have any more psychic overload?"

She heads over to one of the display racks holding crystal earrings and necklaces and arranges them by color. "Yeah, Charlie will be fine. My sigils should hold for him until he's school age."

"So, why the face then?" I head over to the far-right corner and grab a broom and start sweeping. It was a habit instilled in me when I was a boy to start cleaning right along with Willy whenever she tidied up the shop.

"The woman, Zara—she's a blood wizard."

"Yep. Remember I told you about her? She was at Damon Blackbird's house."

Willy rubs her chin, deep in thought. "I sensed a connection between her and Damon. I think she's—excuse the pun—a blood relative of his."

I sweep up the accumulated dust and debris, using the

dustpan to deposit it all into the waste basket. "I figured she had to have some kind of connection to Damon."

When Lucas and I met Zara, she had been little more than a maid in Damon's fancy manor, and out of all the wizards on the island of Scarletwood, she and the dark wizard were the only blood wizards. It makes sense that they're related. Blood wizards also have a reputation for being both powerful and full of themselves, and like True Name wizards, there aren't too many of them running around.

Willy nods as she heads over to the New Age books and begins dusting them with a microfiber cloth she pulled from gods know where. "She seemed reluctant to talk about it, and she clammed up when I asked about Charlie's father, a man named Ben Corani."

I shrug. "Maybe she's ashamed to be related to Damon. He didn't exactly treat her well, either."

She raises an eyebrow. "So, you have a relative who's carted off to prison and leaves you in charge of his mansion, his money, accounts... and you decide to go live somewhere in the human world? And not only that, she went and found Lucas and has got him wrapped around her finger."

"You've got a point there," I say, grabbing a rag and a bottle of cleaning spray and wiping down the countertop. "It's odd how everyone's zeroing in on Lucas—The Cloaked Council, DMA, and Baby Mama?"

Willy snorts. "Just keep an eye out for him. He may think he has people figured out, but in some ways he's as naïve as a child..."

Her lips continue moving and I vaguely hear her voice, but it's muffled, as if I'm underwater. A high-pitched ringing invades my ears, piercing them like a knife. I hiss and cover my ears in reaction to the pain, and Willy rushes over to me.

"Are you okay? What's wrong?" She reaches for my head, but I gently hold my hand out to keep her at bay.

My head throbs with a migraine, and the high-pitched

ringing still skewers my brain. "No, Willy, it could be dangerous. Don't try and read me."

Her eyes fill with worry as she pauses to listen, to try and pick up the sound with her own ears, but she hears nothing. She shakes her head. "What does it sound like, Jack?"

My stomach flips and I force down the bile creeping up my throat. I pour my strength into tamping down the volume of the unearthly sound. My ears are still ringing, but at least I don't feel like my head is about to explode.

"It's like a banshee screeching in my head," I tell her. "Hurts like hell to hear it."

Willy lets out a low breath and scans the shop, reaching out with her psychic senses. "I feel a vibrational pull, but I still can't hear anything." She turns and points toward the hallway. "It's coming from the storage room."

"Yeah, I think it's coming from storage," I say through clenched teeth.

She frowns. "Wait here, I'll go—"

"You're not going in there by yourself," I say, waving a hand through the air. If there's a cursed object or hidden spell, I'm not letting my adoptive mother face it alone.

Willy's eyes take on a golden hue, illuminated by her magical energy. "Then follow me. Let me know if the sound hits you again."

I nod my assent and follow her into the hallway, walking slowly, trying not to puke from the headache. When we make it into the storage room, our first instinct is to reach out with our senses, check for anything tainted with dark magic. If I had to explain it to a normal human, I would say it's like inhaling various scents and then carefully dissecting that one smell that doesn't belong—the one that screams *poison…danger.*

Willy glares at me, and then her gaze travels toward the stack of boxes on our left. She lets out a low breath and gives herself a facepalm. "Of course, that's what it is."

21

I glance toward the African tribal blackwood mask that had earlier caught Samuel Mayhew's attention. "That? Really?"

Willy approaches the mask and picks it up. "It's the blackwood. Very expensive, might I add. It enables its wearer to contact the spirit realm, and it blocks energies. Do you hear anything now?"

"A little, but it's not a strong as it was a few minutes ago. My head is still throbbing, though."

Willy walks the mask over to a section of brick wall, which is actually an illusion. She traces a luminous key symbol into a spot on the wall and a perfect square lights up. The wall within the square becomes transparent, and behind it is a hidden safe.

"You haven't seen any ghosts? Come across any spirits?" She punches in a code on the safe's electronic keypad and opens it.

"Nope," I admit.

After sliding the mask inside, she shuts it closed, and the false brick wall conceals the safe again. "Gee," she says, turning toward me, "do you think it might have to do with the fact that you swallowed a slip of paper with two of God's Names written on them? Huh?"

I gulp and recall how the demigod Calais had told me there would be consequences to doing that, but at the time, it was the only way I could keep two of the Names of God away from a madman.

"Willy, you know I had no choice…"

She shakes her head. "I know, I know. How's your head?"

"Better, actually." It seems her warded safe added a layer of protection. The high-pitched ringing from the blackwood mask is now a mere vibrational pull in the back of my mind. I hope it stays that way.

Willy crosses her arms. "Are you sure you're okay?"

I slowly nod. "If something weird happens again, I'll let you know."

She stares at me in the same way she does when she's trying to determine if I'm being truthful. I learned a long time ago it's next to useless to lie to a psychic. After a few moments, she looks satisfied and waves me toward the back exit that leads to the parking lot.

"Go home and get some rest. I can handle the shop."

"I'm okay," I tell her. "The ringing's gone."

A chuckle escapes her lips. "You're so damn stubborn. Always have been, since I brought you into my home. Go and rest."

I sigh and finally relent. "Fine. I'll see you later."

"And Jack…"

"Yeah?"

"Do you want anything special?"

"Just some rest." My lips curve into a slight smile. I knew she would ask. Halloween, my birthday, is just a couple of days away.

4

I pull into my underground parking space at the historic Blackstone building in downtown L.A. Before getting out, I guzzle a bottle of water and rub my temples, thankful that the dim lighting in the garage doesn't aggravate my headache. As I head to the elevator, I go over the reasons why a spirit mask would cast a signal that only I could hear. A very painful signal, as if it's trying to tell me something. Perhaps I am suffering a side effect of eating two Names of God, and I'm just spiritually sensitive at the moment. Maybe it will wear off soon, especially since Willy placed the blackwood mask in her warded safe.

My fist pounds the janky elevator button and the doors slide open. I step inside and press the button for the eighth floor. There's a pull in my belly as the elevator car rises upward, and my thoughts move toward the demigod Calais, who only weeks ago charged me with the task of finding and protecting the stolen Names of God—and who warned me I would have trouble coming my way.

"Uh..." I say in a low voice, hoping I don't sound like an idiot, "Calais...can you hear me?"

The elevator jolts to a stop, and I get no response.

"I don't know if you're still around and looking out for me, but if you are…" The doors open, and I decide to mentally wrap-up my supplication: *Help me out with this. I don't want it, whatever it is. I was just trying to keep Marco from destroying the world.*

As soon as I exit the elevator, the kid from apartment 815 rushes down the hall toward me with a huge grin on his face. His dark brown eyes light up with recognition, and I can't tell if it's a good thing or not.

"Hey!" he says, reaching up for a high-five. "You're Jack."

I smack my palm against his, still a little confused as to why he's happy to see me. "You know me?"

He gestures with his index finger, indicating that he needs me to get down to his level so he can talk to me face-to-face. I crouch down just low enough for him to whisper something in my ear.

"It's me, Desmond. From 815. Remember?"

I frown and stand tall again. "Of course I do. You left a Hot Wheel near my door the other day and I almost broke my neck. I've been meaning to talk to your parents about that."

Desmond gives me an apologetic look. "But do you remember me from that day? With the monster?"

My heart leaps into my throat and I drop to one knee, my nose almost touching his. "And how exactly do you remember that when everyone else doesn't?"

He shrugs. "I guess whoever those guys were, they talked to my mom and dad, but they didn't ask me anything. Maybe they didn't think I saw anything, so they didn't take my memory away. Were they secret agents?"

Hmm, looks like the DMA was so busy chasing down the three adults who witnessed a monster unleashed in this building, that they overlooked Desmond, who got an eyeful before slipping back into his home.

"You know," I say in a low voice, "I can wipe memories too."

Desmond's eyes widen. "Really? Cool."

I can't help but chuckle. I thought he would actually get scared and promise to keep quiet.

"Listen, kid…how old are you?"

"Ten."

"That's nice. Listen…it's best if you don't go around talking about what happened, especially to strangers. Got it?"

"Don't worry, Mr. Jack, I haven't said anything."

"Good."

"And I'll keep your secret too."

I rise to my feet, keeping eye contact with him, determining the right moment to wipe his memory of that day. "And what secret is that?"

He smiles up at me. "You have superpowers, and you helped save people."

Damn. He actually looks proud of me, like I really am some sort of hero.

Just great.

Guilt overcomes me, and I release the memory wipe spell I had been preparing in my mind. I never liked having to do something like this anyway; tampering with people's minds has consequences, and this was an innocent kid.

I incline my head, indicating the gravity of what I'm about to tell him. "And you know, Desmond, superheroes need friends who can keep their secrets because bad guys are always after them, right?"

He enthusiastically nods. "I already know that. And if you need any help, just let me know."

"Will do, buddy." I tousle his dark hair and head down the hallway to my apartment, 809.

As I unlock the door, my magical senses kick into gear and a monotonous hum thrums in my ears. The steady, rhythmic vibration of my wards lets me know that my protective spells are still strong and haven't been tampered with.

I step inside and head straight for the kitchen and pull out a tupperware of leftovers from the fridge. It was graciously given to me by Carmen, my friend Salvador's mom. As the enchilada casserole is heating up in the microwave, I grab a beer and take a swig. My landline phone's voicemail button is annoyingly blinking, so I reach over and grab the phone to check my messages.

"It's Mayhew," the DMA director's voice coolly states in the first voicemail. *"Listen, I just want to make sure Lucas is all right, and…maybe you can escort him down to the lab. It doesn't have to get messy, Jack. Call me back."*

Ugh. Something tells me that Samuel Mayhew is willing to get as messy as he needs to, in order to secure Lucas. The microwave beeps and I pull my steaming casserole out and grab a fork, digging in and munching on the savory combo of ground meat, cheeses, and spicy sauce. Then, I move on to the next voicemail.

"This is Master Valerio," the arrogant voice announces. *"I've got something here at the Akashic Academy that I believe will be of use to you in your pursuit of Kenneth Cherish—who, by the way, was possibly sighted in Arizona a few days ago. I have an associate who's trying to confirm, so I'll keep you posted. Oh, and I'm certain I don't need to remind you that you are still responsible for keeping Lucas out of DMA custody, so if you let those human agents take him, you might as well hang yourself. Have a good day."*

Screw that guy. Okay, final voicemail, then I can enjoy my meal in peace.

"Mr. Crowley," an Irish male voice says, *"this is Baltazar Maune. I believe Olette delivered my invoice to you. As earlier indicated, I expect payment by October 31st…"*

Okay, time to end this. I finish listening to his demand for money and memorize his phone number. I dial his number and wait through a few rings before Baltazar picks up.

"Jack! Good to hear from you. I can send Olette to pick up the cash, or you can pay by check or card."

I swallow another bite of casserole. "Listen, Baltazar, I didn't hire you for anything, and if I did, it certainly wouldn't be worth $2,000."

A long pause falls between us, and for a second, I wonder if the guy hung up on me.

"This morning," Baltazar begins in his baritone voice, "didn't a group of DMA agents come knocking at your door?"

"Yeah, and my wards sent them packing." I down some more of my beer.

"Well, genius, your wards not only sent those agents running, they also attracted the attention of two people—the old man from apartment 804 and his granddaughter. Your wards are messy, not as refined and subtle as they should be."

"And?" I respond, bristling at his critique. Okay, granted they're not all perfect and fine-tuned, but those wards aren't meant for just humans—they also protect against other wizards and dangerous magical beings, so they *have* to pack a punch and be messy.

"And, Jack, you're lucky I was nearby, sensed your drunken version of a magical ward, and was able to wipe those humans' memories. I even deleted the cell phone footage the granddaughter took, for goodness sake."

"Oh. Well, thanks, I guess. But I'm still not paying you two grand. I didn't ask you to do that."

Three heavy knocks sound at my door, and I pause.

"Jack," Baltazar's tone carries an edge of impatience.

Who does this guy think he is?

I sigh and head over to the door. "If that's you at my front door, or your stupid faerie, you'll regret it."

I end the phone call and toss the phone onto a nearby stand. With one hand, I call forth a burst of wind, holding it steady in my palm while opening the front door with my free hand.

No one is there.

I peek left and right, the unruly wind straining against my will, threatening to escape my hand and blast in all directions. I focus on containing it in a ball, then I reach out with my senses to ensure no one is cloaked near my door or in the hallway. After a few moments, my body shivers, and I command the elemental wind in my hand to dissipate.

"Calais?" I whisper, but only silence greets me.

Hmph. Just like a demigod. Loves sticking his nose in your business when you don't want him to, never around when you need him.

As soon as I hear someone coming up in the elevator, I step back and shut my door closed. For a second, I consider calling Willy and maybe asking her to do a full-on psychic reading, but then my stomach grumbles and I remember that I have to meet up with Salvador and Lucas at The Ruined Oak. I rush back to my half-eaten casserole and finish it off, my ears still perked and my senses on high alert for whatever mysterious force is lingering in the vicinity.

5

I luck out and find a parking space in the lot, thankful I don't have to park down the street or around the corner. As soon as I step out of my Corolla, my phone buzzes in my pocket, and I'm tempted to just turn it off for the rest of the evening. With a sigh, I pull it out to check who's calling—it's Alanna Reid. DMA Agent Alanna Reid.

As I stroll toward the building entrance, I answer the call. "Hey, Alanna. What's up?"

"Hi Jack," she says in an unusually curt voice. "I was just wondering about Lucas. Is he doing all right? You know he needs maintenance from time to time?"

Hmph, she' been ignoring the automaton for the last week or so, and now all of a sudden she's calling me to find out what he's up to?

"Alanna, despite the fact that I'm pretty sure Samuel asked you to call me, I *do* think you ought to speak to Lucas."

There's a long pause on her end, and she finally responds. "When he's ready to help me, to tell me the truth about my dad, then I'll talk to him. You know how important this is...how it feels to lose your father."

I won't deny it, and I can understand why she's pissed at

Lucas. He's the only one who can unravel the memory spell she's under; he can provide the last piece of the puzzle to figuring out why her father took his life that night when she was just a teenager. Well, assuming that's what even happened.

"Yeah, I know. I get it. But Lucas is sad. He misses you, and whether you believe it or not, I think he's trying to protect you."

"Look, I've known him my entire life, and just because you spent the past few weeks bonding with him—"

"Hey," I interject, halting near the front door of the worn, historical building that has long since lost its charm. "We're not bonding...I'm just watching him for a while. I've got a master wizard damn-near stalking me to make sure that I do."

She lets out an exasperated breath. "Are there any alternatives to breaking the memory seal? There has to be *something*. Please."

I nod in greeting toward a couple of wizards hopping out of a Ferrari and they head past me into the building. "Maybe I can consult some of my books, but I can't promise anything."

"Really?"

The hopeful lilt of her voice kind of stabs at me, because I more than likely won't be able to deliver.

"Yeah, no promises though. And don't try to mess with this on your own—memory magic is dangerous."

"Of course. I'll wait for you."

"You know you're going to eventually have to make up with Tin Man and bring him in on this. He memory-holed you and placed the seal, so he needs to be the one to unravel it. But it's clear someone doesn't want that, because Lucas's programming got tampered with. So, we have to be careful, okay?"

"I understand."

I'm just about to reiterate my demand that she doesn't attempt to obtain any rogue spells, but her end of the line clicks and the call ends. I shrug, placing my phone back into my pocket, hoping that she doesn't try to visit a shady wizard or charlatan claiming to have the power of restoring lost memories.

I turn and spot Lucas heading toward me. The goofball smiles at me and I wave at him, scanning the parking lot and noting that he didn't drive or hitch a ride. So, looks like Zara lives within walking distance of The Ruined Oak.

"Hey, Tin Man, everything okay?"

Lucas nods. "Zara and Charlie are safe at home."

How sweet.

I pat Lucas on the shoulder and head inside with him. "Just be careful, okay? Remember what I said about humans and how they can be bastards."

The magical robot who looks like a 6-foot-plus model arches a brow at me. "Even you, Jack?"

I smirk in response to his question. "*Especially* me."

My sneakers squeak against the marble floor as we approach the reception desk. Everyone knows to stop here and check in with Poppy Grimm, even if it's just to say hello. She's an Enforcer who's been running security here for as long as I can remember.

"Hey, Poppy." I give her my most charming smile.

The dark-haired wizard isn't wearing her usual thick-rimmed glasses, and her hair is pulled back into a bun. Instead of browsing a fashion magazine, she's typing on a laptop. My grin fades when I realize that the cute blonde chick sitting next to Poppy is her female automaton, Betty. And she is nothing like Lucas.

Poppy shuts her laptop. "Good evening, Jack. Heading downstairs?" She motions across the way to the left, where the doorway leading down to The Ruined Oak stands.

I gaze in that direction and give a respectful nod to the other two Enforcers, Darryl and Miki, who stand guard at the door. "Yeah, if you're going on break soon, maybe you can join us?"

I must've asked Poppy out for drinks about three times now, and each time she threatened to send a hexwielder to curse me. This time, though, her shoulders shake with laughter. I'll take that as progress.

"I think I might actually miss you," she says, leaning forward and studying me.

Her automaton, Betty, stares at me with her hazel eyes, which lack the warmth and light that I usually see in Lucas's. "Miss Grimm, Chief Blaise expects you at the Council Hall in twenty minutes."

Poppy nods. "Yes, I should get going."

"Ooh, what does the head of the Cloaked Council want with you, Poppy? And why, exactly, are you going to miss me?"

She rises from her seat and slips her laptop into a sleek, black messenger bag. "I'll have you know, Mr. Crowley, that as of 8:00 p.m. tonight, you're looking at the official new Human-Wizard Liaison of the Cloaked Council."

Lucas breaks into a wide smile. "Congratulations, Miss Grimm. Or, I should say, Councilwoman Grimm."

She winks at him. "Thanks, handsome."

"You deserve it," I tell her in earnest. She's one of the few people I know who actually cares about her job and about doing what's right. When I asked Poppy to help me take down a dark wizard just a couple of weeks ago, she did it without hesitation.

Lucas's gaze goes from Poppy to Betty. "I assume you'll be taking her place here?"

Betty, wearing an expressionless face, gives a curt nod. "Just for a day or so until her actual replacement arrives. However, be assured that I am knowledgeable about human behavior and interaction and will appropriately greet guests. I speak all languages and can scan and monitor everyone who enters the building. I am a logical and fitting choice for face-to-face interaction."

Yeah, sure, and I'm the pope.

"Congrats, Poppy." I nudge Lucas to follow me toward the door to our left.

"Thanks Jack," Poppy says from behind me.

Darryl, one of the two Enforcers guarding the door, nods at me and smirks. "What's up, man? Staying out of trouble?"

His friend, Miki, gives me a dubious look. "When is Crowley ever trouble-free?"

"I swear, guys, just going down for some drinks with my pals and maybe see Jamie Chamberlain."

Miki mutters something in Korean and chuckles before opening the door for me and Lucas. "Have a good evening."

"Thank you," Lucas says. He then leans in toward me once we're out of earshot and heading downstairs. "By the way, Miki just said in Korean that visiting Jamie *is* going to get you into trouble. Shall I go back there and explain to him why you're seventy-five percent more likely to do that on your own?"

I shake my head. "Nah. Let's keep that between us."

We make our way down to the bottom of the staircase and through the next door which opens up to the dungeon area. With its tile floors and black leather furniture, this area reminds me more of a swanky hotel lounge. Archways with transparent glass doors stand to our right, leading to the club proper, where the silhouettes of patrons dining or dancers moving to the beat of music can be seen. To our left, just ahead, is the bar, where my favorite bald man is serving drinks to my pal Salvador Barraza.

"Starting without us?" I ask, feigning offense.

Sal chuckles, scratches his short dark beard, and holds up a martini glass containing a swirling, neon-blue liquid. "Just taste-testing for you, man." He turns to Roy, the bartender. "What's this called again?"

"Scriostóir," the bald man answers with glee as he prepares a rum and Coke for me. "It means 'destroyer' in Gaelic."

Sal, the toughened ex-Marine that he is, simply shrugs and takes a sip.

"Now that we're all here," Lucas says, "let's sit, so that you and Salvador can enjoy dinner."

Sal takes another sip of the scriostóir and motions toward a table across from the bar. "Mmm. I already ordered for us. Roy's got our seats warded."

"And remember that'll cost you an extra sixty." Roy hands me my drink and I follow Sal and Lucas over to the table.

As soon as I pull out my chair, I feel a magical *whoosh* rush through me—a firm, protective ward to keep unwanted ears from overhearing our conversation. A non-wizard might question why we'd do this, but most wizards down here ward their booths, VIP rooms, and tables. Many of us have business with Jamie Chamberlain, and sometimes he's on the Enforcers' naughty list. And the rest down here work for or with Mishka Tarasov; he's the equivalent of a magical mafioso, and he owns the building.

I settle into my seat as Sal pulls out his cell phone and hands it to me. After browsing the names on the screen, I nod, wondering if he will ever fess up to the DMA about keeping a list of Los Angeles occultists to himself. These are humans who play around with magic, not knowing the full consequences of it...or do they? Samuel would love to go after those guys, and maybe then it could give me some breathing room. I hand him his phone and cross my arms, fighting the temptation to scold him like a teacher for messing around with this list. It got his brother killed, and I would hate to see him meet the same fate.

"Sal..." I begin, "you don't need me to tell you—"

"That this is dangerous, I know." He slips the phone back into his jacket pocket. A waitress strolls over and sets down a tasty platter of seafood and some plates. We thank her, and once she's out of range, Sal speaks up. "I'll eventually give a copy to DMA, but not yet. I want to figure out what made this list so important to my brother, and what the people on this list stand to gain. I was thinking maybe you can help me track down some of them."

I munch on my buttery shrimp and swallow, nearly choking. "Or you can just hand that list over to the agency and let them take care of it. We already caught the wizard who killed your brother. Those occultists, they're just roleplaying. They're like the people who walk into Willy's shop, buying crystals and books, thinking they've found an easy answer to their problems. They have no clue what the *real* world of magic is like."

Sal leans back and finishes off his scriostóir. "Maybe you're right, but you know Mayhew and the others will just wipe their memories and steal anything of value. I feel like there's more behind it. Otherwise, dark wizards wouldn't be hanging around them."

Lucas, having neither a need nor desire for food, leans forward and clasps his hands. "It is a point of concern that Damon Blackbird spent time with these humans. What did he reveal about our world to them? Do they know about Grey Haven? The Cloaked Council? It may be worth looking into."

Sal perks up. "See? Lucas has a point."

"Well, I can't go around playing detective. I've got a lot on my plate already."

"You're going after the Dark Coven?" Sal asks, his fork stuck in a piece of grilled salmon.

"Hmm," I say, as if I'm really considering it. I take another bite of buttery shrimp. "I know I'll have to, eventually. But before I get into all that, I actually wanted to talk to you, Lucas."

The automaton's blond eyebrows slowly rise. "Oh? About what?"

"You know damn well about what. Alanna's been bugging me about memory magic, and she's getting desperate. I'm surprised she hasn't tried casting a spell on herself. You hold the key to that night, so, between us, what happened? Why did her father kill himself, and why are you so keen on keeping it buried?"

Sal lets out a low breath and strokes his short beard. "Damn, I thought we were over that."

Lucas shakes his head, his bright eyes betraying a steely resolve that annoys the hell out of me. I swear he's the most disobedient robot ever.

"Jack," he says slowly, "I wish I could explain. Every time I see that ouroboros tattoo on her arm, knowing that my spell locked her memory of that evening…"

"So, just unravel it. Open it up for her, she's a big girl. She can handle it." I clasp my hands together and observe Lucas. A touch of fear flashes in his eyes.

"It's not that I don't want to help, but my programming—"

"I know, it won't let you, because someone screwed with it, but Lucas, I've seen you do amazing things. You can't override it?"

"It's corrupted, Jack. I remember bits and pieces from that night, and I know I'm responsible for altering Alanna's memory, but how and why…I don't know."

"Man," Sal says, placing a hand on Lucas's back in a conciliatory gesture. "Why didn't you tell us?"

Lucas's expression fell. "I'm ashamed. If there is a flaw I possess, this is it."

I roll my eyes. "Yeah, maybe your creator should've sharpened up that metal brain of yours instead of focusing on your chiseled face."

Sal shakes his head. "Don't be an ass, Jack."

"Not being an ass, but Tin Man, you know what this means, right?"

The automaton raises his gaze to meet mine. "Someone else was there that night, Jack. Someone powerful, and dangerous, and who is more than likely responsible for Martin Reid's death."

"Again," Sal interjects, "why didn't you tell us, Lucas? You know we'd help you."

"I know I need to repair my programming and recover that night, but I must be prudent about it. Whoever went through such trouble to conceal everything—they'll destroy you, Alanna…everyone I care about."

The pieces of this puzzle finally start to fall into place. I nod in understanding. "You wanted to find out who it is before letting anyone know. You *want* Salvador to go through that occult list, because it could lead you to the murderer. You'll finally be able to give Alanna the answers she's seeking."

Lucas closes his eyes. Damn, he's good at emotions. "I say nothing, and my friends hate me and think I am keeping secrets. I speak, then we are all dead. I would rather you hate me than for a murderous magic-user to cut you down."

My first thought is to tell Lucas that he can put on his big boy pants and get his programming fixed so we can help Alanna restore her memory. If we can face dark wizards and monsters, we can face whoever broke his metal brain. I *hate* when people, robot or not, tamper with human memories. It's like warping someone's heart and soul. You just don't do it. Besides, Alanna deserves the truth. I'm just about to tell him this when I feel my phone vibrate in my pocket. I pull it out and see that it's a text from none other than Jamie Chamberlain.

Bro, the merchandise is here.

I type back into my phone, *Okay. And don't call me Bro.*

"Lucas," I say, rising to my feet. "This conversation isn't over, but for now, I have business with Jamie."

Tin Man gives me a sad look, and Sal orders another drink. I'll leave them to it. As I turn and head toward the entrance to the club area with its transparent glass doors, I nearly stumble when a distinct chill rushes down my spine and past my legs. It's the same chill I had when I got that mysterious knock on my door earlier. I slow my pace and look around, mentally reaching out again to the demigod Calais, just in case it's him. After a few seconds, I figure it's not.

What the hell?

6

I weave my way through a small crowd of wizards on the dance floor, some cavorting with dates, while others hold enchanted drinks in their hands and stand chatting. The steady thrum of music fills my ears, and a couple of guys who recognize me shout out my name, trying to wave me over and bribe me with a martini or two. My lips quirk into a smile, and I softly shake my head. As much as I would love to join them for a round or two, since other wizards actually treating me nice is a new thing—a good thing—I don't have time to socialize. I've got to meet with Jamie and grab what I need from the street-hustling alchemist.

As expected, he's holed up in his swanky VIP room that's located just past the dance floor. The burgundy curtains are drawn, which allows me to catch a glimpse of him sitting inside. That old man, Xander Pettway, slips past the curtains, having finished his own business with Jamie, and heads out in my direction. The last time I spoke with Xander, he had sworn he knew Alanna's father, Martin Reid, and asked about a magic sword. She had no clue about it, and I had no patience to figure out what he meant, but perhaps...

"Mr. Crowley, how are you?" Xander's clear gray eyes study me as he slows his pace and stops in front of me.

"As well as I can be, old man. So, you really knew Alanna's father? A human DMA agent?"

He nods with pride. "Saved my life. Did you tell her about the sword? Witchbane?"

I chuckle. "I still don't know what you're talking about. I'll ask her, though."

Xander rolls his eyes. "Just have her come see me about it. I'll explain everything."

"Hey," I say, lightly touching his arm. "Do you know anything about the night Martin died?"

"No," he says with a sigh tinged with regret. "But I know where Witchbane was supposed to go, and I had hoped it had reached Alanna by now."

"Well, I'll tell her to stop by and speak with you, gramps."

He smirks. "You do know I can read auras and trace lineages?"

"Yeah?" I hope he doesn't try to pull some type of psychic bullshit on Alanna.

"Your aura is off, by the way. Just thought I would let you know."

"Yeah, thanks, Xander. I'll catch you later." Grandpa does not need to know I ate a couple of divine Names of God and am probably screwed because of it. Of course my aura's gonna be off.

Xander takes his leave, and I head toward the burgundy curtains. Although they're already open, I halt at the threshold. As soon as the familiar whoosh of magic passes through me, I step inside the room. I quickly turn and close the curtains then face Jamie, who's seated in his cushioned booth and drinking from a bottle of beer. He breaks into a large smile when he sees me, gesturing for me to sit across from him at his walnut table. A tall glass, filled with an enchanted Mirthmaker cocktail sits at the table, already prepared for me. I have a seat and gratefully take the glass and lift it toward him in salute, taking a long sip.

"Okay, bro, I know you're about business…"

I roll my eyes, but this time, not as hard as usual. Sometimes I want to tell him he's not my friend, but when other wizards hated me and thought I was a criminal, Jamie always gave me a fair shake. Well, probably because *he's* a criminal, though not as tough or vicious as Mishka Tarasov.

I pull out a wad of cash and dangle it. This is his language. "Let's see it, Jamie."

With a dramatic flair, he pulls out a black bag; it's the size of a man's palm, but when you reach inside, it's much bigger. One day I'm going to stick my arm in there, maybe a leg, and find out just how bottomless it really is. He retrieves a satchel of faerie dust from the black bag and slides it toward me, then reaches back in and pulls out the honing crystals Willy had ordered. Psychics love using those to enhance their powers.

"It's good, huh?" Jamie grabs the cash I had placed on the table and retrieves a ring for me, something I need to enhance my elemental magic. The silver feels cool to the touch as I slide it onto my right index finger. The engraved flaming dragon symbol glows with a subtle, soft light.

The grand finale is the Memoriae, a spell book that I think will help Alanna finally unlock her memories from the night her dad died. Of course, I'm going to look over it first, and she won't be able to use it without me. Playing around with minds and memories can be tricky…tragic. I don't want to screw this up, and I don't want to screw *her* up by handing her something that could incapacitate her. Or worse.

"Yeah, this is good. Thanks, Jamie." I grab the book and flip it open. It's about five inches wide and eight inches in length. The pages are crisp and a dingy off-white, but they don't reek of age. The Memoriae's cover is hard, but with a velvety green texture on the front, and swirling gold vines and leaves decorating it from top to bottom. It's pretty, and the latent magic in the book fills my hands with warmth, which means it's the real deal.

"Anything else you need, Jack?" Jamie slides another Mirthmaker drink toward me.

I happily accept and take a sip. The elixir slides down my throat, leaving a trail of warmth and magic. My ears tingle, and I hear a faint, female voice. I turn my gaze toward the exit, thinking another of Jamie's clients has shown up a little early, but no one's there. I scan the dance floor area, where wizards are still socializing and drinking; no one's near the VIP room, but the voice sounded as if it was right here with us.

Weird.

I swirl the Mirthmaker in its tall glass, watching the bright gold and blue hues mix. Then, the hairs on the back of my neck raise as the female voice returns, just mere inches away from me. I glance around again and place the drink down on the table.

"What the hell did you put in this thing, Jamie?"

"It's a regular old Mirthmaker."

This time, the female voice is louder. "Jamie…little one…"

"Did you hear that?" I jump to my feet and scan the VIP room.

The redheaded alchemist frowns, then looks at me as if I'm crazy. He extends his right hand and brushes his left thumb against the back of his right hand, where there's a tattoo of an All-Seeing Eye. Flecks of light shimmer around the tattoo, and he raises his right hand, palm forward.

When he turns his palm toward me, his eyes widen and he lets out a gasp. "The hell…?"

"Should I be worried?" I erect a protective mental shield around myself.

Jamie's eyes water and I'll be damned—he looks as if he's about to cry.

Jamie Chamberlain. Cry?

His lower lip quivers. "Nana, is that you?"

My gaze zips to my right, where Jamie apparently sees his nana standing. "Your grandma's here?"

He nods enthusiastically. "Nana. H-how are you? You up above, or down below? 'Cause I know you could be a real handful..."

For crying out loud, I just want to grab the items I paid for and go home. "Jamie, I've got to go. I don't know why your dead grandma's here."

Nana's voice chuckles, right next to my ear, and I shiver. "Tell my boy that he has a lot of nerve jesting with me like that..."

Jamie looks to me, his expression perplexed. "Jack, I can see her, but I can't hear her. What did she say?"

I cross my arms. "She said you're an ass and to give me a discount next time."

He lets out a sigh, his gaze slowly lifting toward the ceiling. "She's gone, Jack. Gone to be with the angels."

The tingly feeling in my ears fade, and the creepy sense of an otherworldly presence disappears. I let out a low breath. "How long ago did your nana pass away?"

"Ten years ago, bro. And tonight...I saw her. Did you see her too?"

I shake my head. "I only heard her."

Jamie smirks and grabs another bottle of beer from his bottomless bag. "She looked beautiful. Happy. Hair redder than mine and a hell of a personality."

"Okay, you're not going to go all soft and squishy on me. Should I call Lucas in so he can hug it out with you?"

Instead of taking offense, the alchemist actually grins at me. "Talk all you want, but I know what's really beneath the surface. You're not so bad. Thanks, man, for bringing her along."

I shrug. "Don't know how that happened, seeing that I'm not a psychic and I don't mess around with spirits, but...you're welcome."

I have no interest in playing medium, but I've got to admit, it feels nice getting to help someone connect with a lost loved one. I had become so guarded over the years because of the false murder accusation against me that I had given up hope of actually belonging, of having any kind of friends.

Is Jamie a friend? Maybe. We'll see.

But now, my attention turns toward this newfound ability and its origin. The headache. The skull-splitting pain I had experienced earlier at the shop with Willy. Could this be the cause of me hearing spirits? Will it eventually fade, or will I be stuck with it? The demigod Calais had told me there would be consequences to swallowing two Names of God, written on paper by an arrogant wizard who thought he could use them. Perhaps this ability is one of these consequences.

I'll have to go to the shop in the morning and ask Willy about it, since she's our resident psychic. She'll know what to do; hopefully she'll have some type of remedy, because I'm not interested in spirits hanging around me or talking to me.

"Okay, I gotta go." I give Jamie a solemn nod.

His smile fades, and he takes a swig from his bottle. "Be safe out there, Jack."

I pocket the faerie dust and crystals, flex my elemental ring on my finger, and clutch the Memoriae. As I head toward the exit, of course the two wizard bouncers, Miki and Darryl, step in and motion for me to join them.

"Crowley," Darryl says, "Mishka wants to see you."

A sharp rush of adrenaline fills me, burning my stomach and causing my fingers to tremble. "He wants to see me? Now?"

Miki nods. "And you know how impatient he can be."

The two men turn around and head out without even waiting for an answer. They know I'll follow. They know I'll be right behind them. If I try to run, they'll probably kick my ass and haul me upstairs to Mishka's penthouse anyway.

I gulp and turn my gaze toward Jamie one last time. At least he could testify in court where he last saw me and who I was with? Bah. Who am I kidding? He'd probably tell the police he doesn't even know anyone named Jack Crowley.

One thing I've learned though, when facing Mishka, is that

showing fear will get you killed. So, I have to at least look like I have a backbone when I go face him. I have a pretty good idea as to why he wants to see me, which means I'm useful to him; overall, it's never good when a magical crime lord summons you, but I have no choice. Just great.

7

"So," I say, breaking the awkward silence in the elevator, "when Mishka asked to see me, did he look happy, or pissed?"

My grip tightens on the Memoriae, as it's the only item I couldn't conveniently slip into one of my denim jeans pockets. My loose black t-shirt hangs just past my waistband, and I glance at Miki's crisp white shirt which is tucked into his. Though he's wearing a gun in a holster at his waist, it's mostly for show—he's one of the most skilled Enforcers I know and could take out most wizards with his magic.

Darryl, Miki's partner-in-crime, gives me a wry smile. "I would say neither, Jack. But don't say or do anything to get on Mr. Tarasov's bad side."

The elevator comes to a halt and makes a loud *ding!* The metal doors slide open, and the lean-framed Miki steps out first, and I follow, knowing Darryl will stay in the rear and keep an eye on me. As we head down the hallway toward a set of double doors, I clear my throat and tap Miki on the shoulder.

"What is it, Crowley?"

"Hey, you studied Theoretical Magic, right?"

Miki slows his stroll and allows me to fall into step with him. "Yeah, I did four years at the Akashic Academy and two more at

Elliteu in Korea, since my parents are from there. Why do you ask?"

I hand him the Memoriae. "I'm gonna help a friend unlock some memories. Any advice or tips?"

Darryl's interest is piqued, and he sidles up to me. The tall, muscular Enforcer scratches his deep brown chin as he gazes at the book. "Crowley, are you sure you want to play around with that?"

"My friend is desperate, and I would rather help her...or him...than for them to try and do it on their own."

Miki arches a suspicious eyebrow. "Is this for that woman? Alanna?"

"No," I say.

Darryl's brawny chest rumbles with laughter. "Yep. It's for her. What's up with her?"

"Nothing," I insist. "Really."

Miki thumbs through some of the pages. "This looks good— stable. Just remember to use the safeguard spells on page twenty, okay?"

"Got it." I take the book back and commit the page number to memory.

Miki halts with us at the double doors, and instead of knocking, he turns to me and stares me dead in the eyes. "You know how to pull someone out of a memory trance, if they need it?"

I shake my head. "The instructions are in the book, right?"

He reaches into his pants pocket and pulls out a slip of paper with a phone number on it. "I was saving this for that cute waitress down at the bar, but I think you need it more than her."

I accept the piece of paper and slip it into the fold of the Memoriae's pages. "Aww, I'm flattered, Miki, but I don't think you're my type."

His expression grows serious. "If that spell book is for Alanna, I would rather her be safe. I may not like who she works for, but for a human...she's okay."

I nod. "Thanks."

Darryl lightly knocks on the left side of the double doors. "Mr. Tarasov, it's us. Crowley's here."

The ornate doors open of their own accord, and without another word, the two Enforcers turn and head back down the hallway, leaving me to face Mishka Tarasov alone. I step across the threshold and take in the full view. The last time I was up here was when I was in Mishka's infirmary. This section looks to be a lounging or dining area; it has a large fireplace with a white marble mantle, floor-to-ceiling windows that overlook part of downtown Los Angeles, and a pure white sofa set which I'm pretty sure Mishka would never let anyone sit on.

My attention snaps to the left, where the aroma of roasted beef, herb-infused vegetables, and enchanted dark wine waft toward me. I slowly approach Mishka, who sits at a rectangular glass table, digging into his meal with methodical cuts. My mouth waters as my gaze falls on the second plate apparently set out for me.

"Jack," he says in his Russian accent without even looking up from his plate. "Please, join me."

I let out a nervous breath, remembering to keep up a nonchalant appearance so he doesn't detect any fear or worry. I slip into my seat and place the Memoriae on another seat to my right before picking up the knife and fork, reminding myself that Mishka probably has better things to do than poison little ol' me.

"Miki and Darryl said you wanted to speak with me." I cut into my steak and take a bite. Holy hell, that's tasty. The tension in my shoulders ease, and I gather the courage to take a sip of the dark red wine in front of me.

The magical crime lord wipes his mouth with a cloth napkin and studies me with his dark brown eyes. "Your automaton is downstairs, *da*?"

I shrug. "He's down there, but he's not mine. He belongs to the Department of Metaphysical Affairs."

For now, at least. Sort of.

I'm still working on getting him under Master Valerio's protection, assuming that's what the wizard wants. But then, if it were up to me, Lucas wouldn't belong to anyone; I would just let him be. I would feel like a shitty friend if I turned the automaton over to either the Cloaked Council or the DMA. He should decide where he wants to go.

Mishka looks neither pleased nor displeased by my response, but he prods further. "Have you been able to use the robot to find Kenneth Cherish? Assuming Kenneth is alive."

"Noooo, no. I haven't."

And believe me, I'm curious as well. Kenneth is like a freaking rockstar to many wizards, and I would love to meet him in person and pick his brain. However, he disappeared decades ago, and a smattering of "sightings" from random wizards doesn't necessarily confirm he's alive and well.

Mishka sips his wine then addresses me again. "Do you know why I haven't made a move to take the automaton?"

The stinging tension in my shoulders return, and I feel like a mouse in reach of a cat's claws. Mishka's the predator, and I'm the prey. I need to tread carefully. "I don't think the DMA or the Cloaked Council would like it. I think they all have the same goal as you—use Lucas to find his creator, Kenneth Cherish. His skills were extraordinary, and he could be useful."

Mishka smirks. "Smart man, you are. I suppose you're not as foolish as I thought."

I bite my tongue, lest Mishka removes it for my backtalk. I gave him a few crumbs, maybe he's willing to do the same for me. "Thanks, I actually had a question about Kenneth. Do you think the DMA whisked him away to their black site prison? If such a place exists, where do you think it would be?"

The crime lord takes another bite of his steak and chews and swallows before answering. "If they had Kenneth, we would know by now. Those humans love stealing our magic, especially when it's combined with technology. They would plunder his mind and take all, then they would use what they know and turn it against us."

To my surprise, I nod in agreement. Granted, there are a few decent DMA agents, but the suits who run the secret government organization…I neither know nor trust them. "Mishka, do you think—"

The rotund man waves his hand in a gesture, indicating that he wants me to shut up. "Let's not waste more time. I summoned you because I am calling in my favor."

Ugh. There it is. Against our laws and customs, I sneaked Alanna past the Gateway separating our wizard city, Grey Haven, from the human world, and Mishka found out about it. He said instead of reporting me to the Cloaked Council, he'd simply call on me one day to do a job for him. I guess this is that day.

I take a gulp of wine to hide my frown. I hope it's not something that will land me in jail, but saying no to Mishka presents its own set of problems as well.

"What's the job? And remember, I may have been found innocent by the Council, but it doesn't mean they're not watching me."

Mishka snaps his fingers and a man in a black suit and turquoise tie enters the dining area from an adjacent room. The guy has tattoos similar to Jamie's running up his neck and across his bald head. It's kind of cool. He must be an alchemist.

"Eli, give Mr. Crowley the information."

The alchemist approaches me and reaches into an inner pocket in his suit jacket and hands me an envelope. "Thanks," I say, hoping it's not a dossier on some unfortunate wizard he wants me to assassinate. I open the envelope, and Eli turns on his heel and heads back through the doorway.

Mishka clears his throat. "It's my nephew."

Hmph. There's actually a tinge of worry in the crime lord's voice. I pull out the small picture of Nicolai Tarasov, a dashing young man, early 20's, who looks like he could've been Mishka in his younger days. I also grab the other contents from the envelope: a spare house key and a slip of paper with Nicolai's address.

"What's going on with your nephew? I've seen him around The Ruined Oak, and he seems like an okay guy."

He leans forward and frowns, which only emphasizes his smile lines. "I want you to find him, Wayward Wizard. Can you do that?"

"He's been kidnapped?" I slip the home address and key into my pocket but place the photo onto the table. Nicolai's dark, piercing eyes stare back at me, but his expression is kind. What sort of trouble did he get into? And who would be bold enough to kidnap Mishka's nephew?

"Nicolai went missing over the weekend," he explains in his Russian accent. "We've tried scrying spells, tracking his phone… nothing has helped."

"And why do you think I can?" I make sure to keep my tone measured, because I don't want to come off as disrespectful, but at the same time I was genuinely curious. I'm not a private investigator, nor have I ever worked on tracking down a missing wizard.

Mishka rises from his seat, and for a moment my stomach twists into knots. Did he take offense at my question? I finally release a small sigh when he folds his hands behind his back and begins pacing, deep in thought.

"Based on a magical examination of Nicolai's apartment, my security team has determined that he was abducted by a hexwielder. You are one of the few wizards I know who has gone up against a hexwielder and…how do they say it? Lived to tell the tale."

Suddenly I have the urge to stab myself with the dessert spoon.

Hexwielders are the absolute worst. Many of them work as shady bounty hunters and even traffickers. Their power lies in slinging curses at people and taking what you magically throw at them and hitting you right back in the face with it three-fold. They fight dirty, they're dangerous, and the Cloaked Council would gladly throw a wayward hexwielder into prison for simply stepping on an ant. Needless to say, they're not well-liked. The only reason I got into a battle with one is because he worked for a dark wizard I brought to justice, and I barely survived that encounter, with the help of Lucas and Sal.

"Mishka, you can't get Miki and Darryl on this? The Enforcers would help out. This isn't necessarily my area of expertise." Though, it does puff up my ego to know that the man thinks I'm somewhat of a badass for having fought a hexwielder.

He emphatically shakes his head of dark hair. "No. No Enforcers. This stays between us."

"Oh. I see." I begin wondering if Nicolai did something to warrant his capture, but I don't dare voice the question to Mishka since I like living. "And you're certain Nicolai is alive? Sorry, I just have to ask."

He gives me a dismissive wave, either to let me know he understands or for me to shut up. "I have many enemies—ruthless ones. Believe me, if he was dead, I would know. Whoever took him wants something from me, but I haven't received a ransom note."

My gaze follows the heavyset man as he finally goes back over to his chair and slides back into his seat. I finish off my yummy steak before speaking again. "I'm assuming this is a job I can't refuse?"

Mishka snarls. "I'm assuming you still want the ability to sire children. And don't forget that you owe me a favor. Are you not a man of honor?"

Ha! *Man of honor,* says the magical mobster who should probably be sitting in a cell next to a hexwielder. The only reason he's able to do what he wants is because he's useful to the Cloaked Council, in their own twisted way. I wouldn't be surprised if he either had powerful connections or blackmailed the right wizards.

"Okay, I'll do it. Do I get a stipend or something?"

"Of course," says the millionaire. "And my security team and their resources will be at your disposal. I suggest you start by visiting Nicolai's apartment and continue from there."

Well, I guess this isn't all bad, though I'll have to let Willy know that she'll be flying solo at the shop until I get this side job wrapped up. "I'll start tomorrow morning, Mishka."

"Very well."

He finally looks content now that he's strong-armed me into finding his nephew. He takes a long sip of his red wine then pulls a business card from his front pocket. I raise a questioning eyebrow, thinking perhaps he intends to slide it toward me, but I'm caught off guard when he sniffs the card as dramatically as he would his glass of wine.

"I can still smell her perfume," he says, quirking a smile then re-pocketing the card.

Ew. Creepy.

I had forgotten about the "business card" Alanna handed to him when she first met him. He apparently still doesn't know that her info was printed on scrying paper, which allows her to spy on him as long as it's in his possession. Both Sal and I warned her to never do something like that again, but she can be a defiant little daredevil when she wants.

Mishka's smile fades. "Is Alanna Reid single?"

I inwardly cringe. "I…never asked. I'll add that to my to-do list."

Note to self, sever the scrying link, or steal that card. Alanna, what were you thinking?

A knock on the double doors grabs my attention. The way Mishka casually waves his hand and magically opens the doors indicates that he's been expecting another guest. I watch with interest, until I see who steps across the threshold.

Baltazar Maune.

I'm still not paying this guy for a task I never asked him to complete. Besides, I've got a crime lord's nephew to un-kidnap.

8

Baltazar stands at a full five feet tall, dressed to the nines in an immaculate high-collared shirt, royal blue vest and tie, and leather shoes that probably cost more than a month's rent. He inclines his head toward Mishka in a gesture of respect, then saves a scathing look for me. His amber eyes bore into me, and I swear if this guy was a hexwielder, I would be dead.

"I see that Mishka has you on board for this mission as well?" Baltazar asks in his Irish accent.

I grunt. "Well, it's nice to see you've found a new client. Will you finally leave me alone and stop harassing me about paying you?"

Baltazar approaches and takes a seat at the far end of the table. With a wiggle of his fingers, Nicolai's photo rises from the table and flutters toward him like a butterfly. He catches it between his index and middle fingers and stares at the image. "Mr. Crowley, I assure you, I'm worth every penny. My services are top tier. I wonder what Mishka sees in you."

"Hey, Baltazar, I think I left a pot of gold at the end of the rainbow for ya." I stand and then slightly squat to match the shorter man's height and mimic dancing around like a leprechaun.

Mishka growls. "Enough! Both of you. Jack, I will pay whatever fee you owe Baltazar."

"That's the point, Mishka, I don't owe him anything!"

Anyhow, I could pay the guy if I wanted. I'm not filthy rich, but neither am I strapped for cash. But it's the principle of the matter. Baltazar can't go around charging people for services they didn't ask for. Besides, I don't want another reason to be indebted to Mishka.

Baltazar pockets the photo of Nicolai. "You are too kind, Mr. Tarasov."

The magical mob boss gives him a curt nod. "I suggest you and Crowley learn to be kind to each other, since you will be working together on finding my nephew."

Oh, hell no.

The short Irishman chuckles. "I hope he's half as good at tracking down missing wizards as he is at avoiding his financial obligations."

Mishka slams his palms down onto the table, making the wineglasses rattle. "Let me be clear on this: I know what my image and reputation is among the wizarding world, and that means this issue of Nicolai's kidnapping must be handled discreetly. People won't fear me, and this will only open me up to more attacks by my enemies, if this gets out. Understood?"

"Of course," I say. "You don't want this to get out to the public."

Mishka continues. "Baltazar, you are my fixer. At times, you will have to accompany Jack while he's on duty and ensure that my rivals, and the Enforcers, and especially those meddlesome DMA humans never find out."

The "fixer" rises from his seat, as if he's about to skip out of here and get started. "We will find Nicolai, sir. You have my word."

Mishka gives us both a somber glance then starts giving us some final instructions. However, his voice is drowned out and my attention is seized by the hazy image of a beautiful blonde woman with sad eyes, standing behind Mishka who's still seated, and looking down on the stern man. The hairs on my arms raise, and a chill runs down my back. Just great, another ghost.

"...do you understand, Crowley?" the heavyset man asks with a curious expression.

"Yeah, I got it." I reach over and grab the Memoriae. "Baltazar, meet me at my place, 8:00 a.m. I'm sure you remember my address."

"Of course," the Irishman says. "See you in the morning, partner."

"You're not my partner."

I say goodbye to Mishka, though he's staring at me as if I'm insane. He's probably second-guessing his decision to hire me for this, but it's too late now. The sooner I get this job done, the sooner I'm free from whatever leverage he would have over me.

I take off, passing through the double doors and down the hallway, retracing my steps from earlier. I make it to the elevator and slip inside and smack the button for the dungeon level. I'll need to see Jamie again before going home. I'm fairly certain he has a charm to ward off spirits. Screw this mess—between dealing with Baltazar and finding Nicolai, preferably alive, I just don't have time to play psychic. Besides, I don't like dead people.

The elevator jolts to a stop and I step back into the familiarity of The Ruined Oak. I stroll down the hallway and make a right turn, and approach Jamie's VIP room; there are only a handful of wizards still in the club, schmoozing and drinking at a table while the DJ plays a smooth R&B song. I catch Jamie just as he's exiting his room. He's wearing a black backpack and pulling the burgundy curtains closed.

"Hey, Jamie. Got a second?" I help him close shop, carefully adjusting the long, velvety drapes and making sure not to trigger his magical wards.

"I thought you'd be gone by now, bro. Something wrong?"

"I had another ghost episode upstairs with Mishka, but this time I saw the spirit and didn't hear her."

Jamie cocks his head and gives me a questioning look. "Really? Interesting…"

"I'll pay you for a charm to ward these spirits off. I need to keep them away from me, at least until I talk to Willy and find a more permanent solution."

He runs a hand through his bright red hair. "I think I got something. Came in yesterday, in fact."

"Thanks." I cradle the Memoriae spell book in my right arm and use my left hand to grab my wallet from my back pocket. "How much?"

"For you? Sixty bucks."

"Sixty dollars for a charm?" I sputter.

"And that's *with* a discount." He slings his backpack around and unzips a side pocket, pulling out a silver lion pendant dangling on a black leather cord.

I'm just about to tell him to screw off, but then the air feels like static, and a deathly chill runs down my arms. Damn it. "Fine. I'll take it, even though I could probably get this for a lot cheaper elsewhere."

I hand him the cash and take the pendant, quickly slipping it on and tucking the cord comfortably beneath my black t-shirt. The weird static in the air dissipates, and the chill that nearly numbed my limbs suddenly vanishes.

"All right, I'm out, Jack. Stay safe."

"Thanks." I'm glad he has enough sense not to stick around asking questions about what happened during my meeting with Mishka. Anyway, I couldn't tell him even if I wanted to.

As the alchemist makes his way toward an employee exit on the other side of the dance floor, I head back over toward the bar area where Roy is wiping down the bar counter and enjoying a final drink alone. Sal is gone, and I make a mental note to call him and check up on him tomorrow. He may be a former Marine but stepping into this world of magic and paranormal danger… it's something altogether different.

Lucas, though, is still here. Despite myself, I smile a little. He's rather loyal for an automaton. "Ready to go, Tin Man?"

He's seated at the table, hands folded and eyes staring into I don't know what. He seems happy, though. He turns his gaze toward me and nods. "Yes, I'm ready."

"Have a good night, Jack," Roy says before finishing off his drink. "You too, Lucas."

The automaton rises to his feet, and I can't help but imagine Baltazar standing next to him for comparison. "Good night, Roy."

I gesture for Lucas to join me, and we head over to the doorway that opens to the stairwell that leads up to ground level. Tin Man and I climb the stairs and enter the front lobby, where Darryl and Miki are standing sentinel. Well, at least Miki is. Darryl's chowing down on a lettuce wrapped burger.

"Still eating keto, I see." I wink at the dark-skinned Enforcer.

Darryl wipes his mouth with a napkin then nods. "See you later, Jack."

"Don't forget about what I said, Crowley." Miki's eyeing me like a stern teacher who's just waiting for his student to screw up.

I tap the Memoriae in response. "I'll call if I need you."

As Lucas and I pass the reception desk, I wave to Poppy, who's swiveling in her chair and reading some novel with a bare-chested man on the cover. Her automaton, Betty, sits next to her, staring at me and Lucas.

"Good night, Mr. Crowley," Betty says in a tone that makes me suspicious she would let a bus hit me without even blinking. Though, that shouldn't be in her programming. Hell, who knows what her programming is? It also doesn't escape my attention that she barely acknowledged Lucas.

As soon as we're out the front door and in the parking lot, I slow my pace. "So, Tin Man, what makes you different from Betty?"

Lucas gives me a thoughtful look. "She's the property of the Cloaked Council. I know that there are very few automatons in existence because of strict regulations, and nearly all of them are kept within the Council Hall. Jack, they don't let us out, certainly not this close to the human world."

"Then they must really trust Poppy to give her Betty, huh?"

He raises an eyebrow. "Or they gave her to Poppy to assist in some special task."

I'll have to keep my eyes and ears open for that. Poppy was just elevated to the Cloaked Council as the human-wizard liaison, but I can't figure out how Betty fits in with that. And why doesn't she seem to like Lucas? Or me?

"So, you don't feel a connection with Betty?"

He shakes his blond head. "The Theoretical Magic wizards of the Akashic Academy made her. Kenneth Cherish made me."

"Plus, you have a freaking human heart beating inside your chest, protected by gold wiring. I'm sure Betty Bot doesn't have *that*."

"Indeed, she does not."

"Here," I say, tossing him the key to my Corolla. "You can drive."

He breaks into a surprised grin. "You know, there's something different about you."

"Because I'm letting you drive?" I open the passenger side door and hop into the seat, stretching out my arm and placing the Memoriae on the back seat.

Lucas settles into the driver seat and starts the car. "I think you know what I mean. Give it some time, and it will come through fully. Then, you can learn to control it."

Great, even this guy can sense my weird new ability. Nope. Still don't want it. I don't want to give it time, nor nurture or use it. It's not mine—it's God's. Besides, I've heard horror stories of wizards unable to control such powers and going mad, or worse…getting possessed. Also, if there's one way to piss off a deity, try hijacking one of their powers and using it.

As Lucas smoothly reverses out of the parking spot and heads to the parking lot exit, he makes a left-hand turn onto the street and annoyingly drives at the speed limit, though there are barely any other cars on the road. I grab the leather cord around my neck and pull out the silver lion's head pendant. I clutch it in my right hand, hoping that its magic doesn't wear off too soon. This ought to do until I talk to Willy about this; I have ninety-nine problems, but I'll be damned if a desperate ghost is one of them.

9

My eyes slowly open as the morning sunlight hits my face. It's inviting, warm, and I adjust myself on my living room couch as I contemplate sleeping in a little longer. However, the Memoriae slides out of my lap, and I catch it just before it hits the floor, and then the mouthwatering scent of bacon and potatoes fills my nostrils.

"Good morning, Jack!" Lucas shouts from my tiny kitchen. The sound of dishes clanking and food frying in a pan fills the morning silence.

"Good morning, Tin Man."

I stifle a yawn and sit up, browsing the page with the trance instructions. I would really prefer not to call Miki for help, so I spent all last night studying the spell book, and I'll probably spend a good chunk of today doing the same. Some of the rituals look promising, like the Locality spell, which can help Alanna build a type of memory palace for her to walk through, as if she were right there back in the desired time and place. This could work. The only thing that worries me though is that she can only spend five minutes inside it before it crumbles and dissolves— and her mind right along with it if I don't pull her out. Yippee.

I wish Lucas could fix his programming and recover what he

knows from the night Alanna's dad died; it will also allow him to unleash Alanna's memories that are in lockdown. If Samuel Mayhew wasn't stalking us and trying to lure Lucas back into DMA custody, I would take Tin Man down to the DMA lab and ask that scientist, Dr. Baker, to repair him. I shut the Memoriae and slide it onto my coffee table when I see Lucas bringing over a plate of hot bacon, fried potatoes, and eggs.

"Thanks." I grab the plate and fork and dig in.

The automaton sits next to me and nods toward the Memoriae. "You're going to use that with Alanna?"

I savor the taste of buttery eggs and juicy bacon, chewing and swallowing before responding. "It's kind of our last resort. I think it will be way easier to fix your programming and have you undo that ouroboros tattoo. It's safer than doing memory spells and rummaging through her head."

"Are you willing to take on that danger, once we discover the truth? Can I protect her from what will come our way?"

I inhale another forkful of eggs and potatoes. "Listen," I say before quickly swallowing, "sometimes the truth is going to be dangerous. I care about Alanna too...as a friend, you know...I don't want anything bad to happen to her. But think about how much more dangerous it is for her, you, or any of us to be left in the dark."

The robot slowly nods, a slight smirk playing around his lips. "It seems there is still much more I need to learn about humanity. My programming, every fiber of my being tells me to protect her...to protect you and Salvador, at all costs. I perceive that chasing this thread and unraveling it is akin to stalking a hungry lion. There will be consequences."

I scarf down the last of my breakfast. Man, I wish I had gotten an automaton sooner. "And we'll face those consequences together, buddy. Do you know if Dr. Baker is ironclad loyal to the DMA? Would he be willing to meet with us secretly? He at least had experience with tweaking your programming and fixing anything that's out of whack."

Tin Man runs a hand through his blond hair. It tickles me how he has little tells when he's thoughtful or nervous. "He has never disobeyed an order from Director Mayhew and does everything the agency asks. He wouldn't help us without telling Mayhew or getting his approval."

I figured as much, but thought I would ask just in case. "Well, if we can't get Dr. Baker, the only other option we have in repairing whatever was stripped from you is Master Valerio at the Akashic Academy. Fair warning, he might want to keep you for *further study*."

He frowns. "I may have to take that chance. Or we can go with the Memoriae. As you said, Alanna deserves to know the truth."

I place my empty plate onto the coffee table and grab the spell book again, along with a pen. I open the tome and start going over the Locality spell again, scribbling a few notes in the margins. Looks like I will more than likely use it; I'm not keen on taking Lucas down to the academy. Either way, we'll help Alanna. There are very few people in the world I believe are watching out for me, and her, Sal, and Lucas are among them. I at least ought to return the favor.

An impatient knock at my door has me glancing at my digital clock sitting on my coffee table. It's 8:00 a.m., and I groan, knowing who's standing in the hallway.

"Ugh. Baltazar is here."

"I heard that!" the Irishman's voice shouts from the other side of my apartment door.

Lucas's silver-gray eyes glaze over for a few seconds, and I can tell he's accessing my magical wards in order to check that it is in fact Baltazar Maune at the door, and he's alone. "All's clear, Jack."

"Thanks, Lucas."

I rise from my seat and approach the door, opening it slowly then standing there, staring at the dark-haired wizard with his unusual amber eyes. My attention is momentarily captured by his annoying faerie, Olette, who's in the form of a hazy amethyst ball of light, zipping back and forth near Baltazar's head.

The short wizard is dressed in an expensive black suit, like a high-powered lawyer. He arches a dark eyebrow as he stands across from me, looking me up and down. If he thinks I'm gonna dress up for this job, he's got another thing coming.

"Jack, can you please lower your ward, so I don't have to wait outside in the hallway? Haven't we learned about keeping a low profile?"

"And that faerie of yours is low profile? Can't she hang out in your pocket or something?"

The amethyst ball of light flickers and lands on Baltazar's left shoulder. The faerie says something to him in her native language and he chuckles. "Now Olette, he is our partner—for the time being. You most certainly shall not."

I grit my teeth and restrain myself from reaching out and swatting Tinkerbell.

Lucas approaches and stands next to me. "Good morning, Mr. Maune. May I interest you in breakfast?"

The short wizard grins and he glances at the ball of light on his shoulder. "Well, look at that, my dear. At least there's someone here who knows how to treat a guest. I would love some breakfast and a cup of tea."

"Sorry Lucas, he can't stay. We've got work to do." I spin on my heel and rush over to the couch, grabbing my black jacket just in case we're out until evening. I also scoop up my phone and keys (including the key Mishka gave me), and slip on the elemental ring I got from Jamie last night. I'm still wearing the silver lion's head pendant, to keep spirts at bay. "Go through the Memoriae, make sure we've got all our bases covered…just in case. And please, call Sal and tell him to be careful about that occult list."

Lucas nods. "Will do. And if I go out, I'll be sure to use a deflection spell so that the DMA can't track me."

"Good. See you later, Tin Man."

I clasp the robot on the shoulder in a parting gesture then head out, closing the door behind me. Baltazar quickens his pace to keep up with me, and Olette, still a ball of light, finally melds into Baltazar's neck and disappears. As we make it down the hallway and into the elevator, I turn my gaze toward the man and give him a questioning glance.

"You're wondering where Olette went?"

"Yeah, I've never seen a faerie hanging out in this realm, especially with a wizard."

I spot a gleam of pride in his eyes as he loosens his tie and pulls down his collar to reveal a rather impressive tattoo. It's Olette, silver hair, purple flowy dress, and her figure stretched as if she's leaping into the air. To any onlooker, she's just a gorgeous tattoo, outstretched arms just a few inches below his left jawbone and her delicate toes grazing his shoulder blade.

"Nice," I say, taking in the view. I wonder if this tattoo magic is similar to the ones the alchemists use.

"Thank you. She's been with me for quite a while, and I'm proud to call her my friend."

As the elevator lurches to a stop at the underground parking level, I ask, "My car or yours?"

"Mine," he replies as he slips on a pair of sunglasses.

"Okay, let's go to Nicolai Tarasov's place and see what we can find."

I sure hope the guy is alive. Whatever clues we can glean from his apartment will be a good start on tracking him and finding out who took him and why. As I mull over what to do once we gather intel, my phone vibrates in my pocket, and I pull it out. It's a text message from Lucas, telling me that he's scrutinized Baltazar's DMV records and has determined that the wizard is an excellent driver. I quickly reply with a thanks, though I'm tempted to tell Lucas that he should remain in my apartment for the rest of the day under the protection of the wards, though I know he hates that.

He may be an automaton, but he's also had a taste of

freedom, and he likes going out and doing things, especially if it's with his human friends. I don't blame him. My apartment isn't necessarily the best place to be holed up in. However, a nagging feeling keeps poking at me, reminding me that the DMA can be shady bastards when it suits them. Up until this week, the agency had been nudging me about bringing Lucas in —until they got tired of it and Samuel Mayhew showed up at Willy's shop with a pair of hellhounds. Now, they're ready to knock me out of the way to get Lucas back. Looks like they've finally run out of patience, but they neglect to consider that I have as well.

10

I roll down the tinted window of Baltazar's black Jaguar XF, inhaling the salty scent of the nearby Pacific Ocean. It brings back memories of when I was a kid and Willy would take me to the beach to swim and play. My lips curl into a soft smile as I recall how I had at first refused to go into the water because I was convinced the ocean would sweep me away. Like any good adoptive mom, Willy told me that was nonsense, and that I was more likely to be eaten by a shark. She then bought me an ice cream and had me sit with her as she used her psychic abilities to read people, which I found fascinating.

I barely notice when the car slows and Baltazar pulls into a guest parking spot. I lift my gaze and take in the view of a tall white apartment tower overlooking the shore. Fancy, expensive, and not quite the place to kidnap a grown man without anyone noticing. I twist in my seat and face Baltazar.

"Mishka said Nicolai lives on the tenth floor. How do you suppose someone could just take him without causing a scene?"

The dark-haired wizard tucks away his sunglasses, slips out of his suit jacket, and adjusts his embroidered black vest. His crisp, white shirt collar conceals his Olette tattoo perfectly. "I suppose we can answer that once we take a look at the apartment, Jack. Shall we?"

We get out and approach the lobby door, which has a security guard stationed out front. I spot a couple of well-positioned cameras and question again how someone could drag Nicolai out of here. Or, perhaps, they escaped through a portal?

I follow Baltazar into the lobby, which of course has orange and black confetti littering the furniture and a huge "Happy Halloween!" sign hanging on the wall near the elevator. The holiday is just a couple of days away.

Baltazar halts at the first elevator and hits the upward arrow button. He wastes no time in turning toward me and studying me with his amber eyes. "Your birthday is in two days."

"Yeah? Are you planning on buying me a gift?"

The metal doors slide open, and we step inside. He presses the button with the number "10" then crosses his arms. "What sort of things do you like, Jack? Clearly, we don't share interests."

My eyes narrow. Who does this guy think he is?

"Maybe I don't go around driving flashy cars or wearing fancy suits, but I'm a pretty well-rounded person."

He barks a laugh. "That's debatable."

"Hey, why don't we focus on our job? The sooner we're done with this, the sooner you can get out of my life."

The elevator comes to a stop, and we exit, heading down the hall to apartment 1023. We slow our pace and make way for a woman carrying a noisy chihuahua. We nod to her in greeting. She smiles before shushing the fawn-colored puppy and strolling toward the elevator. Once she makes it inside, Baltazar and I approach Nicolai's apartment door.

"He may still have residual wards," the Irishman warns as he carefully holds an open palm just inches away from the teal door. He closes his eyes and utters a spell in Gaelic. The area on his neck where Olette melded into his skin glimmers with an amethyst light, and the ground beneath us shifts like an earthquake.

My senses heighten and I plant my feet firmly into the ground, readying a counter spell, just in case. However, Baltazar gestures toward me, indicating that the wards have been broken. Hmm, makes me wonder if he could've easily done that at my place this morning. I bite my tongue, not wanting to get into another squabble with Lucky Charms. I pull out the key that Mishka gave me.

"Here," I say, handing it to the wizard. "Use this."

He unlocks the door, and we slip inside. My first order of business is to flip on the lights and check his fridge. I'm thirsty. I go over and rummage inside until I find a cold wine cooler, offering a second one to Baltazar. Who says I don't like to share?

"Really, Jack? We're on duty."

I shrug, set the unwanted bottle aside, and open my own. I take a long gulp before following Baltazar over to the fireplace mantle on the other side of the living room. By the look of the place, with its overturned furniture, scattered knick knacks, and broken vase, it's clear a struggle took place.

I take another swig from my bottle. "I'll check his bedroom."

The other wizard grunts, as if giving an annoying toddler the go-ahead to do something else other than hang around him. I pass through the short hallway and open the door to Nicolai's room. The scent of a milky sandalwood cologne wafts toward me, the notes of spice and vanilla tickling my nose. My feet carry me over to his dresser, where I find the matching cologne bottle. I dig through a few drawers and find the typical items a young, wealthy wizard would possess—stacks of cash, a passport, a satchel filled with glittering magic crystals that would make Willy jealous, and a few pricey alchemical potions.

My attention then turns toward the array of framed pictures on top of the dresser. Nicolai, smiling with friends on a yacht, another one of him hiking in the mountains with an attractive brunette, and a large photo of him blowing out candles on a birthday cake. Not a bad life if I do say so myself; I hope Sal and Alanna don't think I expect a cake or a party for my birthday. I mean, I wouldn't say no if they insisted, but...

The familiar sound of fluttering wings fills my ears, and I sigh. "Did Baltazar send you to babysit me?"

Olette flits past me and halts just above the pictures, her ever-changing little face taking in the view. She makes a comment in her native language, which she knows I don't understand.

"Do you speak human? Heck, Latin?"

She rolls her eyes, at least for the three seconds that I see them, and she points toward the birthday cake picture. Before I can reach for it, the quick little faerie zooms toward it and touches the glass surface protecting the picture. Her head turns toward me in a panic, her eyes widening, and she tries to disconnect her hand from the surface, but it's stuck like glue.

"Are you okay?" I move toward her and set aside my drink.

"*Eeeeep!*" she squeals, as the frame's surface becomes like ripples of water and begins pulling her in.

"Hold on!" My heart pounds in my chest as she's elbow-length deep into the picture. If I don't get her out, this thing will swallow her whole, and I doubt Baltazar would accept an apology for that. I wrap my right hand around Olette's tiny waist and pull against the force of the rippling surface, which earns me a few curse words from her. I ignore her protests and place my left hand on the surface, and it immediately starts pulling my hand inside.

"*Speculum, partem e converso...*"

The temperature in the room drops and a flash of light nearly blinds me. The pull of the picture's glass surface reverses and pushes us backward. I stumble, nearly falling over with Olette still in my grip. I breathe a sigh of relief then release her before she decides to bite me. The silver-haired faerie flits around the room like a possessed bird, and I just let her be. I grab an obsidian crystal from the satchel I found earlier and slam it against the glass surface, and it cracks and peels like old parchment, revealing a hidden picture behind the birthday photo.

The concealed picture looks like a surveillance photo, taken of a cute twenty-something woman, with white-blonde hair and dark eyes. I flinch when Olette settles on my shoulder and takes a seat. She tilts her head to the side and studies the picture before making a noise in what I interpret as some kind of compliment.

I grin. "So, you're thinking we need to find this girl and see if she knows anything about Nicolai's kidnapping? Maybe who he pissed off and why?"

The magical creature nods.

She can be kind of cute when she's not flying around being a little demon spawn.

"Let's go show this to Baltazar." I turn and head out with the photo, Olette still perched on my right shoulder. I make it back into the living room, but Baltazar is straight up gone. Damn him. I go and check the bathroom—empty. I head toward the exit, but he opens the front door and pokes his head in from the main hallway.

"Ah, I see that Olette is starting to tolerate you." He smiles at the sight of the little ball of amethyst, now buzzing and glowing above my shoulder. She zips over to Baltazar and melds into his skin, once again taking on the form of an intricate, beautiful tattoo.

"Where were you?" I ask.

"I didn't find much here, but I slipped out to talk to a few of the surrounding neighbors. There's no way a hexwielder could have carried an unconscious Nicolai out of here without anyone seeing."

"Agreed, but wouldn't talking to neighbors draw attention to us? Which we don't want?"

"If you do it the right way, my boy, talking to people and winning their trust can bring a multitude of benefits."

An elderly man's voice from down the hallway calls out to Baltazar.

The wizard smiles as if he's just proved his point then turns toward the other person down the hall. "*Sí, Señor Vargas. Un momento, por favor!*"

Baltazar disappears.

I'm just about to follow him when of all things, my head starts throbbing as if someone had hit me with a hammer. I shudder and grit my teeth, trying to push away the pain. In the background, I hear Jamie's dead grandma whispering.

"Hey, Jack-O!"

Ugh. I'm gonna punch Jamie into next week. This spirit ward pendant is garbage. "I'm not supposed to be hearing you. Besides, I'm not your grandson. Why don't you go haunt Jamie?"

"Pffft!" Nana responds. "That lion's head pendant works better on weaker spirits. Those of us who are stronger can find our way around its power and grab your attention."

I rub my temple and curse at her in my mind. "And why do you want my attention? Can't you see I'm busy?"

"Hmph. Since you're Jamie's friend, I thought you'd like to know that there's a vial beneath the couch that your friend failed to find on account of him being distracted by Nicolai's *indecent* magazine collection."

Why am I not surprised?

The pounding headache I had moments earlier has now subsided. "A vial, you said?"

"Right over there."

I go over and kneel next to the gray leather couch, stretching out an arm and sweeping it across the floor. My fingertips brush against something and I retrieve it and rise to my feet. It's just as Nana said, a glass vial that's been emptied of its contents. I turn the dark green vial at an angle, hold it up, and sniff it.

Blech. Like vinegar with a dash of red wine.

Having worked with Willy in the shop since I was a kid, I was familiar with this concoction—reverie serum. This alchemical brew places a person into a sleepwalk or drunken state. This whole time we all thought Nicolai would fight and make a scene with anyone who tried to abduct him. Now, it looks like the fight happened here in his apartment, he was forcibly given the reverie serum, and he most likely walked out of here with his captor. Onlookers would just assume Nicolai had a little too much to drink. I slip the vial into my pocket.

"Jack! Come!" Baltazar's voice calls from down the hall.

I exit the apartment, close the front door behind me, and join Baltazar a few doors down. He's standing in the hallway with a gray-haired man who I assume is Mr. Vargas.

"Hi," the old man says, holding out a hand. "I'm Ignacio Vargas."

I reach out and shake his hand. "Nice to meet you. I'm Jack, a…friend of the family. You saw Nicolai leave?"

"Yes, I was just telling Baltazar I saw him Saturday night walking to the elevator with a pretty young woman, white hair. She seemed very affectionate with him. I don't want to gossip, but his girlfriend has dark hair…so, you know…"

Oooh, clue time. I pull out the picture of the mysterious platinum blonde. "Is this her?"

Mr. Vargas gazes at the picture and nods. "That's the girl."

Baltazar's eyebrows shoot up and he gives me a furtive glance. I smirk at him. I can talk to people too.

The other wizard clears his throat. "I guess we know what our next lead is." He faces Mr. Vargas and says something to him in Spanish. The elderly man bursts into laughter and pats him on the back.

"Please, Baltazar, when you return, I must insist you join me and my wife for dinner."

The Irishman clasps him on the shoulder. "I would be delighted. Until next time—" he pauses to grab a handful of crisp bills from his wallet. "My friend, there may be others coming around, asking questions. You see, Nicolai's uncle is an important man, and he hired us to look after him. Can I rely on your discretion, *Señor*?"

Mr. Vargas gently pushes Baltazar's hand away. "No, I can't take that. It's fine."

"I insist, for your trouble, my friend. I won't take no for an answer."

The elderly man sighs and takes the cash, resigned to the fact that Baltazar won't take no for an answer. "Very well. But promise me you'll join us for dinner? Next week?"

Yeah, assuming he, or I, will be alive next week if we can't deliver Nicolai safe and sound.

The wizard places a hand over his heart. "On my life, I wouldn't miss it. Thank you."

I slip my hands into my pockets and remind myself to tell Baltazar about the vial. "Time to go."

Baltazar and Mr. Vargas exchange goodbyes once more and then we head back down the hallway to the elevator. Once we're inside, I hand him the vial.

"You're full of surprises today, aren't you, Jack?" He sniffs the vial like I had done earlier, except he goes a step further and touches the vial opening with the tip of his tongue.

I pretend I didn't see that. "It's—"

"Reverie serum," he says, finishing my sentence. He licks the vial again. "And each brew is like a distinct brand of perfume, with its own notes and blends."

I give him a quizzical look. "So, you know who made it?"

"There's only one shop where this particular brand would come from."

"Good to know, because the white-haired girl he walked out with Saturday night gave this to him. She's our hexwielder."

The elevator comes to a halt, and we stroll into the lobby and head out toward Baltazar's Jaguar. We hop inside, and he turns to meet my gaze. "Why did you have her picture?"

"Olette and I found it hidden behind one of Nicolai's photos. It was boobytrapped, like he didn't want anyone else to access it. I don't understand, if he had this image and knew about her, why didn't he say anything to anyone? Why was she a secret?"

He starts the car and puts his sunglasses back on. "Excellent question. More breadcrumbs for us to follow."

As he pulls out of the parking spot and we take off, I ask, "So where did the reverie serum come from?"

"The Pits of Hell."

"Seriously?"

"Yes, the Pits of Hell. It's a potions shop in Scarletwood."

I groan as the car barrels down the busy street. "Scarletwood? We can't go there. DMA agents are monitoring the Gateway, thanks to Damon Blackbird's antics. And on top of that, they hate us."

He grabs a can of sparkling water from the console, pops it open, and takes a sip. "Correction...they hate *you*. I'll arrange safe passage for us. Just give me a day."

I doubt it, but then again, Baltazar Maune knows nearly everyone worth knowing and where bodies are buried. If anyone can get us through the Scarletwood Gateway, it's him.

"I'll drop you off at home," he adds, making a right turn.

"Just take me to the shop. I have an 11 a.m. shift and Willy hates when I'm late."

He snorts a laugh. "That's cute, you working a day job."

I shrug. "Well, we can't all be overpaid, perverted private investigators."

"Did you hear that, Olette? He's besmirching my good character."

I smirk. "There are lots of things I would attribute to you, and *good character* isn't one of them."

Instead of showing offense, he actually smirks at me. "Delightful."

11

We pull up to Willy's Whimsies twenty minutes late, and I can already tell that the shop has been opened for business. That was supposed to be my task this morning. Willy must've decided to come in earlier than planned. I groan inwardly, dreading a lecture from my adoptive mother on how I need to haul ass in the morning and get to work on time. And she won't just threaten to fire me—she'll send a poltergeist to harass me for a week.

"Mmm..." Baltazar leans forward and gazes at the store front. "I haven't seen Willy in a while. How's business?"

"It's great!" I put on a fake smile and open the passenger side door. "Don't forget to call me tomorrow about Scarletwood, okay?"

"I wouldn't dream of moving forward without you, Jack. Mishka made it perfectly clear that I'm to stay by your side as needed."

Wonderful. Just what I wanted to hear.

I step out and close the car door, waving to Baltazar as he drives off. My mind immediately goes into how I'm going to explain my tardiness, but that all goes out the window when I enter the shop and see Zara standing behind the counter. She's ringing up a customer at the register, her head tilted upward as she smiles at a tall, lanky guy with glasses.

"Thanks, Zara," he says. "Nice to meet you." He grabs his bag of goods and heads in my direction, giving me a nod of acknowledgement before exiting the shop.

Zara brushes a wisp of dark hair away from her face and smiles at me. "Good morning, Jack."

I look left and right, then straight back at her. Since when did Zara Wilson ring up customers? "What are *you* doing here?"

She places her hands on her hips. "It's obvious I work here. Willy offered me a job."

"Huh. Did Willy slip and hit her head?"

"Oh please, stop being so petty." She sucks her teeth then reaches for a *Yer A Wizard, Harry!* mug and takes a sip.

No. Not my favorite coffee mug.

I approach the counter and grab the mug as soon as she sets it down. "This is mine. Get your own."

Okay, maybe I am a bit petty.

"Jack, really, I already apologized to you. You're going to treat me this way because I'm related to a dark wizard? Is that it? Let Damon pay for his sins, not me."

"Speaking of relations, where's baby Charlie? Who's watching him while you're here?"

Her cheeks flush red and suddenly she's at a loss for words.

As if on cue, Lucas comes in from the hallway to my right, holding the curly-haired Charlie who's munching on a piece of fruit. That's a bad idea. Lucas has a target on his back, and it's best he's not holding an infant if DMA agents decide to aim their weapons at him.

"So, you tricked Lucas into becoming your nanny-bot?"

Lucas grins like it's a compliment. "Interestingly enough, I first met Agent Reid when she was a newborn. I can take care of children, if needed."

"It's just for today," Zara says. "I found a babysitter who's starting tomorrow. I know that you and Lucas and Salvador are working on important things."

I glare in Lucas's direction. "Yeah, and one of those is not getting captured by the Department of Metaphysical Affairs. Weren't you supposed to be holed up at the apartment working on the Memoriae?"

Charlie squeals happily at I don't know what, and Lucas keeps a firm but gentle grip on the kid while keeping eye contact with me. "I've added a few extra notes, and the information Miki gave you will also help. You can proceed with the spell. I would only caution that you—"

"Yeah, I know, I'll be careful with it." The last thing I want is to screw up my mind or Alanna's. "Is Willy in her office?"

Zara grabs a second mug from behind the counter. "Yeah, and while you're back there, could you be a *gentleman* and pour me a cup of coffee, since I can't use your dumb mug?"

I take the bright pink mug with a bare-chested man on it. Clearly, it belongs to Willy. "Sure thing."

"Thanks," she says with a grin.

I take the man-chest mug with me and head down the hallway to Willy's office. The door's ajar, so I don't bother knocking. I slip inside and head over to the French press and begin pouring a hot cup of joe for Zara.

"Hey, Willy." I throw in a couple of sugar packets and a dash of powder creamer. "That's a cool Employee of the Month you got there."

The psychic raises her steel gray eyes from her laptop and stares at me with her *Don't-Give-Me-That-Mess* type of look. "Do you have a problem with me hiring Zara? Unlike you, she actually got here on time."

Okay, she's got me on that. And this isn't my first time being late. "Sorry, Willy. It's just that I don't trust her the way I trust Sal and Lucas. *And* she took my favorite mug."

She chuckles and runs a hand through her short, white hair.

"Just be patient with her. She needs a second chance. Isn't that what I gave you, hun?"

I stir everything in the mug with a stirrer stick. "Yeah, I get your point. I know I can't tell you how to run your shop anyhow. I'll try to get along with her."

"Good. She needs someone to look out for her, at least for the time being."

I begin wondering if my adoptive mom has a soft spot for Zara because Willy herself had to "start over" when she came to America and left behind her past.

"So, you expect us to work shifts together?" I ask.

She closes her laptop and shakes her head. "I'll call you on an as-needed basis. I gave her the 11:00 a.m. shift, so you don't have to worry about it. Besides, I know about your little side job with Mishka Tarasov. Seems like that's going to either keep you busy or get you killed."

I wave a dismissive hand through the air. "I can take care of Mishka and this job he's got me working. As soon as I'm done repaying his favor, I'm done with him, and I'll be free."

"I should hope so," she says, pulling a mahogany box from her desk drawer. "Come over here."

I grab the pink man-chest mug and hop into the seat across from her. Having seen that box a thousand times, I already know the drill.

I'm mesmerized by the intricate faerie images carved into the top; it reminds me of an old-fashioned jewelry box. Willy clicks it open and reaches inside, pulling out a red jasper stone that looks like candy. The only giveaway is that its surface glints in the light, and as a wizard I can drink in the powerful hum of magic emanating from it. We've got imitation ones sitting out front for humans to purchase. All of the authentic stuff, the powerful artifacts and charms, are either here in the office or in the back storage room.

"Hold out your right hand," Willy commands as she closes her eyes. I do as she says, and she sets the jasper crystal on my palm while still keeping hold of it, like how a doctor would press a stethoscope against a patient's chest.

"I haven't had a headache since this morning," I tell her, knowing she's still concerned about my episode from yesterday. I had even told her about Jamie's dead grandma speaking to me.

"Shut up, hun." She screws her face up in concentration, and the low hum of the crystal's power spreads in a warm embrace through my arm, torso, neck, and head. "That's weird."

I hope she doesn't think she's going to bench me and tell me to go home. "What's weird? I mean, besides the usual."

Her eyes snap open, and she purses her bright red lips. "You've clearly been in contact with spirits, but this odd ability of yours isn't purely psychic in nature. Not like mine."

"I'm starting to get used to it," I assure her.

She takes the crystal and returns it to the mahogany box. "What I think we're dealing with is a form of divination—spirit magic."

"That sounds like a lot more commitment than simply being psychic."

"Ha! You're telling me. That demigod Calais wasn't kidding, was he? Just promise me you'll be careful, okay? Maybe I can find a remedy for this before it gets out of control."

"I'm not a baby, like Charlie," I tell her. "You don't have to build wards and walls around me."

"Son, there's a reason why psychics train so hard with their abilities, even though wizards of other disciplines look down on us. The magic is as strong as the mind that wields it, and if that mind is weak and confused, the person won't be in control…the magic will. Get it?"

I nod. "Yeah, I've heard about wizards who get too many voices in their heads at once and they have epic meltdowns. That sucks."

I silently promise myself, and to Willy, that it won't be me.

"You know what sucks more, Jack? When you get the *wrong* voice in your head. Take it easy, will you?"

"Come on, you know I will."

She opens her mouth to speak, but my phone rings in my pocket and I gesture for her to hold that thought. I rise from my seat and pull out my phone and answer.

"Hey Jack," Sal's voice says. "You at work?"

"Yep, but Willy's got Zara covering my shift. What's up?"

"Damn. Better watch your back."

"See? That's what I tried to tell Willy."

Willy skewers me with a look, but I turn around and head out into the hallway, still clutching the man-chest mug.

"Meet me at my parents' house. we've got lunch ready, and I can hand over the catalogue to you."

Sweet. He actually did it. I had asked him to compile a list of any magical artifact in Pandora's Box that had belonged to Kenneth Cherish. Pandora's Box is the DMA's storage room of stolen wizard goods. Whenever they raided a wizard's home or business or whisked someone away who happened to be carrying potions and charms, best believe the agency confiscated it all and threw it into Pandora's Box. I had been in there once, with Alanna. Now? They probably wouldn't even let me through the front door. Not unless I was dragging Lucas along.

"Are you finally going to tell me why you want it, brujo?"

I quirk a smile at the nickname that had once been an insult. "I'm cross referencing it with Kenneth Cherish's research. I have a nagging suspicion Lucas's creator may be in the DMA's clutches, despite the so-called sightings in Paris, or London or Vegas. If I can find him, I can get master Valerio *and* the agency off my back."

"Okay, just know that you owe me big."

I exit the hallway and approach Zara at the counter, handing her the mug. She mouths a "thank you," and I grunt in response. I turn my attention back to my phone call. "Thanks, Sal. I'm on my way."

I end the call and wave to Lucas and Charlie. "I'll call you later, about the Memoriae."

He nods. "Stay safe, Jack. And tell Alanna that I'm willing to help in any way I can."

"Will do."

I swipe across my phone screen and order myself a ride, since my car is still parked at my apartment's garage. After waiting a few minutes outside in the sunshine, I hop into a white sedan, and we take off toward Sal's parents' home. I'm looking forward to getting an edge on the DMA. If those asses can keep tabs on me, then I can do the same. I'll get to the bottom of Mayhew's technomancy research, and ultimately the truth of what happened to the genius wizard who created Lucas—Kenneth Cherish.

12

"I hope you know what you're doing, man." Sal slides a flash drive across the dining table to me, and I waste no time in snatching it and placing it into my pocket.

"Thanks." And I mean it. I know he's taking a risk sharing this list of magical items stored in the agency's headquarters. I hope he knows that if our positions were reversed, I would do the same.

"You saved my life, Jack, helped me get justice for my brother —it's the least I could do. Just try not to get yourself killed, brujo."

Everyone keeps telling me that. "I'm fine. I can handle the agency, and I can handle Mishka and this side job."

Sal wags his finger at me. "You need a team to back you up."

"That's the ex-Marine in you talking. I'm used to working alone. Anyhow, how's Alanna holding up at the DMA office?"

Before he can answer, the doorbell rings. Sal's mom, Carmen, strolls past us in the dining room and heads for the front door. Carmen loudly announces Alanna's name and exchanges a few words with her before laughing and ushering her over to us. As quickly as she entered, Carmen disappears back into the kitchen. Alanna scans the dining area then waves at me. She's in a dark gray pantsuit and her auburn hair is tied back into a ponytail. Her expression softens with a sense of relief when she sees it's just me and Sal. No Lucas.

"Hey, Alanna." Sal grins and pulls out a seat for her.

"Hi, Sal." She takes the seat next to him. "Mayhew expects you down at the office soon. He wants to go over a pending case with you."

"Hmm," I say, grabbing a chip and scooping a chunk of guacamole dip onto it. "Does this case have anything to do with Kenneth Cherish? Or Lucas?"

She crosses her arms. "Have you gone through the Memoriae? Am I clear to take it?"

I shake my head. "I will take you to it, and I'll help you with the spell, but there's no way in hell I'm giving you that book for you to just play around with and memory hole yourself."

Sal's dad, Leonardo, comes in from the kitchen with a steaming platter of roasted chicken. It smells heavenly. Carmen follows him, carrying a bowl of steamed veggies. We all thank them, and Carmen leans over and gives me a tight squeeze.

"And I packed some leftovers in the kitchen," she says with a gracious smile.

"You're an angel," I say.

"I'm off to work." Leonardo approaches Carmen and plants a kiss on her cheek. "I'll see you all later." Alanna and I say goodbye to him.

"Bye, Papá." Sal grabs his plate and starts heaping chicken onto it.

Once Leonardo's gone and Carmen's upstairs, my attention turns back toward Alanna. "Oh, and another thing, James Bond...you need to break the link to that scrying paper you gave Mishka."

"He's figured out it's not just a business card?"

"No, not yet at least. Why did you give it to him?"

She places a few spoonfuls of veggies onto her plate. "Simple

—I'm building a dossier. He's a powerful wizard, and we need to know everything we can about him."

"Brilliant," I say.

"Jack, he strong-armed you into some crazy mission. Wouldn't you like to know his weaknesses and secrets?"

"That's beside the point," I respond. "Just…quit spying on him. He's not the type of wizard you want to cross. And he sniffs the card you gave him and asked if you're single."

She wrinkles her nose. "I know. Yuck."

I'm kind of on a roll with this admonishing stuff. I devour a piece of chicken before addressing Sal. "And as for you, what are you going to do with that occult list from your brother's old files?"

His brother Ramón died to protect that list. It contains the names of humans who make up a group of occultists in Los Angeles. They know about the existence of magic and magic-users, to the Cloaked Council's and the DMA's chagrin.

Sal downs a glass of water before answering. "I'm giving the occult list to Mayhew today when I go in. I just needed to look at it first, see if there were any personal connections, anyone who knew my brother or my family."

"Fine," Alanna says. "But if you don't do it today, I'll tell Mayhew myself. The agency needs to know who these occultists are and make sure they don't expose people like Jack."

Sal nods. "Understood. It's just that some wizards' names show up, too. My best guess is that they're working with the occultists, because Damon Blackbird's on the list."

Now that's interesting. Damon tried to kill us all and is locked up in a wizard prison, the Obelisk of Qaveus. And his cousin Zara is drinking out of a *Magic Mike* mug and standing just feet away from Willy. I don't like that.

Sal pulls out his phone and points to a few candid photos of occultists he's apparently been stalking. He draws my attention to the zoomed-in images of silver rings they all wear on their right middle fingers: a sigil displaying a cluster of seven circles enclosed in right-side-up and upside-down triangles, all contained in a hexagon, at which six more circles are at each point. It's the symbol of the most powerful angel in existence.

"Hey," I say, nearly choking on a chip. "That's Metatron's symbol. Jamie showed it to me before."

"They call themselves the Society of Mystics," Sal explains.

Alanna grabs the phone and swipes through a few more pics. "So, now we have a name to go with their organization. Good. These people are meddling with forces they don't understand, even if they fashion themselves as students of the esoteric." She makes a few more taps, sending copies of the pictures to her own phone then hands the phone back to Sal.

"I should let Willy know." I rise from my seat and head into the living room for privacy. I call Willy's cell instead of the shop's landline.

"Hey, hun. How's Salvador and Alanna?"

"Great, but it's you I'm worried about right now."

"Why?"

"Zara's cousin not only worked with the wizard who framed me for murder, but he also rubbed elbows with the Society of Mystics, the human occultists. Zara may be connected to these freaks too."

"I didn't think the occultists were that organized, or that well-connected."

"Yeah, so you need to fire Zara and kick her out. We can't trust her or trust that the Society won't find their way to her."

"Listen," she says, "I know about Damon Blackbird all too well. He deserves to rot in prison. However, what has Zara done except escape his house and try to start a new life with her baby?"

Why do I feel like I'm being made out to be the bad guy? I'm just showing some healthy skepticism and looking out for Willy. Damn her stubbornness.

"Keep your eyes open. *Please*?"

"I always do."

I end the call, knowing that at least Lucas is still there to lend a hand if needed. Anyhow, Willy's set on protecting Zara and Charlie. Hopefully she doesn't regret it. With a sigh, I resign myself to returning to my friends when I catch movement outside the front window from the corner of my eye. I take in a deep breath and exhale, reaching across the living room and past the window with my magical senses. In return, I get a sledgehammer of magic, whacking me straight in my face and knocking me onto my ass. All I see are stars, and it takes a few seconds for me to refocus my vision.

"Guys!" I shout. "We have a problem!"

I *hate* hexwielders.

Sal and Alanna rush into the living room, no doubt wondering why I'm on the floor and looking stunned.

"It's a wizard..." Alanna reaches for an enchanted fire ring and slips it onto her right index finger. She can do a lot of damage with that, seeing how she punched me with it a couple of weeks ago. Her hand then hovers near her gun in its holster.

"Hold on," Sal says, rushing to the hallway then returning with a rifle.

Just as I get back on my feet, Carmen comes rushing downstairs. "*Mijo!*" she says in a harsh whisper to Sal. "A woman was floating outside my window, and before you tell me I'm crazy, I am not crazy. Why do you have your rifle out?"

Alanna turns toward the staircase. "I'll check upstairs. Sal, stay with your mom. Jack, go around the house. I'll yell if I need you."

Sal settles into an arm-rested standing position with his rifle as he watches the front window like a hawk. "Mom, there's something I need to tell you about me and my friends."

Carmen snatches a bronze angel statue from a nearby stand, holding it like a bat. Her eyes widen. "Is it drugs? Is someone after you?"

"No, Ma...no. It's *not* drugs, and put that down, we're going to protect you."

"I'll go around outside," I tell him.

Alanna and I give each other a quick nod, and she quietly goes up the staircase while I head out the front door. I tap into my elemental magic, my secondary skill, and the dense presence of nitrogen and oxygen flow across my hands as I gain control of the wind. I figure using the power of Air would be less messy with the hexwielder, since a blast of fire toward her would only give her the fuel to sling an inferno right back at me. I would hate for Carmen's house to become burnt toast.

I tiptoe past a few plants and bushes and make a left turn to the side of the house. The fence separating us from the neighbor's house is taller than me and would obscure their view, but I still listen for any innocent bystanders. My nose wrinkles as I make my way past the garbage bin, and I make another left to the back of the house. My gaze is immediately drawn upward, toward the second-story window where the white-haired woman from Nicolai's photo is hovering like a ghost.

I raise my hands and send a blast of wind toward her, while at the same time closing in on her so I can catch her when she falls. But instead of losing her balance and hurtling toward the ground, the veins in her right hand turn black and she sticks to the edifice. My wind spell buffets her, and she dangles as she opens her mouth and sucks in the powerful gust of air.

Uh oh.

As if blowing out a candle, the hexwielder rounds her lips and blows hard, sending a jagged stream of wind right at my head and knocking me against the patio furniture. She then turns the stolen air toward the window she's been hovering at and breaks the glass. She wastes no time in hopping inside the house. I prepare another air spell and use the force of the wind to propel myself toward the broken window. I dive through and fall into a roll, just as a silver blade whisks past me. I jump to my feet and quickly scan my surroundings; we're in a bedroom.

The hexwielder swivels toward the doorway as Alanna forces the door open, her hand blazing with fire from the enchanted ring she's wearing. The white-haired woman parries a fiery hand strike from the DMA agent, but then Alanna makes a jab to the hexwielder's torso, and the wizard grunts as she backs away and quickly pulls out a whip, cracking it and looping it around my neck. She pulls me in while simultaneously backing away from Alanna, using the force of the whip to place me right in front of her as a human shield. Alanna draws her gun and trains it on us, but we both know she won't take the shot unless I'm out of the way. Well, at least that's what I'm betting on.

"Let my friend go," Alanna commands.

"I have no quarrel with you." The hexwielder tightens the loop around my neck, and I grab onto it to keep it from strangling me. "I only want to deliver the Wayward Wizard a message—to stay out of this."

"Why? What's your name?" I ask.

The hexwielder sends a hard knee against the back of my right leg. I bite my tongue and nearly lose my balance.

"I know you're a True Name wizard," she says into my ear. "I'm not stupid enough to tell you."

"Hey!" Alanna says, taking a step forward. "Let...him...go."

As Alanna's speaking, I'm whipping up a subtle, thin stream of fire in my hands. I shoot the stream of fire along the line of the whip. My own elemental spell won't hurt me, but for the hexwielder, she's gonna get a nasty jolt. As soon as the stream of fire reaches her hands, she yells out and immediately disengages me, turning me loose from the whip's loop.

"Jack, get down!" Alanna cocks her gun.

"We need her!" I stand between my friend and the hexwielder, facing the wizard because there's no way I'll turn my back on her. "I need to know if Nicolai's still alive. Just tell me where he is, hexwielder."

The woman glares at me and clenches her jaw. Her gaze goes between me and Alanna, sizing us up. With a frustrated grunt, she turns and runs for the broken window, and I give chase, nearly catching her by her white braid. The hexwielder launches herself through the window, exuding a black mist to obscure our vision. My eyes burn and Alanna coughs into her elbow, but we both approach the window and look out. She's gone.

"I'll put out an APB with the agency, just in case they're able to intercept her." Alanna places her pistol back into its holster and pulls out her cell phone.

"She must know that I'm working for Mishka, trying to track her down." I make a mental note to tell Baltazar when I see him tomorrow. Hopefully, he's able to deliver on his promise to gain us passage to Scarletwood.

Alanna turns toward the open door with her phone at her ear and steps into the hallway. "Sal! We're clear! She's gone."

"Roger that!" his voice responds from downstairs.

While Alanna's talking with Agent Bardwell on the phone, I squeeze past her and head back downstairs. Carmen is sitting at the dining table, subdued, with a glass of Tequila cradled between her hands. I don't blame her. I sit down next to her and give her an apologetic grin. She probably thinks I'm a troublemaker who shouldn't be allowed back at her home.

"Carmen, I'm sorry about this. I never meant—"

She slides the glass over to me with a trembling hand. "Drink, Jack."

I obey, wondering why she's not freaking out. "Thanks."

She leans forward and pats my cheek. "Salvador told me everything about you. I still don't understand all this, but it's okay…we're going to be okay."

Sal's still standing guard with his rifle, despite what Alanna told him. He's a soldier through and through. "Jack's a good guy, Mom."

His statement feels more like a punch to the gut than a warm, fuzzy compliment. Running around with Baltazar, working for Mishka of all people, isn't necessarily something a "good" guy would do. And what if I screw up and prove myself unworthy? I spent half my life being an adopted kid who no one but Willy wanted, and after being framed for murder, I was a black sheep among wizards. How do I bounce back and show that I am something more?

I guess my first step is to protect those closest to me.

I rise from my seat and give Carmen a grateful squeeze on her shoulder. "I can lay down protective wards around the house, to keep out any wizards wishing you harm."

Carmen stands. "I'll walk with you." She lifts her left foot and takes off her slipper. "Let's go."

Sal rolls his eyes. "Not the chancla, Mamá! These are *real* wizards!"

Carmen waves him off and retorts at him in Spanish.

I hide a chuckle behind my hand. "Well, today's the day you get to see a wizard at work, Carmen."

And hopefully it will be the last. I never want a murderous magic-user thinking they can come here and lay a finger on Sal or his family. Because whoever does, they'll have hell to pay.

13

After warding the house and keeping watch a couple of hours, we decide the place is as secure as it would ever be. Sal grabs his badge and pistol, preparing to head out to DMA headquarters to meet with Mayhew and turn in the Society of Mystics list. And of course, he makes Carmen promise to call him if she even hears the slightest noise. Since Alanna had offered to drop me off at my apartment, I knew now would be the right time to crack open the Memoriae with her.

After saying goodbye to Carmen and Sal and hopping into Alanna's car, we spend a half hour in traffic before pulling up to the Blackstone building. Alanna finds a parking spot near the front, beneath the canopy of a large tree.

As soon as she shuts the car engine off, my gaze meets hers. "Are you ready to do this?"

She nods. "I have to know the truth. And this may be bigger than just me and Lucas."

"Okay, I'll do my best then."

We exit her car and head into the tall building, walking at a steady pace as we make our way through the 1930s-style lobby. I imagine the place was something to behold back in the day. I catch Alanna admiring the décor as we wait at the elevator.

"How long have you lived here?" she asks.

The elevator doors open, and we step inside. "About four years."

As we go up to the eighth floor, my phone dings with a text message. I check and see that it's from Lucas. He's already at the apartment.

"He's there, isn't he?" She's reading my face and watching for my response. She's probably had DMA training on how to catch someone lying. Though Lucas isn't her favorite automaton at the moment, there's got to come a point where they both reconcile and work together to get this memory thing taken care of.

"Yeah, but he's with us on this," I assure her. "He even helped with the Memoriae."

The elevator stops at my floor, and we step out. Alanna frowns, but she doesn't complain or offer any objections. Since Lucas is already inside, I simply knock on the door. The vibrational hum of my wards rise and fall like waves as the automaton opens the door and welcomes us in with a flourish of his hand.

"Please, Alanna and Jack, come in."

"Hey," Alanna says with an awkward smile.

My first thought is I hope Zara and her baby aren't here. "Oh, I see you're alone, Tin Man. That's great."

Lucas shuts the door behind us and smirks. "That was sarcasm. Zara is at home with Charlie, and I promptly came here, as promised."

Alanna spots the Memoriae on the couch and rushes over to it. "This is it? Can I…?"

"Go ahead," I say. "Open it."

Her lips curve into a smile as she sits on the couch, delicately turning each page like she's reading a sacred text. This whole memory unlocking must mean a whole lot to her. Tin Man picks up on it as well as he slowly approaches Alanna and sits on the couch next to her.

"You must know," the automaton says, "that I am sorry. I've known you your entire life, and I promised your father that I would always protect you."

She leans toward him and presses her forehead against his. "I know. I'm sorry for being mad at you and avoiding you."

"Aww. How sweet, guys. Now turn to page twenty so we can make sure your brain doesn't turn to mush." I hadn't forgotten Miki's instruction to cast the safeguard spells first, so that we'll have a protective buffer.

As Alanna thumbs back over to the indicated page, I come around and sit to her left on the couch. Lucas is at her right, intently studying the safeguard steps. "We need to cast two protective wards: one for Integrity of Mind, and the other for Integrity of Memory," he says. "After we cast these, we can activate the Locality spell and let her walk through the memory palace."

"You can do the Mind one," I tell him. "And I'll do the Memory."

We both hold out our hands, palms facing upward, and they light up with magical energy. The Integrity of Memory feels like a cold, heavy weight in my palms. I steady my arms and feed more power into it to keep it stable. I cast a quick glance over to Lucas, who seems to hold the Integrity of Mind spell with ease. His hands are aglow, and determination fills his piercing eyes. Alanna's sitting between us, wide-eyed and probably second-guessing herself. I don't blame her for doing so.

"You ready?" I ask her, my arms straining to keep the weight of the spell in place. "We can stop at any time."

She takes in a deep breath, as if she's about to plunge herself into the ocean. "Let's get this over with."

I offer her my right hand, and she grabs it. She then takes Lucas's left hand. As soon as she's physically connected to us both, a gasp escapes her lips, and her blue eyes are consumed by white flames, which neither hurt nor burn her. She's as still as a statue, her mind finally sinking into the Locality spell.

"Alanna," I say in a firm voice, "you should be in the memory palace. You've got five minutes, then you need to haul ass, so you don't get stuck in cuckoo-land. Got it?"

"Yeah, I got it." The white flames dance in her eyes.

It's up to her to wade through the irrelevant memories accumulated over the years and reach the one she needs—the night her father died.

After two minutes pass, I clear my throat. "Alanna? What do you see? What's going on?"

Her lips curve into a smile. "Jack, Lucas…I see Dad. He looks just the way I remember him."

Lucas nods. "And are you in the memory as well?"

Alanna nods. "Yeah, my fifteen-year-old self. And my dad's partner Walter is there too."

"Keep talking," I say. "Let's hurry up and walk through this before our time is up."

Her smile fades. "He's holding up a key. It looks antique. Lucas, you're with us as well."

"What is he doing with the key?" he asks in a low voice.

Alanna's face screws up in concentration. "My dad's using it to open a long chest. He's pulling out a sword."

"Shit," I say. "It's Witchbane. Old Man Xander was right."

"It's beautiful," she says with a sense of awe. "I'm touching it. I feel its magic. It's…like it's seeping into me."

I furrow my brows. "That's weird, for a human, at least. What does Witchbane look like?"

"Wait…" her grip on my right hand tightens. "I see a silhouette. Someone's approaching."

Lucas's gaze meets mine. "Jack, our five minutes is nearly up. We need to pull Alanna out of the memory palace."

She squeezes her eyes shut and vehemently shakes her head. "No…no, I need to see this. I need to see who's coming."

"Now," Lucas insists.

"No!" Alanna shouts.

I go with Lucas on this one. I gradually start peeling the

Locality spell away, letting the protection of the Integrity of Memory ward keep Alanna's mind intact.

"Jack, I see someone!" she shrieks.

"You can't stay," I say in a soft voice. I start unraveling the spell, just the way Miki had told me I should, and the ebb and flow of energy surrounding Lucas indicates that he's doing the same.

The dancing white flames fade and leave Alanna's eyes. They return to their normal blue color, though they're now filled with tears.

"I almost had it…" her voice is broken, riddled with disappointment. Tears trail down her cheeks.

Not gonna lie, this is making me feel slightly uncomfortable and a little bit guilty, but if I didn't yank her out of there, she'd be insane by now.

"Sorry, Alanna." I give her hand a squeeze, but she snatches it from my grasp and wipes her cheeks.

"I just needed a few more seconds. You couldn't have given me that?"

Lucas studies her crestfallen expression. "Alanna…"

Her cell phone rings, and she quickly pulls it out and answers it. "This is Agent Reid…yes, sir, right away."

She slips her phone back into her jacket pocket.

"Let me guess," I say. "That was Samuel Mayhew calling you down?"

She nods. "Looks like Sal finally turned in that Society of Mystics list. The director wants all hands on deck."

She rises to her feet, and I do the same. Lucas is still seated, looking as if he's calculating how to make Alanna happy again. Poor guy.

"Sorry we didn't get far enough." I escort her over to the front door.

"How soon can we do the memory palace again?" she asks.

Hell if I know. I thought we'd get our answer in one round

and be done. Looks like I have a little Memoriae homework to catch up on.

"A week, at minimum," Lucas says. He's still on the couch looking like a sad puppy. "This type of spell can be dangerous, and it was never meant to be used repeatedly."

"Then we'll have to make our next session really count. I'll know what to do next time, and I can get to that memory faster. Thanks for helping me, guys."

"See you later." I open the door for her.

She gives me a curt nod then slips out, heading down the hallway and back to the elevator.

I shut the door and sigh. "I *hate* this memory crap. And you know she's going to be hounding us in a week."

"I've disappointed her," Lucas says.

"Hey, Tin Man, don't be too hard on yourself. We gave her five minutes and took her out before the palace crumbled. We did our part."

"I wish I could've done more."

"Hey, you want to help a friend out? Why not come with me and Baltazar to Scarletwood tomorrow. It'll be fun. Promise."

A glint of amusement sparks in his eyes. This automaton loves danger, apparently. "Scarletwood? For what?"

"We're going to nab a hexwielder. It beats babysitting."

Lucas smiles. "Yes. I'll go with you. I'll help you catch a wizard."

14

Monsters with razor sharp teeth chasing me through alleys, hexwielders raining curses down on me, and a pissed off Alanna swinging Witchbane at my neck all roll into a heart racing nightmare that forces me to eject myself from a fitful sleep and wipe the sweat from my brow. I sit up, clutching my sheets and taking a few seconds to realize that I'm in the dark, in my chilly room. It feels like a refrigerator in here. I'll have to talk to Lucas about his use of the air conditioning.

I shiver, but not because of the cold. In the left corner across from my bed, despite trying to cloak itself in the dark, a shadowy figure stands there, watching me with its silver eyes. The hairs on the back of my neck raise as I quickly discern that though the figure stands on two legs and has a torso, arms, and head—it's not human. At least, not fully.

My throat is dry and scratchy. "What do you want?"

I reach out with my senses and check my wards. They're tighter than a jar of pickles. So, how did this figure get in here without Lucas or my wards detecting it? The answer comes to me as my head is bombarded by the all-too-familiar spirit headache. The shadow figure is another ghost. I suck in a quick breath and bury my face in my hands. The pounding and throbbing is worse than the headache I had gotten at Willy's shop. The sharp pain goes on for what seems an eternity before it subsides, and I raise my head to speak to the shadow ghost again. It at least ought to tell me what it is and what it's doing here. But, as quickly as it appeared, it's gone. Good riddance.

I grab the silver lion's head pendant that's still dangling around my neck, and I'm tempted to remove it. Nana's ghost said that the strongest spirits can work their way around the charm, but it does well at keeping weaker spirits at bay. Well, if I'm having this much trouble already, I would hate to double or triple it. My hand falls to my side; I decide to keep the pendant on for now. Although it annoys me to admit it, Lucas is right. This charm is merely a band-aid on a huge wound. I can't run from this new ability, and Nana and the shadow ghost have certainly proven that I can't hide. I'll have to accept this and control it before it controls me.

I sit up in my bed and concentrate, remembering the psychic meditations Willy used to have me practice with her when I was a kid. She mostly did it to get me to shut up, but I actually learned a thing or two about quieting my mind and keeping it anchored. Before I know it, I fall asleep again, and it isn't until a ray of sunlight hits my face that I stir and get out of bed.

After showering and slipping into a pair of black jeans and a dark gray t-shirt, I head out to the living room, where I inhale the scent of bacon and pancakes wafting toward me. I grab the Memoriae and take it over to the dining table with me. I smile at Lucas, who brings over a plate of food and a hot coffee. I give him a grateful smile.

"Thanks, Tin Man." I take a sip of coffee. "You know you don't have to cook every day, right?"

He nods then takes the seat across from me. "I do, but it's my choice. My way of thanking you for taking me in and being my friend."

I start browsing through the Memoriae, wondering if I don't deliver on this if Alanna really will come hacking away at me with that enchanted sword. "That's right, Tin Man. We've got each other's backs."

A rather impatient knocking at my front door tears my attention away from the Memoriae. I shut the book closed and hand it to Lucas, who takes it to my room without question. I go over and take a look through the peephole, my magical senses already poised to activate a ward if needed. When I see who's standing on the other side, I groan, and reluctantly open up for Master Valerio Magnus.

"Master Valerio...come on in," I say, as the dark-haired wizard crosses the threshold without so much as a glance in my direction.

He plops down onto my couch. When he sees Lucas return to the dining area, he motions toward the automaton. "Bring me food."

"Of course, Master Valerio."

I shut my door and approach the asshole. "Is there something you needed?"

Lucas serves the man my untouched plate of bacon and pancakes, which makes me grit my teeth. Valerio isn't just the headmaster of the wizarding academy I attended, he's also a member of our governing body, the Cloaked Council. It would be tough to toss him out my window and pretend it was an accident.

"Jack," he says, cutting into the fluffy stack of pancakes, "you've been avoiding me."

I throw my hands up in frustration. "I haven't been avoiding you, I've just got a million other things to take care of right now."

Valerio's dark, bushy brows furrow. "And they all need to take a back seat to you and Lucas finding Kenneth Cherish."

"I'm getting around to that, okay?"

Lucas leaves for the kitchen then comes back with a glass of orange juice for the man. "It's true, Master Valerio. We are working on finding my maker. It's just that we have a task or two to complete, but finding Dr. Cherish remains a priority."

Valerio gulps down his orange juice. "It wouldn't hurt to call me, Jack. Just to keep me updated."

Lucas smiles. "I've marked it in my programming to contact you every other day with an update, if that's acceptable, Master Valerio."

He chomps down on a piece of bacon then swallows. "Very well. Because if you don't treat this as a priority, Crowley, then I may as well take Lucas back to the Akashic Academy with me."

Lucas's smile falters. "Sir, I…"

"You're not taking him anywhere," I say with enough force that makes the master wizard narrow his dark eyes. I quickly adjust my tone before he decides to whack me with a spell. "Master Valerio, what I mean is that he'll be useless at the academy, and he works better with *me*. We're…a team. I promise you we can handle this."

"Oh? Is that so? And what about the DMA?"

I wave a dismissive hand through the air. "Mayhew wants him back, as expected, but does he have him? No. I do. Because I've got this."

The master wizard stares at me for nearly a minute before fishing off his juice and stuffing his face with another pancake. "Very well. I have something that may aid you." He rises from his seat and approaches me, handing me a slip of paper with what looks like geographic coordinates.

"What's this?" I ask, examining the note.

"I found this among some items and notebooks left behind by Kenneth at the academy. This may lead to a safehouse or a dead end. The way the coordinates are listed, they don't correspond to an actual physical place on earth, so I'm quite sure this is an enigma which Lucas can unravel. I want you both to check it out."

I walk over and hand the note to Lucas, so he can take down the info and determine the coordinates. "We're on it. Anything else? Perhaps another round of pancakes? A foot massage? My first-born?"

Valerio smirks. "Sometimes I don't know if I want to laugh with you or send you to the Obelisk of Qaveus."

Black tower prison for wizards, by wizards? No thanks.

"Have a nice day, Master Valerio."

"Good day, Crowley. And answer your phone when I call."

I walk him to the door without saying another word. Once he's out and gone, I roll my eyes and grunt. "Okay, that guy's banned from my apartment. Remember that, Lucas."

"Certainly," he says while still studying the mysterious coordinates.

I motion toward the sheet of paper. "And what's up with that? If Valerio thinks these coordinates can lead to Kenneth, I'm pretty sure he has professors at the academy who can crack the code. Why does he want us to do this?"

In some ways, the master wizard reminds me of Mishka Tarasov—he loves having someone else do the dirty work or the hard parts but will be there to take all the glory. Willy had told me that Valerio could have ulterior motives for wanting to find Kenneth. Maybe she's right.

Lucas folds the note and sets it on the coffee table. "I will say that Master Valerio and Kenneth Cherish were close at the academy. Perhaps he wants to find his friend."

"Pffft! That guy isn't even thinking about friendship. It's something else." I just gotta stay a few steps ahead of him and find out what that is.

"Thank you, Jack."

I shrug. "For what?"

"For standing up for me when Valerio threatened to confiscate me."

I take a seat on the couch. He tries to bring me more coffee, but I gesture for him to just sit and join me. "Listen, Tin Man, I know you don't want to be dragged into the Akashic Academy. You want to be free, and you want to be with me, Sal, and

Alanna. Besides, all they'll do at the academy is dissect you and tinker around with your programming. I can't let that happen."

His eyes brighten. "I appreciate it."

The rhythmic rapping of a tiny hand at my door lets me know that it's Baltazar Maune. I let out a low breath and go answer the door. Before I can even greet the short man, he steps inside and shuts the door for me.

"Jack," he says dramatically as if he's about to tell me some salacious secret, "the hexwielder came for me last night. She must pay for her audacity."

"She came after me too. I guess I should've given you a heads up, but then I remembered that I don't like you."

Baltazar narrows his amber eyes at me. "Well, in case you're interested, I managed to stalk her. She's been using an unstable, illegal Gateway between Los Angeles and Scarletwood. We won't even have to bother with the DMA agents guarding the one at Griffith Park."

"Okay, so what's the plan?"

"Olette has been watching the Gateway, so I know our little hexwielder has yet to pass through to this side again. We're going to ensnare our white-haired friend. Shall we go?"

"Hell yes."

Lucas rises from his seat. "I'm coming as well."

Baltazar grins. "The more, the merrier. Come, my little automaton. We will either catch her or die trying."

I grab my keys, wallet, and phone. "Yeah, but hopefully not that last part."

15

Just my luck. Baltazar neglected to tell me that the hexwielder's illegal Gateway is at the freaking Hollywood Forever Cemetery. As soon as we drive onto the property, I squeeze the lion's head pendant in a silent plea of protection, hoping that the spirits swarming the place are weaker than Jamie's nana. I groan inwardly and lean back a little in the passenger seat of the Jaguar, swallowing my pride and finally deciding to ask The Fixer for help.

"Baltazar, can you enhance the strength of this pendant?" I pull the leather cord and hold up the silver lion's head image.

He parks the car and turns off the engine, eyeing me with interest. "I can already sense that the pendant is meant to repel spirits. Is someone haunting you? Have we been a naughty wizard?"

Lucas pokes his head through from the back seat. "Jack saved the world. He ate—"

"That's enough, Lucas," I quickly interject. "Can you do it or not?"

The Irishman holds out his right hand, and I place the pendant on his palm. His eyes flicker a brilliant gold before returning to its usual amber color. He utters a string of words in

Gaelic, in a rhythmic tone that flows to my ears like a song. The pendant glows with a soft silver light, and once Baltazar ends his incantation, the brightness of the pendant fades.

"There you are, partner. Anything else you need?"

I slip the pendant back under my t-shirt. "I'm good, thanks. I owe you one."

"Oh…you most certainly do."

Lucas pokes his head through again. "I just wanted to say that I think we make an efficient team so far, Mr. Maune."

The dark-haired man chuckles. "Indeed, Lucas. I hope to forge a lasting relationship with you and Jack."

"Okay, let's find this Gateway and grab the hexwielder." I exit the car and my gaze sweeps the area, from the polished headstones dotting the landscape to the manicured lawns and statues.

A frown pulls at my mouth as I spot the on-going Dia de Los Muertos festivities, with participants dressed in colorful clothing setting up candles, offering fruit baskets, and even dancing to a live band's performance. I catch a few spirits among the crowd, but they don't seem to notice me, which is exactly what I want. I just hope the living humans stay distracted and out of the way, so we can nab the white-haired hexwielder and make her tell us where Nicolai is.

Baltazar and Lucas flank me as we head down the nearest pathway. My stomach tightens as I glance at a mournful female spirit in a flowy white dress lingering in front of a dark granite headstone, but I exhale a relieved breath when she looks right past me, as if I were the ghost. I guess hanging with Baltazar can have its perks, though I don't plan on making it a habit.

"There," Baltazar says, pointing to the Cathedral Mausoleum. "Her Gateway's in there."

As we head toward the mausoleum, I scan the area again. Only a couple of families visiting grave sites, but most of the people today are gathered at the Dia de Los Muertos event. I look to my right and give Lucas a knowing look. He responds with a nod. He's probably equally concerned with how messy this could get, though one thing I know Baltazar is good at is shielding magic from the human world. Fixer indeed.

We step a little lighter as Baltazar leads us across the threshold into the Cathedral Mausoleum. It's easy to see why it's named such, with its vaulted ceilings, stained-glass windows, and immaculate marble flooring and statues. A heavy silence falls upon my shoulders as I follow the wizard down the corridor. My fingers tingle in response to the magical shield Baltazar is placing around the mausoleum.

"We don't want this spilling out into the open," he mutters as he feeds more energy into the shielding spell.

Lucas's eyes glimmer. "I feel the Gateway's magic. It's in that crypt just ahead."

Baltazar takes the lead as we head toward the crypt. A familiar amethyst ball of light flutters toward us and zips in a circle around my head.

"Hey, Olette," I say. "Staying out of trouble?"

The fluttering faerie playfully shoves the side of my head before flitting over to Lucas and asking him something in her native tongue.

The magical robot smiles. "Yes, I've been well. Thank you for asking."

Her amethyst light fades as she approaches Baltazar and lands on his shoulder. She takes a seat and shakes her silver hair; her ever-shifting facial features whir in a blur, though I can tell she's looking straight ahead.

Baltazar glances down at her like a father full of pride. "You did a marvelous job, keeping watch."

Lucas slips past us and cuts us off, stopping at the crypt entrance and holding up his right hand. He emits a pale-yellow light from his palm, and it swirls toward the entryway. His yellow magic clings to what looks like a spider's web, lighting it up like a Christmas tree. We patiently wait for Lucas to break down the hexwielder's ward on the crypt, and once the web turns into mist and floats away like ash, Lucas faces us and gives a goofy thumbs up.

"It's safe to proceed," the automaton says.

"Thanks, Tin Man." I pat him on the shoulder.

We enter the large crypt, which looks unused, though it has a white marble sarcophagus sitting in the center. I step closer to look at the engraved images on the outside of the marble burial box, a bunch of mythical monsters, some with grotesque faces staring back at me. I'm sure this is a pleasant spot to spend eternity.

"Let's open it," Baltazar says, rolling up his sleeves. Olette resumes her form as a ball of light and hovers above his shoulder.

"Okay, take the other end, Lucas." I get into position with Baltazar, and with the automaton's super-human strength, we slide the top of the sarcophagus right off.

I peer inside, and instead of a swirling magical light, my gaze is met with a pool of blackness, which throbs like a heartbeat. It reminds me of tar. "Damn, that girl is dark. Even her DIY Gateway has to be creepy."

Baltazar snorts a laugh. "Did you expect sparkles and butterflies?"

"It's pulsating faster," Lucas notes. "She may be coming through."

"Good," Baltazar says as he backs away and fills his hands with silver magic. "Let her come."

Lucas and I take a few steps back, each preparing our own spells. Lucas forms an electrical circle of light, which I can tell will be used to bind the hexwielder, and I fill my hands with a blaze of elemental fire. The flames feel like warm water running past my fingers, but to the white-haired wizard, it will burn like hell.

Olette says something to Baltazar and dims her amethyst light. The sarcophagus vibrates, filling the crypt with a loud pounding noise. The vibrations increase in intensity and speed until a feminine figure rises from the inside, covered in an inky substance. She holds her arms out at her sides, and the black liquid peels away and falls back into the sarcophagus, revealing the white-haired hexwielder in a skin-tight jumpsuit.

Baltazar eyes her appreciatively, and Olette smacks him upside the head.

"Halt!" Lucas shouts as he launches his electrical binding spell at her.

She flips backward like an acrobat and lands on her feet as gracefully as a cat. She takes hold of Lucas's binding circle like a lasso. She swings it and slings it straight back at the automaton. He dodges with ease, but I jump sideways to avoid being knocked on my ass and having my magic muted.

Baltazar's eyes turn gold, and he sends a blast of silver light toward her middle. I simultaneously launch a stream of fire toward her as a distraction, reminding myself that we have to take her alive, or else we'll never find Nicolai. The hexwielder crosses her arms into an "X" shape in front of her, capturing both Baltazar's spell and my fire, holding them suspended in mid-air. While she's occupied with our spells, Lucas sneaks around behind her and wraps his arms around her torso. She screams out in a shrill tone.

Lucas falters, damn it, and with a worried expression he loosens his grip. Her lips quirk into a sly smile and she uses her hold on my fire and Baltazar's silver magical energy, slamming them both against Lucas, who loses hold and stumbles backward. She swivels and delivers an uppercut to him, but her fist hits his chin with a crunch, and she recoils in pain.

Baltazar and I move in. I deliver a sweeping kick to throw her off balance and Baltazar begins weaving a silver mist around the hexwielder's head. She tries to duck and dodge, but Olette zooms right toward her and emits an amethyst spark of light which temporarily blinds her. Lucas grabs hold of her from behind again.

"This time, I won't let go," he tells her. "Stop fighting."

The hexwielder shakes her head, as if trying to force herself to concentrate. Baltazar's silver mist surrounds her face, shimmering each time she attempts to mentally resist. Looks like she won't be able to sling another curse at us.

"Let me go!" she demands.

I scoff at her. "Let you go? How about you let Nicolai Tarasov go? That's all we want. Tell us where he is, and we'll retrieve him and take him back to his uncle. I'm pretty sure you know who that is, right?"

Her nostrils flare as she gives Olette a scathing gaze. "I know who his uncle is. That's *exactly* why I took him."

Baltazar flicks his wrist, and the magical mist surrounding the woman's head begins to shrink, closing in on her face. "I suggest you answer us, before my silver mist sinks into your mouth, nose, and enters your lungs."

The hexwielder's eyes widen and her breathing quickens with desperation. "You wouldn't…"

"Oh, I would."

"Come on," I tell the woman, playing along with the threat. "Just tell us. My job isn't even to fight you. I just need to deliver Nicolai back to Mishka."

The silver mist around her head turns opaque as soon as it touches her skin, and it clings to her face as if someone's placed a plastic bag over it.

Olette settles back onto Baltazar's shoulder, but his eyes are set on the hexwielder. "Ready to talk? Or do you want to die here?"

I glance from Baltazar to the hexwielder, waiting to see who'll chicken out first. After a few seconds, it looks like she's not relenting, and Baltazar apparently has no problem suffocating her. However, that would be a huge problem for me. I need her alive, and besides, I told Mishka from the beginning that I'm not an assassin.

"Baltazar," I say in a low voice. "She's gonna pass out."

"That's the idea."

Lucas's strong arms are still wrapped around her torso from behind, but he tilts his head so that I can see his expression which gives me *Is he really going to kill her?* Vibes.

"Baltazar," I say forcefully this time. I wonder if I'll have to use my True Name magic and force him to relinquish his spell.

He holds up a finger to shush me. "Wait…"

"Okaaaaayyy!" the hexwielder's muffled voice screeches from beneath the silver film.

Baltazar waves his hand and the substance lifts from her face and disappears. She coughs and sputters, sucking in air and reeling from nearly losing consciousness.

Baltazar steps forward. "Now tell us, or I'll have the automaton crush you."

Lucas doesn't look like he's keen on crushing a woman, even if she is a nephew-kidnapping hexwielder. And neither am I. I'm just about to speak up when a metal object crashes onto the floor and rolls right next to us. And the way it slightly shimmers, I can tell who just threw it.

"It's a magic-muting grenade!" Lucas shouts.

We all dive out of the way as the flash and bang of the grenade goes off. A blaze of light obscures my vision, and my head rings with a high-pitched tone as my body trembles in reaction to the magic-weakening effect of the grenade. Armed DMA agents in full tactical gear file into the room, and the hexwielder takes advantage of the interruption to stumble toward the sarcophagus and throw herself inside back through the Gateway. It collapses, leaving us stuck here with the agents.

I quickly back up and join Baltazar, Olette, and Lucas. My gaze roves across the room, counting the agents and determining any possible escape routes. We're surrounded by a dozen guys with guns and stolen magic.

The agent nearest to the exit moves aside and makes way for none other than Samuel Mayhew. I've got to hand it to the old man, it takes balls nonchalantly walking into a wizard versus DMA battle wearing a gray suit and a smug smile.

He stops just a few feet away from us then stares, sizing us up. His dark brown eyes then confidently scan the room as his tactical team is perfectly lined in a circle surrounding me and my companions. These agents are ready and willing to carry out his orders, whatever they may be. Samuel looks satisfied with the odds, that he could blast us away and take what he wants. However, what he's probably not counting on is that I'll fight like hell to keep Lucas, even if my magic is muted from that damn grenade.

"You know why I'm here, Jack." Samuel extends a hand in invitation to Lucas. "Come with us, and we won't harm your friends."

Lucas frowns and whispers into my ear. "There's an 86-percent chance you'll die if I don't leave with Director Mayhew. I should accept his offer."

Anger churns in my chest. This isn't fair. "No. We stick together, Tin Man."

"Mayhew," Baltazar croons in his Irish accent. "Do you really want to go down this road?"

The gray-haired man gives him a pointed look. "Mr. Maune, the agency has been keeping tabs on you. There are about a hundred charges I could bring you up on. Don't screw with me."

Baltazar smirks. "Oh, but if you don't let us walk out of here, with the automaton, I *will* screw with you. And you won't like it."

Samuel reaches for the gun in his holster and trains it on me.

"Hey!" I shove a thumb in Baltazar's direction. "He's the one who challenged you."

"I'm not going to ask again," Samuel says in a cool, steely voice. "Give me the automaton, or this will be your final resting place."

16

"I can't give up Lucas," I say to Samuel, hoping he understands that for once in my life I'm doing something because I care, and not out of self-interest. "He was never yours anyway, and he wants to stay with me."

The DMA director just shakes his head in response. "How many times do I have to tell you that he's merely programmed to simulate human behavior and desires. Lucas isn't human. You're going to get shot over him?"

I subtly tug at the magic-muting wave of energy the grenade had released, testing its strength to see if I could at least get one good spell in. "I notice Sal and Alanna aren't here," I say, trying to buy some time. "Are you too cowardly to tell them what you're doing today?"

He cocks his pistol. "Hand over the automaton. You're out-gunned, your magic's muted, and I don't like you."

Damn. He's right. I reach out with my senses again, but the invisible wave of energy dampening my powers still flows throughout the room. I won't be able to launch an elemental spell or use True Name magic.

Baltazar clears his throat. "Director Mayhew, your grenade

mutes the magic of natural born wizards. It doesn't mute automaton magic...or a faerie's."

Samuel fires a shot at Baltazar, but Olette weaves a shield and deflects the bullet. I lose my balance and nearly fall over when the faerie grows herself to human size and sends a blast of amethyst energy toward Samuel and five of his men. They fly backward and hit the wall. Lucas pivots and speeds toward three other agents on the other side of the sarcophagus. The automaton's movements are so quick and fluid that they don't even have time to get a shot off. He makes a jab to the first agent's chest and the man heaves and falls backward. Lucas's fist crashes down onto the helmet of the second, stunning him and knocking him to the floor, and an uppercut to the third agent lands him on the ground, knocked out cold.

I rush over to Baltazar to join him behind Olette's magical shield. The remaining four agents open fire on us, but the faerie's protection holds. The bullets halt as soon as they hit the shield, flattening and then dropping to the floor like coins. She brings her hands together in a loud clap, and a deep purple energy wave spreads from her fingers and surrounds the four agents. An invisible force lifts them into the air, and they yell in shock when their weapons are yanked from their hands and clatter to the floor.

"I could use one of those, my dear." Baltazar nods toward one of the rifles on the ground.

Olette, still at normal human height, screws her face up in concentration and uses telekinesis to send the rifle flying toward Baltazar. The wizard catches it with ease then trains it on the four men still floating in mid-air.

"Much better odds, wouldn't you say, Jack?" the Irishman asks with a smirk.

"Agreed."

Lucas is standing over the three agents he had knocked down, his hands glowing pale-yellow. "I wouldn't try and get up, if I were you," he warns them.

Samuel, wiping a trickle of blood from his nose, jumps to his feet and pulls out a familiar pair of shades, and a cold lump forms in my stomach. While I'm glad that Olette and Lucas have got our backs, facing hellhounds is not how I want this standoff to end. Hell, I never wanted this fight to begin with.

I pass through the faerie's protective shield and rush Samuel, tackling him to the ground before he can put on the technomancer shades and summon the hellhounds. He grunts as we both hit the floor, and the shades fall from his grasp. His fist smashes into my right cheek, causing an explosion of pain. For a sixty-something year old government pencil pusher, this guy can hit hard.

With a growl, I wonder how Alanna would feel if I punched her mentor and boss. She probably wouldn't like it, but I know her well enough to also know that she wouldn't take kindly to him trying to take Lucas from me at gunpoint.

I lean over, snatch the technomancer shades, and bash them into the marble floor. I would rather them be useless to everyone than to allow Samuel any advantage. The DMA director shows me just how much he appreciates this by coming up behind me and putting me in a rear chokehold.

Baltazar fires a warning shot. "Director Mayhew, I would prefer not to shoot you, but I will if you don't release Jack."

Samuel backs up a few steps with me still in his chokehold, keeping himself behind me in case Baltazar does decide to shoot. "I doubt you'd shoot me and cause a war between the U.S. Government and the Cloaked Council. Or worse, the government and all wizards."

Three of the agents near Olette try to rise to their feet, but a threat uttered by the faerie in her language makes them think twice and they sit back down, hands raised in surrender.

Baltazar trains the rifle on Samuel. "The problem with humans is that you reject what is different, even to the point of destruction. Did we ask you to force us underground or to make us hide in plain sight? Who ambushed who today?"

Samuel takes another step backward with me. I can tell he's pulling me toward the exit. "And when a dark wizard goes on a killing spree or unleashes unnatural fires, who do you think is there to pick up the pieces? Who will defend the innocent? Or what about that automaton, the only link we have to the most dangerous wizard in the world? Whether you like it or not, the agency is here to stay. We're the only ones standing in between the safety of people and chaos."

We take one more step back, but I feel a tingling sensation in my fingers. The tip of my tongue burns. Hallelujah, the magic-muting grenade's effects have waned, and I can feel my powers again.

"*Samuel Mayhew,*" I say in a strained voice.

"What, Crowley?" he growls into my ear.

"*Dormires…*"

"Motherfuuu…" His grip loosens, and he hits the floor like a bag of bricks. He's lucky I only decided to put him to sleep. True Name wizards like me can also speak the words of death, but it takes a little of our own life force as well. It's not to be used lightly.

Baltazar breaks into a grin. "Ha! Serves him right. Now, what to do with this lot? They're not as valuable as the director." His gaze sweeps the room. The agents, or at least those among them still conscious, all raise their hands in surrender and shout in protest, probably thinking Baltazar's crazy enough to mow them down. I honestly can't say if he will or won't.

Lucas motions toward the exit. "Let's go. We've done enough here."

Olette utters an agreement with Lucas and shrinks back to her miniature size.

Baltazar's expression falls. He looks like the kid who finds out he won't get dessert. His pocket vibrates and he pulls out his phone, reading a text. "Mishka wants to see us…now. We must go."

Both Lucas and I breathe a sigh of relief. Human or not, I

can't deny that the automaton often acts more like a person than some who are made of flesh and blood.

"Let's get the hell out of here," I say, heading toward the exit and stepping over an unconscious Samuel. I pause and turn back around when I reach the threshold. "Your director ought to wake up in an hour."

One of the agents nods. "Okay. We backed off. Just go."

My gaze darkens. "And when he does wake up, let him know that if you ever try something like this again, we'll rain hell down on you and give you your war."

With that, my companions and I take off, exiting the crypt and escaping through the cemetery.

17

I barely notice when Baltazar's Jaguar comes to a smooth halt in The Ruined Oak's parking lot. I'm scrolling through my texts, my stomach tying in knots as I anticipate a message at any moment from Alanna, freaking out and worried over me and Lucas, or, a blistering condemnation of how I handled the confrontation with Samuel Mayhew and his taskforce. I just resolve to tell her the truth, to let her know that I didn't start the fight, but I sure as hell finished it. She can take it up with Samuel if she doesn't like it.

"Gods, I'm starving." Baltazar adjusts his collar and conceals his Olette tattoo. "Want to grab a quick bite after we see Mishka? You seem like the type of guy who'd like an ale and a greasy slice of pizza."

I shake my head. "I'm not hungry."

Lucas leans forward. "I've tried running our hexwielder's appearance through facial recognition so that we can identify her, but I'm coming up with nothing. It's as if she's a ghost."

Baltazar smirks. "Nevertheless, you're quite the hexwielder hunting partner. One day you'll have to tell me everything you know about Kenneth Cherish. Yes?"

I grunt. "Or not. Stop trying to pry, Baltazar. Let's go see

Mishka."

We exit the car and head for the entrance of the historical building, passing through the double doors and walking with purposeful steps across the marble floor to the reception area. As soon as I spot a tall man with salt-and-pepper hair at the desk, I remember that Poppy Grimm had been promoted and now we're stuck with a wizard not nearly as cute.

He offers us a lackluster half-smile before pushing his glasses up on the bridge of his nose. When we reach him, I force myself to keep a straight face upon seeing that he's dressed in a decadent 18th Century style jacket and a ruffled shirt. He might as well grow himself a ponytail and call himself Benjamin Franklin.

"Good afternoon, Mr. Crowley and Mr. Maune."

Baltazar gives the man a good look over then shakes his head. "We're here on business with Mishka, my good man. Have we met before?"

The wizard lifts a brow. "Never, and you know you'd remember it if you did." He tilts his chin upward then points at Lucas. "That one has neither an ocean blue aura like the humans nor yellow like ours. No brown or gray, so that rules out werewolves and vampires. Is he an automaton?"

"Yep," I say. "He's with me. He's been down to The Ruined Oak before."

He jots something down into a notebook. "Very well. I'm Gary, by the way."

Lucas offers his hand. "It's a pleasure to meet you, Gary. I'm Lucas."

The wizard shakes Lucas's hand. "Indeed. You may go with your companions, Lucas."

We head to the left and open the door to the lower level, going down the stairwell and reaching the dungeon area with its velvet rugs and black leather furniture. We quickly greet Roy who's tending the bar, but he doesn't take offense at our hasty walk-through. We turn down the hallway and head for the elevator leading to Mishka's penthouse. As we step inside and make our ascent to the top floor, I turn and catch Baltazar's gaze.

"So, how did you get a faerie like Olette?" I figure asking it that way is more polite than inquiring if he captured her or struck some kind of bargain with her. I've seen faeries in the wizarding realms, like Grey Haven and Scarletwood, but they don't care for us and keep to themselves. This is the first time I've seen one in action, and who hangs out with a wizard.

Baltazar's amber eyes take on a sad, wistful look. "Olette was the faithful friend and servant of my mother. She is my inheritance, and over the years has proven herself to be so much more."

I nod in understanding. "Sorry to hear about your mom. That's kind of amazing though, to have a faerie ready to kick ass and just chill as your tattoo."

He chuckles. "It is, but don't tell her that, it will go to her head."

The elevator comes to a stop and Baltazar steps out. Lucas and I follow, the automaton leaning in to whisper into my ear. "Baltazar speaks a long-forgotten faerie language with Olette. I dare say only a handful of wizards in the entire world would be able to communicate with her."

"Then how do you understand what the faerie says?" I ask.

"It's in my programming to do so. However, it's quite fascinating that Mr. Maune speaks Aes Sidhe, the tongue of faerie royalty."

Faerie royalty, eh? And strange amber eyes. Looks like there's more to the man than I thought.

We end our conversation when we approach Miki and Darryl who are standing at the ornate double doors, waiting for us. The two Enforcers look a little more uptight than usual. Darryl's deep brown face, which usually displays an observant gaze or confident smile, is tight-lipped and serious. Miki shoves his hands into his pockets.

"Gentlemen," Baltazar says, "we have arrived as requested."

"Is something wrong?" I ask Darryl. "Did you quit your keto diet?"

The burly Enforcer shakes his head. "There's been a development in the case, Crowley. Mishka's waiting inside."

I look over to Miki. "Should we be worried?"

The skinny wizard draws up a shallow breath and opens the door for us. "Go, Crowley."

I square my shoulders and look straight ahead, and Baltazar and Lucas flank me as we cross the threshold and approach Mishka, who's sitting at the dining area's expensive glass table, swirling a glass of whiskey. The Russian doesn't even look up at us in acknowledgement. His gaze is fixed on a small wooden box in front of him on the table.

Baltazar clears his throat. "Sir, you called for us?"

Mishka takes a sip from his glass, and his right eye twitches. "Why have you not found my nephew yet?"

"We almost had the hexwielder," I tell Mishka, "but the DMA intervened and she got away. I think I know a way to uncover her identity though, and we're—"

The whiskey glass crashes to the floor near my feet, and a tendril of panic seizes my chest.

"Obviously you're not doing enough," he says in a dark tone. "Baltazar, open the box."

The Irishman's breath stalls, but he does as requested. He goes over and flips the lid open and grimaces at the sight—a severed pinky finger.

"Mr. Tarasov…" Baltazar begins.

"Enough!" Mishka rises so quickly from his seat that both Baltazar and I take a step back. Lucas, on the other hand, watches the entire exchange with a sense of fascination. Not a great time to study human behavior, buddy. We may need to blast our way out of here if this goes south.

Too late. A dark aura fills the space around Mishka and expands from his back, forming into thick, glistening tentacles. Before Baltazar or I can react, the black tentacles whip toward us and wrap around our torsos, lifting us into the air. Another three tentacles slam against Lucas and pin him against the wall. I grunt and hold back a yell as the tentacle not only squeezes me to the point of nearly crushing my internal organs, but also draining me of magical energy.

"Mishka," I manage to say through labored breaths, trying to think of something to tell him that won't get us killed. "I know this looks bad, but this is actually a good thing."

Baltazar frowns and gives me a side eye. Mishka shoots me a venomous look, but pauses.

"Good? Good how?" He says something else in Russian, probably an insult.

"Well," I continue, "just think—the hexwielder sent a finger. Which means she wanted to hurt him but not kill him. Nicolai is alive. This also means that she wants something from you. If we can distract her and lead her to believe you'll agree to her demands, that will give us just enough time to cross over into Scarletwood and retrieve your nephew."

Mishka's chest rises and falls with a deep breath. He still looks pissed, but less murder-y. The black tentacles loosen, and Baltazar and I drop to the ground, quickly jumping to our feet in a defensive stance. Lucas quickly joins us, standing with us in case we need to fight our way out of here.

I continue my pitch, for our sakes. "We know where the hexwielder is…in Scarletwood. We plan to enlist the help of a contact at the Council Hall to identify the woman and get a name and address. We could have your nephew back by tomorrow, if not tonight."

The Russian lets his tentacles fade back into his dark aura and disappear. He looks to Baltazar. "Is this true?"

The Irishman shoves some of his dark hair out of his face. "It is, Mr. Tarasov. But we won't be able to catch her and free your nephew if we are detained here. Do not let emotion cloud your decision."

Mishka rubs his chin and casts another glance at the severed finger. He shuts the box closed. "He's all I have. I promised I would look out for him."

Baltazar slightly bows his head. "And you are noble for doing so. Let us help you in this. Let us bring Nicolai home."

The magical mob boss wags a finger in warning. "But no law enforcement. No publicity. Remember?"

"We got it," I say. "We'll contact my person discreetly. They won't even know this inquiry's connected to you."

"Then, I suppose I won't kill you today." Mishka takes his seat again.

"How generous of you," Baltazar says with a forced smile. "We will update you soon, Mr. Tarasov. Lucas, Jack…let's get to work."

With that, we eagerly take our leave and exit the penthouse. We make our way down the hall, and we spot Miki and Darryl hanging out by the elevator doors, no doubt standing there to catch us in case we tried to leave without Mishka's permission.

Darryl crosses his arms. "So, he let you go. I thought he was going to smoke you and I would have to hide your bodies."

I shrug. "I can understand why he's upset, but we're going to finish this job."

Miki hits the down button for us and stands aside. "You lucky bastard…"

Baltazar looks rather sullen, and his demeanor is stand-offish. "Either lucky or a damn fool."

He, Lucas, and I step into the elevator. Darryl waves goodbye, and Miki's gaze meets mine.

"Hey, how's Alanna? Is she okay?"

Lucas smiles. "She is well. We are still helping her."

The elevator doors close and we start heading down. Baltazar suddenly rounds on me and shoves me against the wall; he snarls at me like an angry animal.

"What the hell?" I jab him in his gut. He retracts his arm so he can deliver a punch to my face, but Lucas grabs his bicep and holds him at bay.

"Mr. Maune, what is the matter with you?" Lucas's tone is absolutely scandalized.

Baltazar backs off in a huff, wresting his arm from Lucas's grasp. "For twenty years, I've built up a professional reputation. People trust me…they *respect* me."

"What does that have to do with me?" I ask, filling my hands with elemental fire just in case I need it.

"Never had I had a client lash out at me and nearly kill me, sitting there with their nephew's severed finger. We failed, Jack!"

"Okay, it was an unfortunate setback, but everything's not going to be perfect or go our way all the time."

His amber eyes glow gold. "Who will hire me if I can't get the job done? I'm supposed to help you deliver Nicolai safely, and losing a finger is *not* safe."

"Hey, I'm the one who's supposed to find Nicolai. Your job is to make sure this isn't plastered over the news—both human and wizard. So far, you're doing your part. If anyone's the screw up, it's me. So, blame me, if that makes you feel better."

Baltazar presses his back into the wall on the opposite side and lets out a deep sigh, one filled with anxiety and weariness. "I tell Mishka not to be ruled by emotion, and here I am ignoring my own advice. I'm sorry, Jack. Just as Nicolai is the only thing Mr. Tarasov has, my job—and how good I am at it—is my everything."

I finally let the fire in my hands subside, and I give him a curt nod to let him know that we're cool. "I get it. I wasn't spinning stories up there with Mishka. I really do know someone in the Council Hall who can help us."

"Really?" he asks.

"Really," I assure him. "And while we're at it, we're going to put in a complaint regarding the DMA. That ought to tie them up for a while."

Lucas grins, already puzzling out my plan. "We're going to see Poppy Grimm, aren't we?"

18

The Gateway to Grey Haven is right across from Roy's bar counter. The few humans who are even allowed this far into The Ruined Oak would only see a bricked-up doorway. To wizards, however, it's the opening to our parallel realm, where we can openly be who we are without fear of reprisal from the DMA or persecution from humans who've decided we're all a threat. We used to have a ton of them throughout the world but, unfortunately, they've been whittled down to a handful. It's partly our fault with our infighting, and partly due to human harassment.

A blaze of light surrounds me, Lucas, and Baltazar as we step through the Gateway and onto the familiar cobblestone pathway leading to the town of Grey Haven. The scent of fresh jasmine swirls up my nose, and the sunshine falls on me like a protective cloak. Now *this* is a real Gate. Not that shoddy, nebulous black hole the hexwielder had constructed for herself.

I glance at Baltazar, who's keeping pace with me to my left. He gazes at the vibrant purple and orange leaves falling from the forest's trees, but I can tell his concentration is elsewhere. To my surprise, Lucas places a supportive hand on my right shoulder, his bright eyes peering into mine.

"Should I talk to Poppy? About the hexwielder?"

I consider whether or not it's a good idea. "Thanks, Tin Man, but I think I've got this. But you can be my backup, since sometimes Poppy wants to whack me with a spell."

He chuckles and lets his hand fall back to his side. "Very well. It seems your communication skills have improved."

My lips quirk into a smile. "Is that supposed to be a compliment?"

Baltazar studies Lucas for a few moments. "Humor me, Lucas. What did you make of Samuel Mayhew's comment about your master? He referred to you as their link to the most dangerous wizard in the world. One—why is Kenneth so dangerous, and two—why did Mayhew speak of him as if he's alive?"

The man has a point. Samuel's comment didn't escape my notice either, though between trying to escape the crypt and nearly getting crushed by Mishka, I haven't had a lot of time to ponder on that.

"Tin Man," I say, noting Lucas's discomfort. "Is he alive? And how dangerous is he?"

We make it into town, the cobblestone path opening into a road. I usually enjoy taking in the view of the art deco style buildings and small-town feel of the shops, but my eyes are set on Lucas.

"I don't know if he's alive," the automaton admits. "I believe the DMA saw him as dangerous because a lot of his experiments were forbidden, by both humans and wizards. He dabbled in marrying magic and technology. That's how he created me."

I wait for a group of wizards to pass us on the sidewalk before speaking again. We're nearly at the Council Hall building. "I wonder if he was working on something big in the 80's, when the agency busted him. And if he's not in their custody and alive, I'm betting they want him badly. No wonder they're after you."

"But they've had the automaton since 1988. Why are they acting like he's the McGuffin now?" Baltazar rubs his chin.

"Correction," Lucas says, "Alanna's father, Martin, was my caretaker from 1988 to 2008 when he died. When I finally did go back to the agency, by then something had changed in me, and Director Mayhew placed me with Alanna and grew strict over who was allowed to examine or run tests on me."

Baltazar gives a thoughtful look as we head up the concrete steps leading to the Council Hall entrance. "They're waiting for something, but it seems they grow impatient. And from what I understand, Alanna has memory trouble from the night her father died?"

I nod. "We're helping her with that. We're going to rebuild a memory palace and have her go through it."

"Fascinating," the amber-eyed man says as he holds the door open for us. "After you, my friends."

We step inside and head straight for the reception desk, where Margaret, whose hair has turned much grayer since I last saw her, sits with her headset on and eyeing us with interest. The last time I came here, she called me "wizard killer" and barely wanted to let me through. But, since I've been proven innocent, now she's all smiles.

"Good afternoon, Mr. Crowley." Margaret flashes her perfectly white teeth. "And what brings you in today?"

I swipe a few pieces of chocolate from a bowl on her desk. Holy hell, I'm starving. I didn't even get lunch. "We're here to see Councilwoman Grimm. Official business."

She gasps. "How exciting. I've been meaning to tell you how much I admire you."

Yeah, right. Now that I'm *not* the black sheep of the wizarding world.

"Thanks, Margaret. Can you let Poppy know we're here?"

"Of course." She taps her headset and waits a moment. "Councilwoman, Mr. Crowley is here to see you. No…no ma'am, he doesn't look injured or in trouble. He's got the Fixer and that automaton with him. Okay, I'll send them right in." She gestures for us to head toward the hallway.

I grab another handful of candy, which makes Baltazar chuckle. I hand him a few pieces. "Done being all mopey?"

He opens a few candies and devours them. Looks like he's just as hungry as I am. "I'll be all right. I always am."

Lucas falls into step with us. "Counseling can be helpful, when dealing with emotional outbursts and sorting out past traumas."

I shake my head. "We don't have time for counseling."

Lucas shrugs. "Perhaps one day."

Our footsteps echo across the wide hallway with its black-and-white marble floors. A couple of Enforcers, battle wizards by the look of the red phoenix emblem on their uniforms, acknowledge me with a nod as they pass. When we make it to Poppy's warded door, with her name placard hanging on the front, I pound on the door with a firm hand.

Poppy opens the door for us, standing there as if she's still deciding whether or not to let us in. Her dark hair, which is usually up in a bun, falls down to her shoulders, and her thick-rimmed glasses and pantsuit makes her look more like a librarian to me than an all-powerful member of the Cloaked Council.

"Hey, Poppy." I look her up and down.

"You're either in trouble or you're here to borrow money. Which is it?"

"Why does everyone assume I have no money?"

"Congratulations on your new position, Councilwoman Grimm," Baltazar says as he smoothly takes her hand and plants a kiss on it. "If you should ever require my services, I am at your disposal."

Her eyes are set on his amber ones. "Oh...thank you, Mr. Maune."

"Hey," I say, "we've got services too, right Lucas?"

The automaton leans in and whispers, "I believe Mr. Maune is hinting at a bit of innuendo. You see, when a man—"

"Okay, never mind."

Poppy giggles and waves us in. She heads over to the large, obsidian desk sitting to the far left and plops down into the leather chair. "Jack, I love my new job!" she gushes.

"You deserve it." And I mean it. She's one of the most honest and fair Enforcers I've ever known, and she even gave me a chance to prove myself when others would've condemned me.

"How are Miki and Darryl?" she asks. "I miss them."

"They're well. I'll tell them you said hello."

She clasps her hands together and straightens her back. "Good. So, let's get down to business. Why are you here?"

I nod toward Baltazar. Since he's apparently charmed her, I'll let him do the talking.

The Irishman takes a seat across from her. "Councilwoman, Jack and I are trying to track down a hexwielder...a thief, of sorts. Quite dangerous. Lucas can't seem to find her by description in any database, and we're trying to match a name to her face. Since the Cloaked Council's resources are vast, we were hoping you could help us in this."

I dig into my wallet and pull out the picture I had found at Nicolai's apartment. "Here she is." I walk over and hand it to Poppy.

She stares at the photo. "What did she steal? And why are you two, of all people, working together on this?"

Baltazar inclines his head toward her. "You know that confidentiality is important to my clients."

"Since everyone thinks I'm a bum, I'm in it for the money," I add.

"Jack is my friend, and I'm helping him," Lucas says.

"I'm sure you are. Please, Lucas, keep him out of trouble." Poppy rises from her seat, photo in hand. "You know, I've heard rumors that you're the automaton created by Dr. Cherish. I have one, given to me by the Akashic Academy, but she's nothing like you."

"None of them are," Lucas says, a slight hint of sadness in his voice.

"Wait here," Poppy tells us. "I'll go run this photo and will be back shortly. Make yourselves at home."

"Thank you, Councilwoman," Baltazar says.

She clears her throat. "Please, call me Poppy."

I roll my eyes in response to their little exchange.

She heads out with the photo and Baltazar jumps from his seat and goes straight for the tall bookshelf, filled with spell books and historical texts. He browses the selection then picks a maroon book with gold foil lettering; he flips it open and begins scanning a page.

"Looking for anything in particular?" I ask.

The door opens and Betty, Poppy's automaton, walks in with a stack of papers. She's wearing a dark gray blouse and black skirt, and her blonde hair is pulled back into a ponytail. She sets the stack of papers on the desk then faces us, looking as if deciding whether or not we're threats.

"Poppy let us in," I assure Betty, whose cold eyes study me.

"Of course she did. I should think you wouldn't be here otherwise."

With a smirk, Baltazar shuts the book closed and slides it back into place on the bookshelf. "Hello, Betty. A pleasant day, isn't it?"

"I believe so, Mr. Maune. May I get you anything?"

"I'm fine, my dear."

Lucas gives an awkward smile and holds out his hand. "Hello, Betty. It's good to see you again."

At first, automaton Barbie eyes him with an air of suspicion, but then she approaches him and shakes his hand. "Likewise, Lucas."

He gently pulls his hand from her grasp. "Do you like it here? Working in the Council Hall?"

"If you're asking if I'm content with my duties and serving Miss Grimm, then yes. This job is sufficient, and I am well taken care of."

"But do you *like* it?" Lucas reiterates.

Her expression grows a little perplexed, but then she tilts her head slightly to the side and places a hand on his chest, right over his heart. "I am curious…what is it like, having a beating heart in there? What is its purpose?"

"I would imagine it's to help me feel like a human, physically and emotionally."

Her hand drops to her side. "Do you not stop to think that it makes you weaker? More inefficient? It may be a flaw."

Baltazar gives her a skeptical look. "Oh, love, we can't all be coldhearted workaholics. Lucas is a fine automaton."

Poppy returns with the photo and Betty steps toward her. "The paperwork you asked for is on your desk, ma'am. Is there anything else you need?"

"That will be all, Betty. Thank you."

The automaton gives Poppy a smile that doesn't quite reach her eyes, and she takes off, exiting the office and closing the door behind her.

Poppy hands me the photo. "I got a name. She's Hunter Bronwyn."

Lucas crosses his arms. "And why couldn't I identify her?"

She raises an eyebrow. "Because Hunter isn't just a hexwielder. She's a prison guard at the Obelisk of Qaveus—"

"Which means her identity and personnel file are protected by the Cloaked Council," Baltazar says, finishing her sentence. "Thank you, Poppy. We'll take it from here."

She places a hand on her hip. "Well, if one of our guards is stealing, I ought to let the other council members know. I've got to alert the warden."

The image of a hulked-out Mishka raining hell down on us for getting the council involved flashes through my mind.

"I assure you this will all be handled, Poppy," Baltazar says. "May I personally keep you updated on developments?"

Poppy blows a huff of air then shakes her head. "Okay. Fine. Get what you need from her then let me know when it's over. I'll have to bring her in for questioning at some point. We can't have thieving prison guards."

Lucas nods. "We can bring her in for you."

"Sounds like a plan. I have a meeting in five minutes, so keep me in the loop. If you guys need anything, let me know. Okay?"

"One last thing," I say, "since you're the new Human-Wizard Liaison, could you tell Samuel Mayhew to leave me and my friends the hell alone? The DMA ambushed us today over Lucas."

She frowns. "I just got this job, and you want me to march into the next council meeting and demand we rein in the agency?"

My nostrils flare. "Yeah."

"I'll…mention it to the others. I've got to go guys, have fun tracking down your thief. And *do* call me and keep me updated."

We all mumble our agreement, and Baltazar gives her a smoldering gaze which makes her blush. Blech. She grabs her stack of papers then rushes out of the office. As soon as the door shuts, Baltazar glares at Lucas.

"Really? Do you think Hunter Bronwyn will go down without a fight? And we can't bring her in, she'll blab about Mishka and Nicolai."

Lucas returns a harsh gaze. "It's the right thing to do."

Baltazar approaches and flicks Lucas's chest. "That squishy heart of yours is going to get you killed one day."

"Guys," I slip the photo back into my wallet then place it in my back pocket, "why don't we swing by the prison, let the warden know that he has a criminal guard on his hands, and force Hunter to tell us where she's stashed Nicolai? Bonus, we can just throw her into a cell while we're there."

Baltazar's lips press into a thin line. "And have the press all over us? And without knowing if this woman is working at the behest of one of Mr. Tarasov's enemies? Are you insane? This is a PR disaster."

"I don't give a damn about PR, I need to find this kid before Hunter chops off another body part and mails it to Mishka. I need to finish this job, so I don't owe the man anything."

The Irishman rakes a hand through his dark hair. "I understand, Jack. But if we just show up at the prison island, she could run, or this could blow up in our faces, which will not help us find Nicolai."

Lucas walks over to the floor-to-ceiling window and looks out, where he could see the tall black tower which houses hundreds of rogue and criminal wizards. Built for wizards, by wizards. "She never made a ransom demand," the automaton says. "It's not about money for Hunter. This is personal, and she wants Mishka to suffer."

An idea comes to me. "Lucas, can you hack into the prison's computer system and get her work schedule? At least that way we can plan this out."

"Of course." He goes over to Poppy's laptop and does his magic.

"Remember the serum she used on Nicolai? I'm willing to bet she doesn't just buy potions in Scarletwood, she may very well live there as well. Let's try there first."

I nod in agreement. "Okay, let's do it. Lucas, do we have a home address for Hunter?"

"I've got it."

Baltazar gives me a quizzical look. "And how are we going to make it into Scarletwood? The DMA agents guarding the Gateway will shoot us on sight."

"I have a friend who'll help us with that." I gesture for them to follow me. It's time to call up Salvador Barraza.

19

Since we had a skirmish with the DMA at the cemetery and I tattled to Poppy about Samuel's ambush, I know that the secret government agency will tell me to screw off if I asked to use the Scarletwood Gateway in Griffith Park. Luckily, I can count on Sal to help us out, since he's one of their consultants and apparently Samuel likes him way more than me.

I check the time on my phone—4:00 p.m., and my belly rumbles on cue, reminding me that all I had were chocolates for lunch, and it's warning me that I had better get in a satisfying dinner. Maybe I can do so after this, assuming I survive another encounter with Hunter Bronwyn.

Baltazar is silent as he drives us up a winding road through the Santa Monica Mountains. After a stretch of time, he slows the Jaguar, parking off to the side. "Do you know much about faeries?" he asks in his Irish accent, unbuckling his seatbelt.

I shrug. "Just the basics. They like to be left alone, by both humans and wizards, but some of them don't mind mingling." My thoughts turn to the faeries in the Scarletwood forest, where they flit about, doing who knows what, leaving orange dust in their wake. Technically, the Cloaked Council forbade us to collect the dust, but some wizards keen on the black market sell faerie dust for medicinal and recreational purposes.

I stretch my aching arms as we exit the car and start our trek down a dusty trail. Lucas falls into step with Baltazar and gives him a curious look. "Mr. Maune, may I ask you a question?"

The wizard grins, and his amber eyes watch Lucas like a hawk. "Of course, and I will answer truthfully if I'm allowed to also ask you a question."

Lucas ponders the bargain. He slowly nods. "Yes. You have a deal."

Baltazar slips on his sunglasses. "Ask away, then."

"Am I correct in ascertaining that you are half-wizard, half-faerie?"

"Yes," he says without missing a beat or stuttering.

I glance at him as we climb over a rock. The grove of trees concealing the Gateway is just ahead. "Shouldn't you be a lot shorter, Baltazar?"

He smirks, taking my question in stride. "There are several races of faeries, and not all are like Olette, or the ones in the Scarletwood forest."

My interest is piqued. "So, where are the others? They left a long time ago, are they coming back?"

He shrugs. "I honestly don't know, though I won't cry over them if they don't."

"Why is that?" Lucas asks.

Baltazar taps his forehead. "Remember, my friend. One question, one answer. Now, I have something to ask you."

"Fair is fair," Lucas mumbles. "Ask me anything you would like."

"Whose heart beats in your chest? A random cadaver? A willing subject or victim of your master?"

Lucas's gaze darts between me and Baltazar.

A flicker of a smile passes my lips. "I would actually like to know as well, Tin Man. Not that I'll judge you for it."

"I'm afraid there's no gruesome or exciting story to tell about receiving my heart. As you know, Kenneth was a master of both technology and magic. He used his friend's heart, or rather, a clone of his heart, and placed it into my chest."

I let out a low breath. "Wow, who'd think that guy had friends. Especially one willing to let him clone his heart. So, was it someone from the academy?"

"He never told me," Lucas answers. "His laboratory partner apparently had a falling out with him right before I had gained consciousness, so I never met the man."

Baltazar takes off his sunglasses and slides them into his pocket. "We're getting to know all sorts of juicy things about each other. Here's the entrance, Jack. You said your friend would be here?"

"I'm here," Sal says in a low voice, stepping from the grove of trees and pushing a low-hanging branch away from his face. "Come on in."

Baltazar, Lucas, and I approach and step inside the grove. A regular human would only see an empty patch of grass in the center, but as wizards, a blood-red marble archway stands in the middle, as clear as day. The Gateway is just as I remember it, a tall strong door with a keyhole, and shimmering with magic. I notice that Sal is wearing a pair of technomancer shades, but they look different from the ones Samuel had.

I gesture toward the Gateway. "You can see it with the technomancer shades?"

He nods, adjusting the eyewear. "We make sure no one comes in or goes out. Well, except for right now."

I frown when I catch a few security cameras hanging from branches or attached to trees. There's a folding table to the left with a laptop sitting on it, along with monitoring equipment.

Baltazar notices the same things and turns to Sal. "I presume the cameras are all off?"

Sal looks slightly offended. "I've got the feed going on a loop so that it looks like the guys are still here with their lazy asses, just watching YouTube videos on the laptop. But, you'll need to go through quickly."

Lucas nods. "Well done, Salvador. Thank you."

"And where are the guards?" I ask.

Sal jerks his head to indicate the east side. "I had the guys break for dinner. Might've bribed them with free meals from my cousin's food truck. He makes these insane cheeseburgers."

"Oof," I say with a faux pained expression. "Don't talk about food right now. I'm starving."

Lucas heads over to the arch and holds up his hand, palm facing upward. A wisp of light manifests and hovers above his hand, and it shifts into a skeleton key. It's the same one he had used the last time we crossed the Gateway's threshold.

"Ready, Jack? Mr. Maune?" The automaton turns the key clockwise, and the shimmering door swirls with purple, blues, and yellows. A strong wind rustles the leaves of the nearby trees, and there's a soft groan as the arch opens to us.

Sal points to the open Gateway. "Oh, one more thing. We made an improvement to the Gateway. You'll land on the beach instead of in the water."

"Thanks." I give him a skeptical look, wondering how the agency was able to tinker with a wizarding Gateway. Lucas passes through, and Baltazar follows. I linger behind and face Sal. "Samuel ambushed us today in the Hollywood Forever Cemetery."

Sal's expression darkens. "So, that's why he had me over here on guard duty today. If I had been at the office—"

"I know. Just be careful with them. You may think you're working with them to keep people safe and go after that Society of Mystics cult, but the DMA didn't hire you just to be nice. Samuel, and whoever his higher-ups are...they have an agenda too."

"I'll be careful. You need to do the same too, okay?"

"Will do."

"And one last thing..." he reaches into his back pocket and

pulls out a metallic wristwatch and hands it to me. "Wear this. When you're done in Scarletwood, hit the button on the side and it'll transport you to a nearby trail here in Griffith Park. You won't have to worry about the guards here."

Transportation tech? My jaw nearly drops. The Theoretical Magic wizards at the academy would have a field day with this. Maybe I ought to start stealing things from the DMA. Would serve them right.

I let go of the thought and refocus on the task at hand. Sal and I fist bump then I turn and jump through the Gateway. My feet flail as the "ground" beneath me shifts and disappears. It's as if I'm falling through a dark cloud. Finally, I land on a sandy shore. The beach waves crash against the island, and just ahead I spot the familiar forest we need to pass through to make it into town.

"Glad you could join us," Baltazar says, observing the thick forest with a sense of admiration.

"The sun will set soon," Lucas warns. "Let's get into town and find Hunter Bronwyn's home."

We trek our way through the forest, climbing over fallen trees and sidestepping murky ponds. The trees are so tall and thick that it almost blocks out the sunlight, but then the otherworldly light from some of the exotic plants, as well as the wisps of light given off by the faeries native to this forest, provides enough illumination to help keep us on our path.

Several of the faeries fly and swirl in a group around Baltazar. They say something to him in their language, and he answers them back in kind. He then utters a few words in Gaelic, and his neck shimmers amethyst. Olette emerges, her bright orb of light outshining the others.

A wide smile spreads across Lucas's face. "The faeries say we are welcome here, and if we need any help, they are at our disposal. How splendid."

We continue trudging through the forest, the curious faeries trailing us and excitedly yapping in their language to Baltazar.

Olette zooms toward me and lands on my left shoulder. I glance down at her little shifting face, which isn't so creepy anymore.

"Are you related to these faeries? Or are they just friends?"

She gives a nod, indicating the latter.

"I guess they're nice, and when you're not trying to collect fees, so are you."

She lets out a laugh, then flutters over to Lucas and hovers next to his head.

We spot a clearing and head in that direction. As we exit the forest, the faeries speak to us again, I imagine telling us goodbye and, hopefully, good luck. Olette shifts from a bright amethyst orb of light as she returns to Baltazar's right shoulder. Her miniature feminine figure stands on him as if on the summit of a mountain, and she points ahead. She then shimmers and melds back into his neck.

"There is still some beauty in the town," Lucas says as we take in the view of the Mediterranean-style city. The buildings are painted white, with terracotta roofs and iron metalwork decorating the windows and balconies. Scarletwood was once like Grey Haven, a wizard city where one could take refuge, but the wrong sorts of wizards took it over, and it hasn't quite recovered since.

My chest tightens with tension as we enter town. My eyes are already roving the area, from the group of guys playing cards just outside the tavern to the drunkard who's taking a swig from his bottle and eyeing us suspiciously. I spot a couple of wealthy-looking wizards exiting a spell book shop, and two tall men who are leaning against the edifice of the trading post are watching me like I'm a criminal. Well, this is Scarletwood, where many of the wizards are criminals and outcasts. Not all, but many.

"Look," Lucas says, nodding toward the large estate to our left. "Damon Blackbird's mansion. It's still shut down."

I glance at the mansion gates, with two diamond shapes wrought in iron, positioned vertically, intersecting at the tips, and with a simple dot at the top, bottom, left, and right. It's the Blackbird family symbol.

"Why doesn't Zara want to live there?" I ask. "Damon's in the Obelisk of Qaveus and that guy's never getting out."

"She wants to be free, Jack. Even if it's in a tiny apartment in a new city."

I nod. Fair enough. "I understand what it's like to want to start fresh."

"Indeed," Baltazar interjects. "Lucas, how close are we to the hexwielder's house?"

"We need to make a right-hand turn at the corner, and it's down that stretch of road, number 423."

We make the turn and head down the road. There's a closed-down bakery to our left, and The Pits of Hell to our right. "We're definitely in the right place," I say.

The road twists and winds downward, to a piece of property where a small, lonely house sits at the end. It looks like it should be in a horror film. The three of us reach out with our magical senses, checking for wards or boobytraps. I pick up on at least three magical wards protecting the front door and the windows.

"How do we get through, without triggering an alarm?" I stop just a few feet from the front porch, just outside of the ward's range.

Lucas's eyes glisten in the daylight. "According to the work schedule, Hunter won't be home for another three hours."

Baltazar taps the side of his neck, where his Olette tattoo shimmers and shifts into an orb of light. "Would you be a dear and slip past those wards, let us know if Nicolai is in the house?"

Olette floats toward the front porch but stops near me. She rises into the air over the house, a crack of silver lightning hitting the front door. Goosebumps run down my arm as the wards bend in response, and Olette is able to slip through like an ant beneath a door crack. She morphs into an even tinier version of herself and goes through the front door's keyhole.

Baltazar turns and faces us with confidence. "If Nicolai is inside, we'll know."

After five minutes, Olette's familiar amethyst light emerges from the keyhole, returning to Baltazar. She says something to him in a disappointed tone.

He frowns, caressing her tiny cheek with his index finger. "Nonetheless, thank you."

"Nicolai's not there?" Lucas asks.

Baltazar shakes his head. "I'm afraid not."

The automaton's eyes brighten, and I can tell he's running some kind of analysis. "What are you thinking, Tin Man?"

"If he's not being held captive at her house, where else would she keep him?" The gleam leaves Lucas's eyes. "I think I've got it."

"Do tell," Baltazar prompts.

"On the day Nicolai went missing, the prison's records show that Hunter brought in a so-called prisoner named Jon Barley. I've just accessed the Council Hall records, and Mr. Barley is a two-year-old in Grey Haven."

Both Baltazar and I exchange glances. "Unless this is a demon child," I say, "it looks like we've got a stolen identity, she probably glamoured his appearance, and Nicolai is stuck somewhere in the Obelisk of Qaveus."

"Smart," Baltazar says. "Definitely not somewhere Mishka and his people would look."

Lucas faces us. "Our next step is to get inside the prison and free him, preferably when she's off duty and not present."

"I'll find us a way in," I say. "When is she scheduled to come home, Lucas?"

"Her current shift ends at midnight, and she has tomorrow off."

"Good," I say. "That'll give us time to get security clearance from Poppy and rescue Nicolai."

Baltazar inclines his head toward us. "Well, I'm going home

for a steak and a Moscato. I'll meet up with you in the morning, yes?"

I nod in agreement. "Sure. And please, update Mishka on this and make it sound good. I don't fancy being strangled in my sleep."

"Of course."

I turn my wrist and press the button on the metallic watch, just as Sal instructed me. A blaze of light surrounds the three of us, and a soft wave of energy passes through me like heat. The ground shifts beneath our feet, similar to passing through the Gateway, and suddenly we're on a dirt trail in Griffith Park, just as my friend said we'd be.

Baltazar shakes his head and steadies his stance, fighting off dizziness. "I daresay they need to tweak their teleportation watch. I feel like vomiting."

"Ew. Please don't," I say.

Lucas grins and waves at a figure approaching us from behind a tree. "Salvador, we're here."

"Great," he says. "Did you find what you were looking for?"

I shake my head. "But round two is tomorrow. We'll be ready."

"Thank you, Sal," Baltazar says. "Now, if nothing further is needed from me, I will get to my car and get the hell out of this park."

He waves goodbye to us and heads down the pathway, whistling to himself.

"Need a ride?" Sal asks Lucas and me.

"I would like to stop at the shop to see Zara," Lucas says.

"After that, we can swing by a fast-food joint and overdose on some chili fries," I say.

"That shit is gross," Sal says, pulling out his car key. "You need to start eating healthy, man."

Lucas chuckles. "He's right, you know. Your cholesterol level—"

"Hey, is this Gang Up On Jack Day? Let's go, I'm starving."

20

Sal mercifully acquiesced to my request for chili fries and I'm in the back seat of his Civic chowing down on my meal. The sun begins to set as we pull up to the front of Willy's Whimsies. I'm still wearing the transportation watch Sal gave me and take a moment to slide it off my wrist. Jamie Chamberlain would shower me with money and jewels if he could get his hands on this. As Sal parks and turns the engine off, I hand him the watch. Lucas is in the passenger seat, waiting patiently.

"Thanks again for the food, and the watch," I tell him.

He takes the watch and puts it on. "No problem, but if I find a single fry back there, I'm kicking your ass, wizard or not."

"Thank you for the ride, Salvador," Lucas says. "Jack, did you want to come in and say hello to Zara?"

"Nope."

"Very well. I will go in to see her, and you can finish clogging your arteries. I'll meet you back at the apartment."

"Sounds good to me. Tell Willy…and I guess Zara too…that I said hi."

Lucas slides out of the passenger side seat and closes the door behind him. We watch him walk into the shop.

"To your apartment, then?" Sal asks.

My phone rings in my pocket, and I pull it out and put it on speaker. "It's Alanna," I say to Sal.

"Hey, Alanna!" he yells.

Her voice is coated with laughter. "Hi, Sal. It's good to know you two are together. Jack, I heard about the ambush today…"

"I don't blame you, or Sal," I tell her. "Samuel really wants Lucas, and I told him to piss off. Something like this was expected, it just came at a crappy time. But I'll take care of it. Don't try to get involved or place yourself in the middle of it."

"Still," she says, "he shouldn't have done that. I'm sorry."

"It's okay."

"Well, the reason I'm calling is because I'll be busy at work all day tomorrow, and I'm not sure I'll be able to see you. I wanted to give you an early birthday present, if that's okay."

A knot forms in my stomach, and it's not because of the chili fries. My family died in a fire on my fifth birthday. It's a day I'm not keen on celebrating, and I don't even think I told her when it was. Willy or Lucas must've told her. Or, knowing Alanna, she probably got it from some DMA dossier.

"Uh, I…"

"Yeah, he's coming," Sal says loudly, leaning in, even though Alanna's on speaker. "Where you at?"

"I'm at my parents' home, in Altadena."

I glare at Sal, but then figure since she's close by, it wouldn't hurt to stop by and grab the gift, especially if she went through the trouble of purchasing it for me. "Okay, we just dropped Lucas off at the shop,"

"I know. I'm tracking Sal's car."

"You're actually kind of scary sometimes," the ex-Marine says.

"Text me the address and we'll be there," I tell her.

"Great! See you guys soon."

Darkness envelops the sky as we make it to the house a little after 7:30 p.m. Lush trees line the quiet street, and the Reid home sits nestled behind a hedge fence and wooden gate. I'm in the passenger seat, gazing at the place, my stomach tightening at the idea of receiving a gift from someone. What if I don't like it? Do I have to smile and pretend I do? What's the protocol? I never wanted to celebrate when I was young, even with Willy. She'd just take me on vacations and excursions, then give me a cake at the end. That was her gift to me. I suppose I'll have to see what Alanna has in store. At any rate, I don't plan on staying long anyway.

"You coming in?" I ask Sal as I stuff a few more fries into my mouth.

"Actually, I'm kind of tired." He does a piss poor job at faking a yawn. "But you go ahead, catch a ride when you're done."

"You can't just wait for me?" My voice is laced with suspicion.

He wriggles his eyebrows. "You might be there for a while, you know?"

I catch on to what he's implying. "Sal, it's not like that. She just has a gift for me."

"Yeah, a *gift*." He smiles.

"I mean, I like her...but as a friend." A very attractive friend. "Did...she say anything to you at the office?"

He just grins in response. "Let me know how it goes. I'm going home...I'm so tired." He fake-yawns again.

"You're an ass and a bad actor," I say with a chuckle. "Goodnight, Sal."

He takes the tray of chili fries from me. "Start thinking about your health, brujo."

"See you later." I exit the car, casting him a critical glance when he grabs a few fries and munches on them.

"*Adios!*" He starts the car and pulls off, barreling down the street and making a right turn.

144

I turn on my heel and approach the wooden gate, opening it then carefully closing it behind me. As I stroll up to the front door of the Spanish style home, I take in a deep breath then exhale before pressing the doorbell button.

It only takes a few seconds for a feminine, warm voice to assure me they're coming, and the door opens, revealing an elderly redhead, with blue eyes and a genuine smile. She's dressed like she's about to go audition for a classic Hollywood film, one of the black-and-white ones, and her hair is neatly curled.

"Hello, I'm Nancy. You're Jack, I presume?"

I smile and offer my hand. "Yes, nice to meet you, Mrs. Reid."

She shakes my hand then gestures for me to follow her inside. "The pleasure is all mine. Have a seat."

I plop down on the teal sofa and accept a mojito from her. I already like this woman. She grabs her drink then sits across from me, her eyes glittering with excitement. "I rarely meet anyone from Alanna's job. Even Samuel doesn't stop by as often, and he promised me he'd come play a game of gin rummy with me."

From the corner of my eye, I spot Alanna coming in, dressed casually in sweats and her hair in a low ponytail. She's carrying a charcuterie tray, and smiles at me in greeting as she sets it down on the coffee table. "Thanks for coming Jack, I know this is short notice."

"No problem," I say.

Nancy leans forward. "Are you Alanna's partner at the DMA, Jack?"

Alanna shakes her head. "You know I don't like partners, Mom. Jack has worked with me before, and he's a good guy."

Mrs. Reid raises her glass to me in salute. "Well, if you can put up with her this far, kudos to you."

Alanna's face tightens. "Mom, not right now."

"She gave me a pamphlet today, Jack." Nancy takes a sip

from her half-full glass and furtively glances in Alanna's direction.

"Oh. Good, I guess?" I watch Alanna frown then backtrack. "Or...not."

Nancy rolls her eyes. "She wants to hire a private nurse for me. It's an insult. I won't be free in my own home."

Alanna leans over to me and says in a low voice, "She has mild dementia, it will be good for her. She needs this, but she's so stubborn."

I nod in understanding and give Alanna a look of sympathy.

Nancy sits up straight. "I'm as sharp as a tack. I bet I could beat you in gin rummy, Jack."

"I bet you can't." I gaze at her in a silent challenge and grab a few grapes from the charcuterie board.

Alanna's lips curve into a smile at our exchange. "Let me go get your present," she says, rising from her seat and heading upstairs.

The deck of playing cards is already on the table, as if she had been waiting for Samuel, or anyone, to play a round with her. She sets aside her drink and slides them out of the package and starts dealing the cards.

"Are you really DMA?" she asks, finishing up her distribution of ten cards each.

I grab mine and take a look at my hand. "I'm more of a freelancer."

One they'd like to put a bullet in, but I'll leave that part out.

"You're a wizard, though." She nods for me to go first.

"Alanna told you?" I take an upcard from the discard pile.

"No. I can just tell. You can't be married to a DMA agent for years without picking up on a few things."

I let out a low breath, not sure if I'm impressed or intimidated. "Point taken, Mrs. Reid."

She takes the top card from the stockpile. "Told you, I'm as sharp as a tack."

Alanna comes downstairs with a wrapped gift box. She sits

next to me on the sofa and hands it to me, while I mentally prepare to smile at a wristwatch or gift card.

"Happy early birthday," she says.

Nancy beams at me. "Happy birthday..." her smile falters, "I'm quite sorry, you said your name was what again?"

A stung expression flashes across Alanna's features, but she sucks it up and puts on a strong face. "Mom, it's getting late. I'll take you upstairs, okay?"

"But I'm not done with my game, and it's rude to just leave our guest."

"I don't mind," I say, carefully placing my cards down on the table. "Maybe I can come by again for another game?"

Nancy sighs and places her cards down. She rises to her feet, her expression a mix of confusion and sadness. "You will come again, won't you?"

"Why wouldn't I? You're an angel." I grin at her.

Nancy chuckles as Alanna approaches and offers her arm. "You hear that, pumpkin? He says I'm an angel."

"You are." Alanna plants a kiss on the top of her mother's head. She stands nearly a foot taller than the elderly woman. "I'll be right back, Jack."

"Goodnight, Nancy."

She loops her arm in with Alanna's and heads for the staircase with her. "Goodnight, my friend. I wish to see you again."

As they head upstairs, my phone vibrates, and I take it out to check if it's Baltazar telling me to escape to the airport while I still can. It's just a text from Sal, asking how I'm doing and if he's interrupting anything. I quickly text him back that I've been playing cards with Mrs. Reid and eating grapes. I also add that I've got my present sitting on my lap. When he replies with a few choice emojis, I bid him goodnight and put my phone away.

My attention returns to the medium-sized gift box, and I pick it up and jiggle it, trying to guess what's inside. Alanna jogs down the steps and I wait for her to re-join me on the sofa. I offer her a sympathetic smile, knowing it must be hard trying to navigate her mom's health issue and things going on with work.

"I'm sorry," she says.

I wave a hand through the air. "Don't be, it's no problem. I like your mom."

She gestures toward the box. "I wasn't sure if you wanted to open it now or tomorrow when it's officially your birthday."

"I'll open it now," I say, unwrapping the yellow ribbon and tearing the wrapping paper.

I open the outer gift box then reach inside to grab a small, sleek wooden box. It has both the phoenix symbol of the Cloaked Council and the DMA logo with the agency's acronym spread across the scales of justice.

"What's this?" I ask with genuine interest.

"Go on," she says. "Open it."

I click the box open and inside are two medals. One in gold from the Cloaked Council, and the other made of onyx from the DMA. A small certificate nestled above the medals reads:

The Supreme Cloaked Council of the United States, and the
Department of Metaphysical Affairs
of the United States, jointly acknowledge Jack Crowley as an honored
civilian and defender
of both wizards and humans. He has saved countless lives through his
bravery
and demonstrated the fortitude, strength, and compassion
for others that we wish to live by, so that we may forge a better world.

I take in a quick breath but can't seem to get it out. I re-read the certificate. Never thought something like this would mean anything to me, but after spending years being treated as an outcast and having been falsely accused of murder, to get

something like this from both the Cloaked Council and DMA…
well, it's a hell of a lot better than a watch or gift card.

Alanna gives a little whisk of a smile. "I put in a request for it
a while ago. I still have Poppy's contact information, and I
begged her for it, and I lobbied Samuel too. You deserve this, an
official recognition that you're a hero, Jack."

"Thanks," I finally get out as I exhale. I wrap an arm around
her shoulder and give her a side hug. "Really, thank you. I
appreciate it."

"I mean, after what happened at the Hollywood Forever
cemetery, he may want to take that back…"

We both laugh, but it's cut short when we hear a thud and
crash from upstairs. Alanna jumps from her seat and runs
toward the staircase, and I get up and quickly follow, hoping
that we don't have a repeat of Hunter Bronwyn stalking me to
my friends' homes. Because if the hexwielder is here, intending
to harm Alanna or Nancy…I just might have to do what Mishka
has been wanting me to all along.

21

We make it upstairs, and down the dark hallway, a light is on in the third room on the left. We carefully approach, stepping lightly. Alanna halts at a stand with a tall vase, reaches behind the stand, and pulls out a combat knife.

I eye her with surprise. "So, you usually have knives hidden around here?"

She shrugs. "Perks of growing up in my family."

We approach the room with its door ajar, and Alanna reaches the door first and pushes it fully open. She lets out a sigh of relief, setting the combat knife aside and gesturing for me to join her. Nancy is sitting next to a pile of boxes, one of which has tumbled to the floor and spilled its contents. Some letters, photo albums, and old VHS tapes litter the floor, but Nancy doesn't seem to care as she's sitting with her legs folded beneath her, admiring an open photo album set on her lap. It looks like her wedding photos with Alanna's dad.

"Mom," Alanna says, "I was worried you were hurt or something. You're supposed to be in bed."

"I'm not sleepy." She wistfully glances at another photo and caresses Mr. Reid's face with her forefinger. "I miss him so much. Jack, you would've loved Martin."

"I'm sure he would've," Alanna says, gently helping her mother to stand. The older woman clings to the photo album.

"I've made a bit of a mess." Nancy glances down at the fallen box and its contents on the floor."

"We'll clean it up, Mom. Please, just get some rest."

Nancy hugs the photo album. "Fine, but I'm taking this with me."

"Goodnight," I say in a soft voice as I drop to my knees and turn the box upright. I scoop up a pile of papers and carefully place them back inside.

"Sweet dreams, Jack." Nancy rebuffs Alanna's attempt to guide her out the room, swatting her hand. "I can find my bedroom. I'm not that far gone."

Once Nancy exits, Alanna shuts the door behind her and presses her back against the door, squeezing her eyes shut and looking as if she wants to curse. "I'm hiring a nurse, ASAP. I've been here with her all week, and I'm afraid to go back to my apartment in Redondo Beach. If something happens and I'm not here—"

"Hey, she'll be okay," I assure her. "She's got you looking out for her, and I'm sure at first she'll be pissed at having a nurse, but if you find the right one, they'll hit it off, play gin rummy, and gossip about stuff."

She smirks. "Let's clean this up so we can get you out of here. I doubt you want to be stuck here all night."

She joins me and grabs the other photo albums, stuffing them back into the box. I swipe one of the VHS tapes. "Ooh, this is old school. This is all your parents' stuff?"

"Mostly my dad's. This used to be his home office. After he died, mom was never the same, and she just threw his belongings here and closed the door. I'm actually surprised she came in here tonight, because we both avoid this room."

I grab a loose photo and stick it into one of the albums in the box. "Too many memories, huh?"

"Yeah."

I turn the VHS tape over and look at the label. "Hey, this has Lucas's name on it."

She nods. "Yeah, back when my dad first took Lucas in, he recorded some interactions and training sessions. He documented it all for the agency."

"These are his copies?"

She opens her hand and I give it to her so she could examine it. "Samuel has official copies in his office. I guess this might be the raw footage he took. I would think he would've sent this off to headquarters."

"Maybe there's a reason he wanted to keep his own copies?" I give her a knowing look.

She gives me a critical eye. "I know you're mad at Samuel, but please don't go conspiracy theorist on me."

"Let's check it out, is all I'm saying. Besides, I want to finish my mojito."

She glances down at the VHS tape. "Well, why not. Maybe it'll help Lucas with those gaps in his memory."

We grab all the tapes and head downstairs to the living room. She has to take a dusty VCR player from the coat closet but sets it up quickly and pops in the first tape. Alanna joins me on the couch, grabbing some cheese from the charcuterie and absent-mindedly munches on it. She's sitting awfully close to me. If we weren't reviewing footage from her father's arsenal of secret government tapes, this would almost feel like a date.

She lifts an eyebrow and stares at me. "Why are you looking at me like that?"

I quickly face the television and stare forward. "No reason. Look, it's starting."

A tall, broad-shouldered man with thick brows and wearing a plaid shirt and a pair of glasses appears on screen. By the look of his surroundings, he's in a garage. "I am Agent Martin Reid of the Department of Metaphysical Affairs, and today is March 5, 1988. And today..." He turns the camera to show Lucas sitting in a chair, watching him with interest. "Today, I got a robot. And it's bitchin', as the kids would say."

Alanna snickers at her father's words, mesmerized by seeing him alive and joyfully speaking.

The camera turns back to Martin and closes on his face. "But it's not just any robot. He's an automaton." He positions the camera on either a tripod or steady surface then grabs a folding chair, pulling it up and sitting across from Lucas.

"What's your name, buddy?"

Lucas blinks and smiles. "I have no name, but I am at your service, Agent Reid."

Martin leans forward, steepling his fingers. "You look human, you talk human, but your maker didn't give you a name?"

"No," he answers.

Martin quirks an eyebrow. "Well, let's give you one. I've got to call you something. What do you think of the name Lucas?"

"Lucas is a good name, sir."

He shrugs. "All right. Lucas it is. So, are the modifications I made okay? Do you feel any pain or discomfort?"

"I don't feel physical pain. I am fine."

"So, you acknowledge me?"

"Yes."

"Okay, good, because I would hate to wake up with a pillow over my face." He chuckles. "What is your purpose, Lucas? Why did Kenneth Cherish create you?"

"To serve my master and help usher in the Great Endeavor."

Martin tilts his head slightly and rubs his chin. "Now what's that?"

"You are not authorized to access that information."

"Okay, maybe we can broach that topic at another time. So, how much robot are you, how much magic are you, and how *human* are you?"

"I'm comprised of metal, artificial but realistic flesh, I have a computerized central core as my brain, and a cloned, beating human heart. I am both machine and magic, and I am primed to absorb, understand, and interact with human emotions and behavior."

"One more question—if I were to let you go today, would you want to leave? Would you like to be free?"

Lucas studies him for a few moments. "I don't quite understand, Agent Reid."

"Perhaps one day you will, Lucas."

Alanna pauses the video and holds up another tape. "Look at the date on this one, I must've been five or six years old."

She ejects the first video tape and puts in the second. This one has a young Alanna, wearing a princess dress and faerie wings. "Come on, Lucas! You're my faerie knight!"

The automaton strolls into view wearing a ridiculous knight's helmet that fits lopsided and he's carrying a toy lance. "I fail to see the purpose of this," Lucas says.

"It's all about using your imagination, buddy," Martin's voice says from behind the camera. "Just think of what it would be like, a knight in shining armor."

Lucas faces the camera with a matter-of-fact look. "If we were really battling dark faeries, Miss Alanna would be a liability. She has no magic."

I chuckle and Alanna pauses the video. "I'm glad you find that humorous," she says with a smirk.

I sort through the tapes and find one that I think might interest us both. "Hey, you said your dad died in 2008?"

"Yes, why?" She gets up and ejects the video tape.

"If this date is correct," I say, tossing it to her, "then this might be the last one he recorded."

She freezes, as if seeing a ghost. Her fingers tighten around the tape. I don't blame her, because her father didn't just have a heart attack or pass away peacefully in his sleep. DMA found him with a supposed self-inflicted bullet in his head, and after that they found "evidence" of his corruption and made him out to be a traitor to the organization and his country. Alanna puts the tape in, slowly approaches me, and plops down onto the sofa next to me, grabbing a throw pillow and hugging it.

The video starts; it's evening, and it looks like Martin's backyard, as I can spot part of this house in the frame. Martin is standing with Lucas and has a long, rectangular case sitting on top of a table and proceeds to open it. Lucas watches with interest.

"Now, as you know my father William served in the second World War, and he brought back something with him, and I was going to keep it in the garage, maybe hang it above my fireplace or something, until tonight…when something triggered it, and it began glowing like a beacon."

Lucas frowns. "Martin, it's a tracking spell. Someone, a wizard, is looking for the sword tonight."

Martin carefully lifts the sword from its case and displays it for the camera, a gorgeous Damascus steel blade with a golden cross-guard, leather-wrapped hilt, and a small emerald in the center of the pommel.

"This is Witchbane, and it looks like someone wants it. Badly. I've just called the agency to let them know I might be having visitors."

"Dad?" A teenage Alanna approaches from the house's back door. "Walter's here to see you."

Martin places Witchbane back into its case and closes it. He pulls out a key and locks it. His thick brows furrow with uneasiness. "Wait here, baby girl."

He goes back inside, and Alanna approaches the camera and turns it toward her face. "What are you guys up to tonight, Lucas?"

"Trying to figure out who's tracking your grandfather's sword, and why."

Young Alanna's making silly faces into the camera. "Hey, Uncle Samuel! If you see this, tell my dad to raise my allowance…by like, a thousand percent."

"Alanna, that's an inappropriate request, we're trying to make an official record of this."

She quickly puts the camera back in place when Martin returns with a short, balding man in a suit.

"Are you sure it's being tracked, Martin?"

He nods. "Are the guys coming?"

Walter eyes the rectangular box and nods. "Yeah, they should be here soon."

"Thanks, Walter."

His lips curve into a wry smile. "I'm your partner. Of course I'll show up to see if a dangerous wizard is coming for your magic sword."

Martin lets out a nervous chuckle. He pulls out his key and unlocks the case, flipping the top open. Young Alanna stares at the Damascus steel sword, which pulses with a light blue aura. She brushes a hand against it and gasps.

"Dad, I feel something. I think the sword is alive."

"Careful, honey," he says.

Walter's face screws up in concentration, and he takes a few quick breaths. He quietly draws his gun while Martin's facing Alanna. "I'm sorry, Martin..."

He aims straight for the back of Martin's head and pulls the trigger, but Martin pivots just in time, the bullet missing his head by a centimeter. Alanna screams and Lucas quickly pulls her into a bear hug and turns around with her, shielding her from another two shots. Martin charges Walter, knocking him to the ground, both men now off camera.

"Why are you doing this?" Martin growls. A physical struggle can be heard. Another shot rings out.

"I'm sorry! She said I had to do it!" The sound of one more shot cuts through the air, and the scuffle and heavy breathing of the two men end. Martin stumbles, disoriented, toward Alanna and Lucas. A wild look takes over his face.

"Lucas, take Alanna, call Nancy at her sister's and tell her to stay in place…" He shudders and swings around, firing a round toward a dark figure approaching.

"I have crushed the heads of human warriors and battle wizards alike. Do you think your gun will stop me?" a female voice, dripping with contempt, says to him.

Lucas is trying to comfort a weeping Alanna, while still shielding her. His eyes widen as he looks over his shoulder and identifies the intruder. "Ora Draper…you should be dead."

A tall, raven-haired woman dressed in black comes into view. Her violet eyes are cold and piercing. "I want my sword. The one your father stole from me."

Alanna's dad trains the gun on her, aiming straight for her face, but then his entire body seizes, and he cries out in pain. His hand trembles as an invisible force makes him turn the gun on himself, the pistol pressing into his temple. He regains control momentarily, a desperate push of his will, but then Ora's control wins out and the end of the barrel is back against his head. His eyes widen in horror.

"Close your eyes, Alanna…" he says.

"Daddy!"

A final shot rings out, and Martin falls to the ground. Young Alanna slumps to the floor, trembling and sobbing.

Lucas's eyes flash with anger. He rushes toward Ora, his hands ablaze with his pale-yellow magic, but the dark wizard makes a diagonal cut with her right arm, and a violet-black energy tears and crushes his torso. He hits the ground, and Ora walks up and presses the long, thin heel of her stiletto straight into his eye.

"Lucas!" Alanna screeches, forcing herself to stand again and lean against the table with the sword case.

Ora twists her foot, and electrical sparks burst near Lucas's injured eye and his mouth. He lays on the floor, motionless. The dark wizard's blood-red lips curl into a grin as she observes Alanna.

"Quit your yowling, you little brat, and I may let you live."

Alanna's grief-stricken face contorts into one of rage. She reaches for Witchbane and grabs it, holding it up in a defensive position against Ora.

The woman laughs at her. "Such tenacity...such a waste." She flicks her hand, and Alanna drops the sword and flies backward, crashing against something and landing on the ground, unconscious. Ora's gaze is fixed on Witchbane though, and she kneels to pick up the enchanted sword. However, the moment she touches it, the light blue aura zaps her like lightning, and she recoils.

Ora rubs her injured hand and sneers. "Listen, you little bitch! I own you."

The light blue aura grows and expands, forming into the silhouette of a woman, who then takes on a flesh and blood appearance: long brown hair, piercing gray eyes, and wearing faerie tribal garments. She hisses at Ora.

"*Neth*," the dark wizard says with an all too familiar authority, "*spiritus Witchbane...*"

Holy hell.

Ora Draper, one of the notorious Three Sisters, is a freaking True Name wizard.

The spirit of Witchbane, Neth, opens her mouth and screeches, sending a whirlwind of magic and blasting wind toward Ora. The dark wizard crosses her arms into a defensive x-position in front of her, and she slides backward, trying not to bend or fall beneath Neth's onslaught. Where Ora's magic is precise and steady, Neth's is wild and unpredictable.

Several sirens fill the night air, and men shouting can be heard. Ora's deadly gaze is set on Neth once more, but the dark wizard seems to weigh her options then decides to bolt. Neth growls, promising the dark wizard another battle should she ever see her again. The spirit finally glances down at Martin, and her eyes fill with tears. She shimmers and turns back into a phantom of light, then seeps back into the sword.

After a few seconds, Samuel Mayhew runs into view with his

gun drawn and wearing technomancer shades. Several DMA agents accompany him. He drops to his knees and grits his teeth, feeling Martin's neck for a pulse.

"Martin…"

"Chief Mayhew!" an agent yells. "His daughter's alive."

"Take her to the infirmary," he says, placing a hand on Martin's head and uttering a quick prayer.

"Looks like he killed Walter Moore," a nearby agent in tactical gear says.

Samuel glares at the man and looks poised to spring to his feet and punch him. "Martin wouldn't do this. This doesn't make sense."

An agent passes across the camera's view with an unconscious Alanna cradled in his arms.

"We should trash the automaton," another agent suggests.

"No, I'll take the robot and that sword." Samuel's eyes water, but he refuses to let a single tear fall. His gaze slowly turns toward the camera. "Is that thing on?"

A female agent grabs it and checks. "Yep."

"I need to review it. Leave it with me, Sheldon."

The screen goes black.

Alanna's curled up against me, tears rolling down her cheeks. Her chest rises as she inhales a deep breath then lets it out. "All these years, they said he killed Walter and himself…but it was her."

I slowly place an arm around her and draw her in. "I'm sorry. Now, I guess you know the truth."

She wipes her eyes with the back of her hand. "Most of it, at least. Now I need to ask Samuel if he's the one who fixed Lucas and had my memory altered. And, I need to find Witchbane. That sword is mine, Jack. And I'm going to run Ora Draper through with it if it's the last thing I do."

22

After hanging out with Alanna for another hour or so and warding the house, I finally say goodbye and order myself a ride home. During the entire trip, all I can think about is how the pieces Alanna was trying to fit together finally fell into place in an unfortunate way. A painful way. And Samuel, he looked genuinely sad at losing Martin; the two men must've been close, at least close enough for teenage Alanna to call him uncle.

I take out my phone and text her, asking her if she needs me to accompany her when she confronts Samuel, or when she even plans to do it. She texts back and reminds me that Samuel is looking to have my head on a pike, and that she'll talk to him about it and try to smooth things over between me and the DMA director. My thoughts also turn toward Ora Draper, the powerful wizard who led the Dark Coven. The disgraced and deceased Cloaked Council member, Marco Welling, had said that the coven was alive and well, but they've been laying low this entire time—with the exception of Ora waltzing into the Reid home and demanding Witchbane. I'm gonna have to talk to Willy about this, since she was one of the Three Sisters, before repenting and escaping her former life.

The car slows to a stop in front of my apartment building. I scroll through my phone and add a tip for the driver, thanking him as I slide out of the backseat. I begin wondering if I even need a car at this point, with all the rides I've been getting. As I approach the building entrance, I cradle my gift box with the medals in my arm, and to my surprise, my mouth widens in a grin. I stifle a yawn as I pass through the 1930's style lobby and enter the elevator, hitching a ride up to the 8th floor.

As I step out and head down the hallway, I spot Lucas standing near #815, talking to my number-one fan, Desmond. The automaton seems engaged in a deep conversation with the ten-year-old kid, and I shake my head and chuckle at the sight. It's kind of charming. For all the data and info that robot's been able to collect on humanity and process, both the good and the bad, he still has this contagious excitement about life.

Desmond turns and greets me. "Hey, Jack!" He then crosses his arms and gives me a wink and nod, assuring me that he's still keeping my secret that I have superpowers.

"Hey kid," I say, approaching and giving him a high-five. "It's kind of late, shouldn't you be in bed or something?"

As if on cue, the door to his apartment opens and his dad pokes his head out. "Desmond, come on! We've got twenty minutes left, then you've really got to get to bed."

Desmond leans toward me. "My mom's working late, so Dad's been playing video games with me all night. But I'm going to jump into bed soon, so she doesn't suspect a thing."

"I've just accessed the building's security cameras," Lucas interjects. "She just parked and is now heading up."

His eyes widen with a glimmer of mischief. He turns and scurries toward his father. "She's coming! She's coming!"

Once their door shuts, I fall into step with Lucas and head toward my apartment. "And how does Desmond know you can access cameras?" I ask, giving Lucas a side eye.

"He doesn't. I just told him that so he would get to bed. Did you know that six to twelve-year-olds need up to ten hours of sleep per night? It's Wednesday, and he has school tomorrow."

We stop at my door, and I pull out my key. "Yeah, but tomorrow's Halloween. He's just going to eat a bunch of candy at school and probably puke."

"Sounds exciting," the automaton says.

I open the door, and the question pops into my head of how Lucas made it back. Did he get dropped off, or did he super-run all the way from the shop? That would be a sight to see. Unfortunately, my silent question is answered when I flip the light switch and step inside—Zara Wilson, along with baby Charlie and apparently a birthday cake, are sitting in my living room.

"Surprise!" Zara exclaims.

Charlie just drools and sticks his hand in my cake.

Lucas shuts the door behind me, and I give him a quick glare. "You let her in? Now the wards won't work on her."

Zara picks Charlie up and places him on her hip. "You ingrate, I'm trying to apologize and make peace. I made the cake myself." She gestures toward it with a flourish of her hand.

"Great, you're trying to poison me." I set aside my keys, wallet, and gift box, and approach the dining table.

"Jack," Lucas says, "she really worked hard on the cake."

"Plus," she rummages through her diaper bag sitting on a chair and hands me an envelope, "I got you a little something."

I accept it from her. "Thanks."

"Really, Jack, I want us to be friends. You and Willy are the only wizards I know out here, at least the only ones who'll accept me."

I consider her words, knowing all too well what it's like to be considered different or even dangerous. I decide to stop being an ass and really give her a chance. "So, you made that cake yourself?"

She smiles and nods. "Chocolate."

After destroying those chili fries and snacking at Alanna's, I'm quite full, but I return her smile and reach for a plate and utensils, so I can cut myself a small slice.

"Oh!" Lucas halts me. "First, we must sing Happy Birthday."

"Really?" I frown.

Zara starts swaying from side-to-side with Charlie. She and Lucas sing to me, and Charlie babbles and hums along with them. At first, I feel a little awkward about it, because after I came to live with Willy, I never really had a proper birthday party. I always kept to myself as a kid and didn't have many friends. But watching my robot buddy, Zara, and little Charlie sing to me, it felt genuine, and like my little tribe might just be getting bigger.

Lucas uses his elemental powers to light the candles, and I let Charlie help me blow them out. After cake and a little chit-chat, the little one gets fussy, and Zara takes it as a sign to wrap up her visit and head out.

"It was nice seeing you, Jack." She approaches and plants a kiss on my cheek while holding Charlie. He tries to lean in and do the same, but he just slobbers on my face, looking mighty proud of himself.

"Thanks," I say, wiping my wet cheek with the back of my hand. "You're going to be at the shop tomorrow?"

She nods. "I'll remember not to use your favorite mug."

I wave a hand through the air. "Nah. It's fine. I'll see you later, Zara."

"I'll walk you down to your car." Lucas shoulders the diaper bag, and it reminds me of the video footage of him taking care of little Alanna and playing with her. Martin Reid did a damn good job with him. I'll have to tell Lucas about the tapes once he returns to the apartment.

After waving a final goodbye to Zara and her baby, I go over and sink into the couch, putting my feet up on the coffee table. What a day. Despite the emotional revelation surrounding Martin Reid's death, and seeing only a portion of Ora Draper's power, I know there's a lot to deal with. Oddly enough, I'm actually in a better mood than I would've thought. I guess that's a perk of having friends, people who I know I can lean on and vice versa.

Maybe my birthday doesn't have to be a painful memory of how I lost my parents and little sister. I can start making new memories, not to replace them, but to add to the joy that I used to feel with them. Getting all nostalgic makes me think of that silver keepsake box Master Valerio gifted me after I faced down the dark wizard, Marco Welling. Valerio had said it contained items from my father. My dad was into Theoretical Magic, always tinkering with machines and magic, even spending weekends in his modest lab in our basement. But that one fateful night, one of his experiments had gone too far, he lost control, and an explosion consumed everyone and everything on our property—except me. Having been born with both True Name and elemental abilities, natural fire doesn't harm me the way it harms non-elemental wizards and humans.

I get up and go to my room, where under my bed sits a sigil on the floor, which conceals a compartment. I bend down and reach under my bed, pressing my hand against the rose symbol drawn into the hardwood floor.

"*Sub Rosa...*" I whisper.

The rose symbol glows softly, and a square of pure light forms, revealing the silver keepsake box. I reach in, grab it, and take it back with me into the living room. After settling back onto the couch, I flip open the box and peer at the items inside: a few pictures of my father at the Akashic Academy, a pair of technomancer shades, a satchel filled with a few enchanted gems, a notebook, and an odd-looking calculator.

My attention snaps toward the front door when Lucas finally enters. I wave him over to the couch. "Hey buddy, looks like we won't need to use the Memoriae with Alanna anymore."

"What do you mean?" he asks.

I tell him everything—about the video tapes, the truth about Martin's final night, and how Lucas had been brave enough to shield Alanna and try to protect her against Ora

Draper, who dealt him a severe blow. Lucas's expression changes nearly ten times as I unfold everything for him, and for a moment it looks as if he's close to crying, which I don't even think I've ever seen him do. Finally having the gaps filled in means a lot to him, and when I finish explaining everything and fall silent, he hangs his head and sits still for a minute, taking it all in.

"Thank you for telling me, Jack. I appreciate it."

"I know, Tin Man."

"Is Alanna all right? Should I call her?"

"She's probably asleep by now, but I placed a ward around the house, so she and Nancy should be safe for now."

"Good." He stares ahead, deep in thought.

"As if that weren't enough, I finally opened that silver box from Master Valerio and found this…" I show off the items in the box then hand him the weird calculator. "Do you know what this is?"

He examines the metallic, rectangular device. It has a small screen and several buttons. Some of them have numbers, and other buttons show mystical symbols. "This is a cryptograph, Jack."

"What does it do? Apparently, it belonged to my father while he was at the Akashic Academy."

Lucas holds up the bottom end of the metallic device, slightly slanted. "Do you see this tab at the bottom? Pull it out."

I follow his instructions and the tab detaches from the device, and I notice a cord attached to the tab. "It's like an adapter or auxiliary cord."

Lucas holds out his right hand and extends his index finger. The tip of his finger partially detaches and opens, revealing a small network of electrodes and sensors. I attach the "tab" to his open finger, which fits perfectly with a click. The cryptograph turns on, and a series of numbers run through its screen until they all end in a row of zeros.

My jaw slackens. "Holy hell. Do you see this?"

"More importantly, why was this in your father's possession?"

I grab the photo from the keepsake box, the one with my dad at the academy. He's in a group photo with about a dozen wizards, but the one who sticks out the most is Kenneth Cherish. I turn the photo over to the back. There's a handwritten note, similar to what someone would scribble in a yearbook. I read it out loud.

"Best wishes to my friend Robert Crowley. May we continue to push the boundaries of science and magic and succeed in the Great Endeavor."

"Jack…" Lucas stares at me.

"And it's signed by Kenneth." And Kenneth called him his friend. Another question comes to mind. "Lucas, didn't you say your heart was cloned from a friend of Kenneth's?"

Lucas's eyes widen. "You are correct. Oh my, I believe what I'm feeling now is awkwardness."

"You're telling me. Now I really want to find this guy."

"Oh! His note!" Lucas hands me the cryptograph and uses his free hand to take the note with Master Valerio's coordinates on it. "Remember Valerio gave this to us? Type the numbers into the cryptograph."

I grab the piece of paper and carefully type in the numerical sequence, a string of fourteen numbers. I hit the ENTER button, expecting a fifteenth number to pop up at the end of the sequence. This would allow us to actually map the coordinates. However, instead of a number, an X shows up.

"Is it supposed to do that?" I ask.

"I know where this is." Lucas's voice is slightly shaky. "It's the Nowhere Dimension."

"Nowhere Dimension? Who the hell would want to go there?"

He shrugs. "Kenneth Cherish, apparently."

The only time I ventured into the Nowhere Dimension was when I was forced into it by Damon Blackbird, and I needed to rescue Sal from there. It's not a Gateway, and it doesn't lead to a city like Grey Haven or Scarletwood. Some wizards have speculated that it's a plane of existence between life and death, temporal existence, and eternity—kind of like the Akashic realm. But it's dangerous. So dangerous that those who've tried to stay there for an extended amount of time have either gone crazy or fallen off the edge of the Nowhere Dimension and disappeared. But these coordinates are telling us to go there. Just great.

"What will we do, Jack?"

I bite my lower lip and think. "Let's get some rest, go rescue Nicolai tomorrow, then we'll figure out what to do about this."

I detach the cryptograph cord and place the device back into the keepsake box.

Lucas's eyes are downcast. "I'm sorry I have your father's cloned heart, Jack. I didn't know."

"Besides it being weird and me still trying to wrap my head around it," I say, closing the box, "I couldn't think of anyone else who deserves it."

"Thank you," he says.

"Okay Tin Man, I need to sleep. We're going to rescue Nicolai tomorrow."

23

Today's Halloween. Happy birthday to me.

After rolling out of bed and taking a shower, I walk into the living room to find Lucas standing at the window near the dining table, watching the sunrise. There's a content look on his face, as if he's at peace. Sometimes I wonder what he thinks about, or what the process of thinking is even like for him. He doesn't eat or sleep, but does he dream?

"Good morning," he says, facing me. "Would you like breakfast?"

"I'm cool." I pull up a chair and cut a slice of Zara's cake from last night. Not the healthiest choice for my first meal, but it's tasty.

I take a moment from chowing down on cake to open Zara's envelope. It's a card from her, wishing me a happy birthday, along with a hundred-dollar bill and a light sprinkle of faerie dust. Sweet.

My phone rings, but it's on the other side of the apartment sitting on a stand near the front door. Lucas's eyes gleam and he picks up the call for me—how, I have no clue—and I hear a loud beep then Baltazar's voice through Lucas's ears, as if on speaker phone.

"Jack! Happy birthday...toooo you..." he sings in an overly sultry tone.

"Thanks, what do you want? Are you on your way?"

"Actually, I think we need to make a slight alteration to our plan."

"What happened?" I take another bite of cake.

"At 6:00 a.m. this morning, our little Jon Barley prisoner was supposedly transferred out of the Obelisk of Qaveus and released to the Yara halfway house. I checked up on it, and Yara hasn't had a transfer from the prison since last month."

"So, Hunter moved Nicolai out of Qaveus?"

"She might have. Or this could be a ploy and he's still at the prison."

"Ah, so you want us to split up?"

"Correct. You and Lucas can go to the tower to see if he is in fact still there, and Olette and I will go to Hunter's house in Scarletwood. We'll keep each other updated."

I nod. "Sounds like a plan, but what about the Scarletwood Gateway? We're still on DMA's naughty list."

"I will find a way, I assure you."

"Okay. Let me know if you need any help."

"I'll keep you posted. *Ciao*."

"Bye."

The loud beep sounds again, and the call ends. Lucas's eyes return to normal. "It's still weird to me how you're able to do that, Tin Man."

"One of the advantages of being an automaton."

I chuckle. "Sure, buddy."

There's a knock on the door, and I groan. It's too early for visitors, and I've got a prison to go visit. "This had better not be Master Valerio," I say under my breath as I approach the door and look through the peephole.

I don't know which is worse—Valerio or Samuel Mayhew.

The DMA director is standing at my front door, alone,

wearing a somber expression. "I know you're home, Jack. I'm by myself. No tricks, no gimmicks. I want to talk."

"Really? Where have I heard that one before?"

He lets out a low breath. "It's about Alanna and Martin."

I guess she went and confronted him already. I open the door, but before he could cross the threshold, I place my right palm against his chest. I tap into the energy of my protective wards, and I grant him entry, this one time only. My hand falls to my side, and he looks in askance.

"You can come in, just for today," I say.

"Fair enough." He steps inside and falters when he sees Lucas. "I've...been trying to catch up with you," he tells the automaton.

Lucas's jaw tightens and his gaze is cold. "I know. I'm not going back to the agency."

Samuel strolls over to the table and takes a seat. "I'm willing to negotiate on that, but you might want to come back, after you hear what I have to say."

Lucas gives him a look as if saying, *I doubt it.*

"Want some cake?" I ask.

"Sure, thanks." Samuel accepts a slice from me.

I cross my arms. "Okay, Samuel, spill it."

He swallows a piece of cake. "First, I want you to know that my job is important to me. I'm here to protect people from getting hurt. You may not like me, and I may very well end up putting my foot up your ass one day but believe that it will be out of justice."

"This isn't helping," I say.

"Jack, Martin Reid was a good man. I joined DMA in the 70's, when some people weren't keen on a black man in the agency. Martin didn't give a damn and hired me, because he said I'm the type of agent they needed. He wasn't just my friend, he was family, and so are Alanna and Nancy. I would do anything to protect them."

"I don't doubt it," I say. "But what happened with Lucas? And Alanna's memory?"

"I had Alanna taken to the infirmary and cared for, and I placed Lucas with Dr. Baker in our laboratory, so he could be fixed. I packed up all those tapes and put them away in Martin's house, because I didn't want the footage at DMA headquarters."

"Why?" Lucas asks, finally taking a seat at the table.

"Walter Moore was a traitor in more ways than one. He went to Martin's house intending to kill him. He had planted fake evidence to make Martin out to be the corrupt one, then left a voice message at the agency claiming Martin was erratic and suicidal."

"Does Alanna know this?" I ask.

"She does now, after we spoke earlier this morning."

Lucas gives him a pointed look. "Did you alter Alanna's memory of that night?"

"Yes, in a way. I didn't want her traumatized and living with the burden of that night, so I had Lucas use that ouroboros tattoo spell to seal it off. From reviewing Martin's videotape sessions, I learned about the Great Endeavor, and I believed...and still believe...it poses the greatest threat to our safety and the unstable truce between our two worlds."

Lucas and I give each other furtive glances. I'm glad he's catching on, regarding when to shut up and just let the other person talk.

"Go on," I say.

"Without consulting Dr. Baker, I tinkered around a bit with Lucas's programming and accidentally wiped some of his memory. That's why he didn't have a full picture of that night or remember that he placed the ouroboros on Alanna."

I lean back in my seat. "And what about Martin's reputation? His legacy?"

"I was a senior agent by then but not senior enough for people to listen when I tried to prove Martin's innocence. So, I had to let it go, and let people believe my best friend was dirty, killed his partner, and killed himself, injuring his own daughter in the process. But I knew sooner or later that Ora or her Dark Coven would resurface."

Lucas observes Samuel, sizing him up. "And where is the sword, Witchbane?"

"If you ask me, the damn thing is cursed. I sent it to an acquaintance for safekeeping."

"And that acquaintance is…?"

Samuel shoots me a sour look. "One of the most powerful wizards alive killed her father for that thing. I'm not putting her in danger by giving her that sword. I've been protecting her all these years, and it makes me sick to think I couldn't do the same for Martin."

Another thing that's been nagging me comes to mind. "Why did you hire my friend Sal as a consultant?"

He points to the cake. "May I take another slice?"

"Go for it," I say.

"Besides Alanna, Agent Bardwell, Dr. Baker, and a few others, I needed someone inside DMA I could trust. Just think— if the Dark Coven got to Walter Moore, who else did they get to? How high does it go?"

A chill runs through me like a dark wave. "The agency's been infiltrated."

Samuel nods. "I'm trying to balance out all this wizard shit and politics, while also attempting to weed out the traitors in the organization. I want to know who they are, the damage they've dealt or could deal, and what their endgame is."

"I don't like the idea of my friends working there if they may become targets," I tell Samuel.

"I agree," Lucas interjects.

"They know the stakes," Samuel says. "I laid it out before them, and they chose to stick with me. I didn't come here only to tell stories, Jack, I'm also here because I could use your help too."

I give him a dubious glance. "You were ready to put a bullet in me."

His expression indicates that he still maintains his position on that. "Listen, we don't have to be drinking buddies, but maybe we can work together to root out these infiltrators. When Alanna spoke to me this morning, she convinced me that at the very least you aren't out to hurt people, and she clearly trusts you. Her trust is not easily won. I still think it's foolish keeping me away from Lucas, because I need to know what he knows, but I'm willing to let him stay with you *if* you're able to tell me everything about the Great Endeavor."

Lucas straightens his back. "It's a deal. I remain with Jack, and we will find out everything about the Great Endeavor and hand the information over to you."

"Okay," I say, "I'm in. We'll do this."

Samuel shifts in his seat. "It will benefit both humans and wizards, and I'm sure the Cloaked Council will want to put an end to the Dark Coven."

I lean back, still studying Samuel, figuring he must be desperate to strike this deal with us. "I'll also need something from you."

"What is it?"

"If I need anything in regard to my search for Kenneth Cherish, I get it without question."

He glares at me, but then relents. "Fine."

"And I want to know about your black site prison."

"Now you're pushing it," he says.

"Beggars can't be choosers."

Samuel grunts and rises from his seat. "Well, looks like we've made some progress. I look forward to working with you. I'll take you off our...problem list."

"Thanks," I say.

I get up and walk him over to the door, opening it for him.

The gray-haired man gives me a curt nod. "Thank you for the cake."

"You're welcome. And I gotta say, you might want to go visit Nancy sometime soon. She misses you."

He steps into the hallway and smirks. "She always beats me at gin rummy. I'll make sure to swing by."

I close the door then turn and face Lucas, who gazes at me from the other side of the room. His face is marred with worry, but he gives me a confident nod. It's time to head for the Obelisk of Qaveus. He probably dislikes the idea of walking into a wizard prison as much as I do, but we have no choice. We've got to save Nicolai Tarasov today, because we're all running out of time.

———

As I'm driving my silver Corolla down to The Ruined Oak, I ask Lucas to message Alanna. "Samuel's good will may not extend to Baltazar," I explain. "So maybe Alanna could help him get through the Scarletwood Gateway. I don't want Sal doing it twice, it might raise suspicion."

His eyes gleam. "It's done."

We ride in silence the rest of the way to The Ruined Oak's parking lot, and my shoulders tense as I think about the dangerous game we're playing, and how a young man's life hangs in the balance—assuming Nicolai's still alive. Lucas and I exit the car and head for the building entrance, and once again we see Gary, cosplaying as one of our Founding Fathers, sitting with his booted feet up on the reception desk and reading a book entitled *Theoretical Magic: How Not to Get Yourself Killed*.

"Good morning, gentlemen." He peers over his book at us.

"Hi Gary," I mumble.

"Good morning!" Lucas says all energetic and positive.

We head over to the left, where Miki and Darryl stand guarding the door leading down to the dungeon level. Miki's dressed in a well-fitting gray suit, and Darryl's wearing all black.

The two Enforcers look bored, but when they spot me and Lucas, their eyes light up.

"You're still alive, my man!" Darryl grins then nudges Miki, who curses and pulls out twenty dollars, handing it to Darryl.

"Well, thanks for your faith in me, guys." I give them a withering look.

Miki opens the door for us. "Go on down, Jack."

Lucas inclines his head toward the Enforcers. "Thank you."

As we enter the stairwell, I overhear Miki say, "We need to get ourselves an automaton…"

I grin at his comment as Lucas and I jog downstairs and open the heavy door at the bottom.

I breathe in the scents of savory, broiled meat, spices, and sweet cakes wafting from the kitchen as we walk along the red velvet rug toward the bar area. Roy, my favorite bar tender, smiles and waves me over.

"Lucas, Jack! Nice seeing ya." He mixes me a rum and Coke and hands it to me. "Happy birthday."

"Thanks, Roy." I take a sip, letting the concoction slide down my throat.

"Any plans for tonight?" the bald man asks.

I shake my head. "I've got so much work, even if I did, I would probably have to cancel. I'm heading through the Gateway."

He nods. "All right, just be careful. A little birdie told me about your…*job* with Mishka."

"Was it Miki or Darryl?" Lucas asks.

Roy winks. "My lips are sealed. Good luck, and don't die, please."

"Thank you," I tell the man. "And thanks for the drink."

Lucas and I head over to the Gateway, opening the entrance and stepping through, letting the familiar mix of magic, mist, and light swirl around us as we pass into this parallel world. As soon as our feet hit the cobblestone pathway, we quicken our steps until we reach the wizard town of Grey Haven. It's full of life this morning, as wizards flow in and out of the shops, smoke rises from the chimneys of nearby homes, and uniformed Enforcers patrol the streets.

We press on, past the Council Hall with its marble pillars and past the stone bridge that leads to the Akashic Academy. Today's destination is the Grey Sea, where we must sail across the glimmering water to the sole island hosting a tall, black tower— the Obelisk of Qaveus. Us wizards pride ourselves on handling our own affairs, which includes administering justice. It's no surprise we have our own system, from the ruling council members to the Enforcers. It's funny how I had feared the tower would be my fate, after being framed for murder, but now I'm seeking to enter it, to save a young man's life.

I scan the pier as we approach a small ferry boat that's docked nearby. The ferry captain, who I doubt is a real captain, adjusts his hat and waves us over. "Going to the Obelisk of Qaveus, friends? I'm Captain Andy, and I can get you there in ten minutes."

Lucas glances at the boat and then at the island across from us. "Very well. Take us across."

I pull out my wallet and pay the captain, knowing good and well that he's overcharging us, but we don't have time to compare prices and shop for other ferry rides.

The boat jolts and lurches forward, taking us toward the island with speed. A spray of salty water from the sea hits the side of my face and I groan, wiping my cheek with the back of my hand.

I'll give Captain Andy credit where it's due, he does get us to the island within ten minutes. As soon as the ferry comes to a halt, I rise from my seat and hop onto the pier, with Lucas in tow. We trek through the sandy beach and step onto the winding stone pathway parting the thick forest. My skin tingles as if touched by static electricity, a sure sign that wards and a magical security system are in place. Lucas walks alongside me and takes in the sight of the imposing black tower.

"Intimidating, isn't it?" he asks.

"Just a little," I say, making eye contact with the Enforcer at the guard station just a few feet ahead.

We slow to a stroll and step into a painted yellow circle on the ground. The Enforcer in his black uniform sports a gold phoenix emblem, identifying him as an Obelisk Enforcer. The ones at the Council Hall wear green emblems, and all other Enforcers wear red symbols.

"State your business," he says, standing just outside the painted circle. The hum of magic surrounding us is subtle but strong.

"I'm Jack Crowley, and this is my friend Lucas. We're here on behalf of Councilwoman Grimm. We need to interview a prisoner...Damon Blackbird."

The Enforcer's eyebrows shoot up. "So, you're the Wayward Wizard, huh?" He looks over his shoulder and gestures to a second Enforcer at the guard station, just twenty feet ahead. The vibrating magic surrounding us in the circle evaporates, and Lucas and I are free to pass.

"Thanks," I say.

He grins at Lucas. "My father is a professor of Theoretical Magic at the academy. I think it's amazing to see you automatons among us."

Lucas looks pleased at his words. "Perhaps I can visit the Akashic Academy again soon."

Or not. Master Valerio Magnus would let Lucas in, but never let him leave.

We stop at the guard station and grab our visitor passes, then move on toward the main gate. It stands at twelve feet high, pure obsidian, with intricately woven sigils and wards to keep uninvited guests out and the prisoners inside. A loud buzz fills my ears as the black gate opens, and Lucas and I cross the threshold. A tall woman in an Enforcers uniform, with short, dark hair and green eyes approaches.

"Crowley. You're here to see Damon Blackbird?"

I nod, hoping that they don't try to call up Poppy to confirm it. I told Poppy we're still investigating Hunter, and I'm telling the tower guards we're investigating Damon. I'm trying to walk that fine line and keep Mishka's and Nicolai's names out of this.

"Yes, there are just a few questions we need to ask him. My automaton friend here will record everything."

Lucas inclines his head toward her. "At your service, ma'am."

"You may call me Erin." She pulls out a card key. "His cell is B124, on the lower level. This key card will allow you access to his cell block and will also track your movements. Please don't stray from your pathway, or we will know. You have twenty minutes."

"Thanks." I take the card key and we follow her through the main Tower entrance.

There's a reception area with three Enforcers, two of whom are observing monitors, and the other one engaged in phone calls and paperwork. Two non-Enforcer guards are also near the station keeping watch. Erin takes us through the hallway on the right to an elevator, and motions for me to use my key card. I wave it in front of the reader, it beeps green, and the elevator opens. Lucas and I step inside.

"Twenty minutes," she repeats, turning her back and heading down the hall back to reception.

As the elevator smoothly glides down toward the lower level, I face Lucas. "Can you poke around in their computer system and find out where Hunter is stationed?"

His eyes gleam, and he's motionless for a few seconds. "She's just below Damon's level, the C-100's."

I flick the key card. "Okay, buddy. Please tell me you can hack this thing so they think we're with Damon Blackbird."

He smirks and take the key card, using that weird finger thingy he did with the cryptograph, except this time an electrical node pops out, and he attaches it to the card. There's a small beep, then he retracts the node, and his finger returns to normal. I take the card back and slip it into my pocket.

Once we make it to C-level, I follow Lucas out the elevator and down the corridor. The prison cells are shut tight, with large, warded glass windows and doors made of iron. Some prisoners in their cells don't give us a second look, while others stare at us with glimmers of intrigue in their eyes. The less stable ones start cursing and begging for us to free them.

Just ahead, I spot a small station, similar to a nurse's station at a hospital. None other than Hunter Bronwyn is sitting there, leaning back in her swivel chair, feet kicked up, and white hair in a thick braid hanging past her shoulder. She's absentmindedly viewing something on her cell phone, but once she hears the commotion of some of the prisoners, her gaze lifts to meet ours, and her eyes widen.

"Councilwoman Poppy Grimm sent us," I say, hoping she doesn't bolt. "We know who you are, Hunter. My friend and I just want Nicolai, okay?"

Lucas and I quicken our steps to close the distance between us and Hunter. Instead of jumping up and running or sounding an alarm, she rises from her seat and comes around to the front of the station, arms crossed in front of her like she's been expecting us. I scan the area for any traps or surprises, noticing that she's already disabled the security cameras.

"What do you know about me?" she asks, her hands filling with magic. "You're not supposed to be here."

"And neither is Nicolai," Lucas retorts. "We know you brought him in here under a stolen name."

She shakes her head. "You know nothing."

Hunter raises her hands and both Lucas and I erect magical shields to deflect any of her attacks. Instead, waves of energy crackle from her fingertips like lightning, and two of the nearest cell doors fly open, allowing a burly man with a goatee and a tall, pale man to emerge.

Hunter smirks. "Have fun."

ALESHA ESCOBAR

Lucas positions himself to face the two men. "The big one is an elemental, and the pale one is a vampire."

Just great. Caught between a vampire and a hexwielder.

"I'll take on Hunter," I tell him.

"Very well." Lucas rushes the two prisoners, and I step toward Hunter.

"Hunter Bronwyn, Ego Magica lig—"

Guess I didn't speak fast enough. A burst of electrical power hits me in the gut and I go flying backward, straight into the vampire. While Lucas is going back and forth in a fistfight of fiery hands with the elemental, the vamp's got a hold of my head and his hot breath is on my neck.

I hate vampires, but not as much as I hate hexwielders.

24

I draw on my elemental ability and fill my hands with the warmth of my fire, enhancing it with the ring I'm wearing. I smash my fist into the vampire's head, just as he's about to take a bite out of me. He screeches more like a beast than a man, and he quickly backs away, as vampires hate fire.

"You bastard," he says with a growl. The left side of his face is bloodied and seared; his fangs peak out, and he backs away and tries to run.

"Oh no you don't!" Hunter pulls out her whip and cracks it, looping it around the vampire's torso and sending a blue blaze of magic along the cord. The vamp shudders and he goes limp.

I take advantage of the distraction and send a blaze of fire toward Hunter. She's forced to drop her whip and she launches herself into the air with a flip. I counter with yanking some of the condensed air around us and creating an invisible wall, which she smacks against. The hexwielder falls to the ground and lands on her ass, and she glares at me, in a silent promise that I'm going to pay for that.

I'm just about to lay another spell on her when Lucas smashes against me and tumbles to the floor with me. Holy hell, it feels like I've just been hit by a car. Sometimes I forget that

Lucas is all metal underneath that human-like flesh. The big guy who threw him lets out a belly laugh.

"Salem," the burly wizard says to the vampire. "Get up, let's get out of here."

The vampire stumbles toward us with a disoriented look on his face, the whip still wrapped around him. Hunter lurches forward and grabs the loose end of the whip. "You're not going anywhere."

She yanks on the whip and sends another crackle of blue energy through it, and Salem the vampire goes down unconscious. She manipulates the whip and takes back control, bringing the other end toward her so that she can use it to lash out at anyone else. Lucas is back on his feet and places himself between me and the big guy. They crash against each other in brute force.

I force myself to stand, though my back is throbbing and my legs wobble. I push the pain away and face Hunter again. She cracks the whip, aiming it for me, but I send a blast of air toward her, and she goes flying backward into the station. I'm just about to cast a True Name spell on her when I notice out of the corner of my eye a third figure observing us from the shadows.

I'm not sure if it's another loosed prisoner or an ally of hers, so I quickly turn and aim a blast of icy wind toward the figure. My spell goes right through the dark figure, as if it's a ghost. As the mysterious observer steps slightly into the light, I notice that it's the same shadowy being from my bedroom, the one with silver eyes. I finally recognize what it is—not only is it a spirit, but it's a werewolf spirit. What the hell?

Hunter sucker punches me and I stumble backward. My gaze goes from her to the werewolf spirit, but it's gone. I erect a magical shield around me and quickly say, *"Hunter Bronwyn, ego magica ligat!"*

English translation—*I bind your magic.*

"No!" she screeches, trying to land another punch.

I call forth the elemental power of air, creating a tight-knit wall around her, so that she can barely move. I swivel around to gauge how Lucas is doing. He's landing a series of successive punches to the big guy's gut, then finally an uppercut which knocks him to the ground. The automaton then drags the man back into his cell. Since I've got Hunter wrapped in air like a sardine in a can, I go over and drag the vampire by the feet and place him back into his cell.

Both Lucas and I approach Hunter, who's struggling against my spell to no avail. In futility she reaches for her power, but she's cut off from it, as long as I have her bound.

"It's no use," I tell her. "*Hunter, ut verum dicas.* Why are you doing this? Where's Nicolai?"

Her clenched jaw suddenly drops, and she chokes. She's fighting like hell against my command. She's heaving and gagging and looks like she's gonna puke at any moment. I feel a little guilty coaxing an answer out of her this way, the same way I would feel dirty wiping someone's memory, but damn it, we need to find Nicolai and end this.

"Mishka had my father murdered." Her eyes fill with tears and her nostrils flare. "He was Ishmael Bronwyn…"

Lucas gasps. "The former sheriff of Scarletwood. He died in a warehouse fire."

"It was Mishka!" Her voice is guttural. "My father found out he was smuggling illegal items that he knew the Cloaked Council would confiscate and was even trafficking people. So, he had my father killed, and I was only twelve. I couldn't do anything."

"And Nicolai is payback." I stare at her, wondering why she didn't use her position and leverage as a guard in the tower to bring this issue to the Cloaked Council. Instead, she went dark.

"It's just the beginning," she says. "Mishka, his money, his so-called business, his family…will burn, like my father did."

Lucas gazes at her, with a touch of sympathy. "You could've easily brought this to the Council."

"I did. As soon as I got this job, I brought it to Marco Welling and he blew me off," she says bitterly.

I step toward her. "Well, turns out Marco was working for the Dark Coven, so he was as corrupt as they come. Not the best person to speak to about Mishka. If this is all true, Hunter, then let us help you. Stop dealing all this damage trying to get revenge."

She scoffs. "Why would you help me?"

"Mishka is not my friend," I say. "If he's responsible for this, then let him answer for his crimes before the Council. Now, can you tell us where Nicolai is? Either way, you're going to answer us. I can call on your name and have you choke on your words, or you can talk to me like a human being. I would much rather you just talk to me instead of having to yank he answer out of you."

She sniffs. "I moved him from here and back to a secret room, beneath my living room floor."

"Great," I say. "Baltazar's probably there now. Lucas, can you message him and let him know there's a hidden room beneath the floorboards?"

Lucas's eyes gleam, but then he frowns. "He's not responding."

"I have a security app," she continues, "where I can view who's on my land." She nods toward the station, and I rush over to it and grab her phone. I remember how she was watching something on it when we came in.

I bring it over, hold it up to her face, and it unlocks. I tap onto the app with her linked security feed. "Baltazar's on her property," I say. "Looks like Alanna got him through the Gateway."

"Then you better call him again," Hunter insists. "Because there's a trap waiting inside."

My stomach ties into knots when I see Alanna join Baltazar on screen. She falls into step with him as they crunch leaves beneath their feet and head down the winding path that will lead them to Hunter's front door Damn it, she was only supposed to get him through the Gateway, not go all the way to Hunter's house with him.

I turn to Lucas. "It will take us too long to get out of here and go to Griffith Park."

Lucas's eyes gleam. "The level below us has an emergency Gateway from here to Scarletwood. We could use that."

"Okay, Hunter. You're coming with us." I loosen the wall of air around her, so that she can move and walk. "Try to run or fight, you'll regret it. Got it?"

"Will you give me my powers back?"

"Hell no. Not until this is over. Now let's go, because if anything happens to Alanna and Baltazar, you're going to see a *very* different Jack Crowley."

25

Hunter gazes longingly at the armory as we pass it and head for the vault door at the end of the corridor. We had to use her security clearance to gain access to this level. She gives me a sidelong glance.

"Visitors only get twenty minutes, and your twenty minutes are up. Erin will come looking for you. And when she does..." she smirks.

"Shut up," I say, the tension crawling up my neck from thinking about Alanna and Baltazar. "Do you have high enough clearance to open up the emergency Gateway?"

We halt at a black metallic door, with a 5-spoke handle, a keypad, and at least twenty different wards, just waiting to ensnare the wrong person who tries to unlock it.

"Oh, now you want me to talk?"

"Tell us!"

"No, only the warden or a Council Member can open it."

Lucas glares at her, and he doesn't glare often. "You could've mentioned this earlier."

"I guess we do need to call up Poppy." I pull out my phone and call her on video chat, which I know she'll hate."

Her image pops up on screen and I can see she's in her office at the Council Hall. "Poppy, I wanted to update you on Hunter Bronwyn."

She arches an eyebrow. "Why the hell are you in the Obelisk tower? On the lower level?"

I tilt the phone to get Hunter into view. "We got her, Poppy, but we're in a rush and need to open the emergency Gateway."

"Jack!" Poppy barks. "Stop holding back from me, what's going on?"

Lucas chimes in. "We're very sorry, Councilwoman Grimm, but we need to use the emergency Gateway to Scarletwood. A few lives are at stake."

Poppy sighs. "Oh my gods...I don't even want to ask who."

"What's the code, Poppy?" I ask.

"If I let you through, you're going to give me something in return. Something big."

"You got it," I say. "What is it?"

"I want a night with Lucas."

My gaze darts toward the automaton. "Say again?"

"Not in that way, bonehead. One night, Betty will assist me, and I get to open him up and study him."

"No way!" I say. "Come on, Poppy! My friends are over there."

"I'm not a vending machine that you can just press a button on and get what you want. If you really want that door open, then agree to this."

I look to Lucas. He should at least have a say.

The automaton squeezes his eyes shut and lets out a low breath. "Fine. Tell her yes."

"He says yes, Poppy."

"The code is 1212489."

Hunter punches in the number on the keypad.

"Thanks," I say begrudgingly, though her help came at a price I'm not keen on paying.

"And Jack," she says, as Hunter turns the spoke and pulls the door open, "don't renege on me, or you'll make an enemy out of me."

"Yeah, and if anything happens to Lucas, you'll make an enemy out of me."

"Good day." She ends the call.

———

We step through the Gateway, which at first blurs our vision with thick, rolling fog. I cough and sputter but keep a grip on Hunter's forearm, so she doesn't get any ideas. She probably won't try to run until after I loosen the binding on her powers. The fog clears and we're now on solid ground, inside an eerily empty administrative building.

"Lucas, how close is this building to Hunter's house?"

The automaton scans the room and seems to look past me as if analyzing the rest of the building. "A five-minute walk. We should head west."

I follow Lucas's directions, finally letting go of Hunter's arm as we walk down the street past some pedestrians. An old woman, a street vendor, calls to us, trying to lure us to her cart with potions and charms. But we don't have time. Once Baltazar breaks the ward and enters, he and Alanna are in a world of trouble.

I give Hunter a little nudge from behind as we quicken our steps. "You can't remotely deactivate your trap?"

She looks over her shoulder and glowers at me. "Defeats the purpose of it protecting my home while I'm away, doesn't it?"

"Your crappy move just put two of my friends' lives in danger. They're just trying to do their jobs."

She catches me in a dark gaze. "It's crappy to take the side of a murderer. The Tarasovs are a crime family, and they killed a sheriff. I only managed to recover a few things from that warehouse."

We make a right turn off the main road and onto the pathway leading down to her house.

"I've got to ask, how is it that Nicolai had a picture of you?" I ask. "Did he know you?"

She bites her lower lip and stares, as if deciding whether or not to answer. "I was just going to use him to get close to Mishka, but I think he got suspicious and tried to follow me and find out who I really am."

"And that's when you decided to drop the charade and just take him by force."

Lucas eyes her critically. "Are you not ashamed of your actions? You attacked Salvador's parents' home, laid deadly traps, and cut off the finger of a young man simply because he's the nephew of the man you hate. Nicolai is near your age, and he would have been a teen like you at the time of Sheriff Bronwyn's death."

My heart drops in my chest when I see Hunter's front door open. "They're inside!"

We dash across the front yard and up the front steps, our feet carrying us as fast as they can. As soon as we cross the threshold and enter the living room, I curse under my breath at the sight. Baltazar, Alanna, and even little Olette are pinned against the ceiling by a whirlwind of deep purple electricity that's emanating from a dark jewel in the center of the floor. Their teeth are clenched in pain and their skin a sickly gray. The life is being slowly sucked out of them.

My eyes go from Alanna and Baltazar to the jewel on the floor, which seems to fuel the trap that my friends are caught in. I relinquish the hold I have on Hunter's powers.

"Deactivate the jewel!" I roar.

"Go to hell!" she says.

Lucas rushes forward and tries to free them, or at least place himself between the blast of the purple electricity and our friends, but he's caught in the web and levitates toward the ceiling right along with them.

"Hunter! Perdere gemma!"

She doubles over in pain and screeches like a mother in labor. There she goes again, trying to fight against my command. Her hands lift in a jerky movement, as if being controlled by a puppeteer, and she walks in stiff steps toward the dark jewel. She sobs as her hands tremble, and she makes a gesture with both hands, forming a diamond symbol with her fingertips touching, pouring her magical energy into a spell.

Cracks of light form across the surface of the dark jewel, and it finally explodes, releasing my friends. I extend my hand and send a quick blast of air to break their fall. Olette flutters into the air, emitting amethyst sparks which descend on my friends. Alanna's and Baltazar's sickly gray skin turn to a warmer, more natural color, and their weakened postures improve. I turn toward Hunter, who quickly casts another spell, but this one's on herself.

"Now I can't hear you," she says. "I lied about the secret room beneath the floor. Now, try and force me to do something."

This woman is getting on my damn nerves.

For my True Name magic to work on a living person, they need to be within hearing range…they need to hear me speak.

I step toward Hunter and raise my fist, and she cowers beneath me. My body shakes with a fury I had never thought possible. I want to punch the hell out of her and make her feel the pain my friends just felt. Even worse, I want to curse her and say the words of death over her, but then I realize that would make me no better than her. I wouldn't be able to look Willy or my friends in the eye after doing something like that, especially my little neighbor Desmond who swears I'm a superhero. Besides, it would just prove to others what they had claimed I was for years—a murderer.

But that's not me.

Instead of focusing on revenge, I rush over to my friends to check on them. "Are you guys all right?"

Alanna slowly nods as I help her to her feet. She hisses with pain as she tries to stand up straight. "I'll be okay."

"I'm fully functional." Lucas stands and assists Baltazar, and he even bends down and scoops up Olette, who lets out a woeful moan. Satisfied that they can at least walk out of here, I turn my attention back on Hunter. She withers under my harsh gaze, perhaps expecting me to strike her dead, but instead, I slip off my lion's head pendant and hand it to Baltazar.

His brows furrow as he stares at me. "Don't you need this?"

I shake my head, concentrating on the one person who could change Hunter's mind. I reach deep down, letting the flood of spirits in the surrounding area connect with me. I focus on Ishmael Bronwyn, until I feel the hairs on my arms raise and the tingle of a spiritual presence.

"Sheriff Bronwyn," I say, not sure how this works or if I can get him to obey me, but I give it a try. "Show yourself to your daughter."

A tall man with brown hair and wearing all white materializes next to me. Hunter's eyes widen and she gasps in disbelief. "Papa?"

Ishmael places a hand on my shoulder. I nearly jump at the sensation, a mix of prickles and ice. "I want justice," the spirit says to me, "but not like this. This is not the daughter I raised." He shakes his head in disappointment.

Hunter's still deaf by choice, but from her father's facial expression and body language, she can tell that he's not on her side, that he doesn't agree with her vigilantism. Her lower lip quivers and she breaks down and weeps.

"I did it for you…" she says in a broken voice.

Ishmael steps toward her and bends his knee, meeting her at eye level. He tilts her chin upward. "You did it for you, out of anger." His words are slow, perhaps so she could at least read his lips. "Hunter…daughter…do the right thing. Fix this."

The hexwielder covers her face with her hands. The sheriff

stands and faces me. "Thank you, for allowing her to see me once more."

I give him a curt nod and watch him turn from opaque to translucent, and then he finally disappears. Hunter inhales a deep breath and wipes her face before speaking to us. "Nicolai is in the bone crypt in the cemetery at the edge of the island. I swear, that's where he is, and he's alive."

Great. Of course we need to visit a cemetery, right after I divested myself of the lion's head pendant. I could grab it from Baltazar and put it back on, but something tells me this new ability will come in handy after all, so I'll just have to deal with it. For now. I grab Hunter by the forearm and pull her to her feet. My gaze sweeps from left to right, gauging how banged up my friends are.

"Are you guys well enough to come?"

"I'm okay, thanks to Olette," Alanna says, rotating her head and shaking out her arms.

"Oh, I'm seeing this through to the end," Baltazar promises. Olette aims a few choice words at Hunter before melding back into Baltazar's neck as his tattoo.

"I will go with you," Lucas asserts.

I nod. "Then let's finish this."

26

The afternoon sunlight bathes us in warmth as we step onto the Scarletwood Cemetery property. My shoulders tense as the familiar tingle of spirits crawls up my back and neck, but I press forward, flanking Hunter on her left and Alanna walking at her right. Baltazar and Lucas are right behind us, and I'm certain Baltazar is just waiting for the hexwielder to step out of line so he can strike her down. I hope she's learned her lesson.

We walk a pathway that slopes downward, past rows of headstones, many with flitting spirits hanging about, and a few of them even wave to me, and I incline my head toward them in acknowledgement. It seems many of them just want to be seen, though an elderly man's spirit does approach and glides next to me.

"Please, tell my family I'm sorry and that I miss them," the ghost pleads.

A little girl, no more than twelve, zooms toward me. "I wasn't ready to go...I was sick and then..."

I let out an exasperated sigh, remembering the mental exercises Willy used to teach me. I exert my will and form a mental hedge around myself, just to give me some space. No wonder wizards like Willy construct guards around their minds.

"Are you all right?" Alanna asks, eyeing me with concern.

"Yeah, it's just…there's a lot of spirits here, and some of them have messages for me." I nudge Hunter with my elbow. "Hey, are you ready to undo your deafness spell?"

She reads my lips and shakes her head. "I don't trust you. It's safer for me this way."

"She's afraid of you, Jack," Alanna says. "Though, she shouldn't be."

"Huh. She's lucky that it's me doing this job and not one of Mishka's goons who'd take her out in a second." I gesture for a group of sprits just ahead to disperse and leave me alone. Just ahead, overlooking a cliff and the blue sea water, is an ancient-looking bone crypt.

Hunter gives Alanna a sidelong glance. "I remember you. You were at the house with Crowley in L.A. Your aura, it's ocean blue. What's a human doing hanging around with wizards? In Scarletwood?"

Alanna faces her. "I'm a DMA agent."

Hunter's expression falls. "DMA?"

"Yes."

The hexwielder's lips press into a thin line. "My father died because he trusted a DMA agent."

"So did mine," Alanna says emphatically.

Hunter's taken aback and lowers her gaze. "What happened?"

A touch of pain fills Alanna's face. "It's a long story. I didn't think a Scarletwood sheriff would be working with DMA, especially since the current one doesn't."

Hunter takes a few seconds to process what Alanna said, still relying on lip reading. Why do I have the feeling the woman has done this spell on herself before, to avoid interrogation or other situations?

"You can thank the Tarasovs for that. I told you they're corrupt. If they can't buy you off, they kill you. My father had accepted a shipment from a DMA chief, and that happened to be the night Mishka and his men struck."

"DMA chief?" Alanna repeats. "Who was he?"

Hunter slows her pace. "Samuel. Samuel Mayhew."

Alanna nearly stumbles and falls. "Jack…"

"Looks like we found Samuel's *acquaintance*," I say, knowing what this means to Alanna.

Lucas sidles up to Alanna. "This means that Samuel sent Witchbane to Sheriff Bronwyn."

A low whistle from Baltazar's mouth fills our ears, along with a deep chuckle. "Well, well…I've hit the jack pot. I mean, *we've* hit the jack pot. Ora Draper's bloody sword, do you know what we could do with it? Do you know how much it is worth?"

"That sword is mine," Alanna snaps. "My father intended me to have it."

"Well, seeing as it's not available on the black market and Mishka hasn't threatened us with it," I interject, "I think it's safe to say that Mishka doesn't have Witchbane."

Hunter is oddly silent, so I place a firm hand on her shoulder. "Hey hexwielder, do you know anything about that? Where's the sword?"

She ignores my question and halts at the threshold of the bone crypt. The entrance is creepy as hell, with a set of rotting wood double-doors, human skulls lining the door frame, and a pungent stench wafting toward us.

"Nicolai's inside," Hunter says. "He's in the warded sarcophagus beneath the Grim Reaper statue."

I pull the doors open and we go inside. My head immediately begins throbbing as I spot several shadow figures moving in the dark corners of the crypt. I push it all away and focus on the one area filled with light, where the sunlight penetrates the stained-glass window and shines down on a bone-decorated sarcophagus, and of course, a life-like statue of Death itself with hooded cloak and scythe poised above the burial box.

We approach the sarcophagus. Baltazar comes around and

stands to my left, and the hexwielder is still wedged between me and Alanna. Lucas stays to Alanna's right, watching Hunter like a hawk. The white-haired woman takes in a deep breath and stretches her hands over the sarcophagus. She does a series of flexes with her hands, forming mystical symbols, and the tight wards on the box shimmer in response before fading.

Lucas leans forward and pushes the heavy stone slab over to the side with a single hand. I peer inside and see Nicolai lying on his side, blindfolded, and looking as if he's in a state between waking and dreaming. He flinches when Alanna reaches for the blindfold, but she manages to pull it down for him.

"Help me!" His gaze darts between us, as if trying to determine who among us may have the compassion or humanity to do so. "She kidnapped me!"

"We know," I say. "Your uncle sent us to get you. I'm surprised she didn't bind your hands and feet."

Baltazar leans over and pulls him up. "Jack, Nicolai's ability is spirit magic. I'm sure throwing him in here, surrounded by thousands of spirits, is more effective than shackles."

"Makes sense," I say.

I've been here for less than an hour, and I'm already anxious and want to get the hell out before I get crowded by hundreds of ghosts—or worse, the shadow figures.

Baltazar gives Nicolai a reassuring smile. "Shall we go to The Ruined Oak? Your uncle's infirmary awaits…as well as the final half of my paycheck."

Nicolai nods, though he shifts his fearful gaze to Hunter, as if expecting her to lunge toward him. The poor guy has dark circles under his eyes, and compared to the photo Mishka gave me, looks ten pounds lighter. He accepts Baltazar's help and carefully gets out of the sarcophagus, still holding on to the Irishman like a clingy child.

I turn and face Hunter. "I think your old man would be proud. You did the right thing."

She finally takes a moment to undo the spell of deafness. "So, Wayward Wizard…what now?"

"Uh, you get turned in to the Enforcers for kidnapping," I say. "It's time to own up to what you've done."

At first, I expect her to scoff and try to run away or cast some sort of spell. Instead, she meets my gaze with a sense of resolve. "Okay. But there's one last thing…"

I raise a skeptical eyebrow. "Hunter…"

"No tricks, I promise." She approaches the statue of Death and places a hand on the scythe, her hand emanating a bright glow. The weapon shimmers and emits a soft blue light before transforming into a Damascus steel blade with an emerald in the pommel.

"Witchbane," Alanna says in a gasp, slowly approaching the statue.

Hunter grabs the weapon and hands it to her. "This is one of the few things I managed to save that night, and I hid it. I hope it serves you well."

Alanna gives her a grateful smile, though her eyes are filled with sorrow. "Thank you."

Lucas approaches Alanna and wraps his arms around her.

Baltazar frowns as he watches them. "What a waste, both the sword and the automaton."

Yeesh, this guy. I face Hunter. "We'll drop you off at the Council Hall and hand you over to the Enforcers. Then, we've got to take Nicolai home."

The hexwielder nods. "Okay, I'm ready."

I breathe a sigh of relief.

It's done.

I don't owe Mishka Tarasov a damn thing.

27

Since Alanna's been permanently banned from Grey Haven, she can't come with us to drop Hunter off. Plus, even if she could join us, she's freaking carrying around the sword of Ora Draper. The wrong eyes would be on her, and envious hearts would plot against her. We decide to split up, and Lucas agrees to escort Alanna back through the Scarletwood Gateway. Baltazar and I take off with Nicolai and Hunter through the emergency Gateway back to the tower prison, where we hand the hexwielder over to Erin the Enforcer.

"I've just called Councilman Marshwick," Erin says, as she shackles Hunter, and two Enforcers take her to a holding room.

"What about Poppy?" I ask.

"Poppy Grimm is the liaison between humans and wizards. Marshwick oversees the Enforcers and tower guards."

I've only met the man a couple of times, and one of those times he sat in judgment over me believing me guilty of a crime I didn't commit. I hope he gives Hunter a fair shake. Despite everything she did, she's not too far gone to be saved.

"Fine," I say. "Can you keep us updated?"

"Certainly," Erin says. "But the next time you want to catch a rogue guard or use our emergency Gateway, do let us know.

You're lucky to have a Councilmember behind you, else I would throw you into our pit and feed you to the minotaur."

I chuckle. "You don't have a...do you, really?"

"Goodbye, Jack Crowley." She turns on her heel and leaves.

"Do I have to keep wearing this disguise?" Nicolai asks. I had cast a glamour spell on him, and he looks like Lucas. We're still trying to keep his identity and the full story of the kidnapping under wraps.

"My boy, if you ask me, it's an improvement!" Baltazar teases.

We head out and exit the prison. I don't know about Baltazar, but my muscles ache, my head and back hurt, and this isn't exactly how I would like to spend my birthday. I pull out my phone and check the time, it's 3:00 p.m. My stomach rumbles and I'm ready for some food, possibly more chili fries, and more of Zara's cake.

Once we make it past Grey Haven and onto the cobblestone path, it's only a ten-minute walk to the Gateway leading back to The Ruined Oak. Baltazar opens it and ushers us through, and we shut the door behind us, greeting Roy who grins with relief.

"Thank goodness, you made it," the bartender says. "Fancy a drink? On the house, birthday boy."

"Soon," I tell him. "We've got to see Mishka first."

His relieved expression suddenly turns into one of worry. "Are you sure?"

Baltazar winks. "We'll be okay, my friend. Have a martini ready for me."

We head left and go up the elevator, to Mishka's penthouse level. I finally command the glamour to fade, and Nicolai turns from a Lucas lookalike to his emaciated appearance with tattered and grimy clothes. As soon as the elevator doors slide open, we're greeted by Darryl and Miki, who quickly steer him to the infirmary.

Baltazar and I head through the double doors and enter the dining area with the glass table, white sofa, and tall windows.

However, instead of Mishka standing there, it's his assistant, Eli the alchemist. The tattooed man greets us and hands us each an envelope.

"Gentlemen," he says, "Mishka's in the conference room. I'll walk you over."

As we leave the dining area and Eli opens another set of double doors, Baltazar opens his envelope and peeks at the check inside. He smiles. "A sum well-deserved." He slips the envelope into an inner pocket in his jacket. I don't even bother looking at mine. Having extra money is nice and all, but when it comes from a scumbag like Mishka, it just makes me feel dirty.

We step into the conference room and Eli closes the door behind us. The dim room has a long, rectangular, black table and twelve matching leather chairs around it. At the head of the table, of course, sits the boss man himself, decked out in a tuxedo, as if he's about to take off to some fancy gala. I catch a glimpse of the female spirit I had seen before here in the penthouse, a blonde woman with sad eyes. I'm curious as to who she is, but I decide to say nothing and refocus on Mishka. His long fingers are steepled together, and his breathing is even, though his eyes are a mystery. I can't tell if he wants to simply talk to us or kill us.

"Thank you," he says in his Russian accent, "for bringing Nicolai back. Your job was well done."

Baltazar opens his mouth to speak, but Mishka's cell phone rings and he holds his hand up in a gesture to silence him. The magical mob boss answers his phone, speaking in Russian and using brief words.

Baltazar's breath hitches as he listens to the conversation. Apparently, he understands Russian. "Shit…" the Irishman says under his breath.

Mishka ends the phone call and smiles. "Now, it is finished. The girl who took my nephew is dead. Jack, your debt is paid."

My eyes pop wide. "What? What do you mean, she's dead. We dropped her off with the Enforcers not even an hour ago!"

My heart sinks in my chest as I remember Hunter's words: *if they can't buy you off, they kill you…*

Was it a lowly tower guard looking for easy money? Or Erin who nonchalantly threatened to feed us to a minotaur? The warden? Who exactly does Mishka have in his pocket? And Hunter…I sent her to her death. I left her with those people, convincing her she'd get a fair trial and that maybe she could redeem herself.

Mishka is a monster for doing this.

And this crime lord is not gonna kill me or buy me off.

I rip my envelope and let it fall to the floor.

"I don't want or need your money," I tell him. "You can go to hell. You didn't need to have her killed. She was already going to face justice and she actually accepted it, which is more than I can say for you. I know you killed her father."

"Partner…" Baltazar says, trying to nudge me with his elbow. "Jack, my boy, are you sure you want to…"

"Maybe he can buy you off, Baltazar, but *I'm* not for sale."

My head throbs with a mix of anger and adrenaline pumping through me. Mishka just stares at me with his cold brown eyes, the scar from his right eye down to his cheek slightly reddening. I know I'm probably next on his kill list but screw him. Some things are worth taking a stand for.

"Sir," Baltazar says, "I'll take him down for a drink, he's had a stressful day—"

"*Mishka Tarasov…*" I say in a dangerous tone, with an air of command that tells him I can speak his name and enact what I want. I'm incredibly tempted to speak in Latin and call something down upon him, but I don't. "I am done with you. Come near me or my friends, mess with me or mine, and you'll end up the same as Marco Welling. I will reach down to the core of my being and speak the words of death on you."

Baltazar slightly loosens his collar, just in case he needs to call forth Olette. "Well, this meeting escalated quickly."

Mishka's chest rises and falls with shallow breaths, and he

leans forward, his palms now lying flat on the conference table. "Go, Crowley. Leave my sight! I may not be able to bar you from downstairs or the Gateway, but step foot in my penthouse, or in one of my warehouses or other establishments, and I will kill you. I will have werewolves savage your corpse and let vampires drink your blood."

My hands quiver with rage, and I'm ready to challenge him, but Baltazar gently tugs on my sleeve. "Not today, partner. Besides, it's your birthday."

I spin on my heel and head out, not even bothering to see Mishka's reaction or to hear him speak again. Baltazar chases after me, exiting the penthouse and following me through the hallway and to the elevator. I pound the down button a little too hard with my hand and hiss at the pain. Damn that bastard. I want to punch *something*.

"Jack, I'm sorry," Baltazar says as he follows me into the elevator. "I had no clue Mishka would do this. I thought this was all done once we handed her over to the Enforcers."

"Did you?" I ask with suspicion, preparing a spell in my mind.

"Hit me, curse me…take your anger out on me, I understand. But do believe that I did not conspire for this to be Hunter's end. I'm just as shocked as you are. I know I didn't particularly get along with Hunter, and I did exert some cruelty toward her, but I would never be dishonorable and help kill a prisoner who's already surrendered."

I kick the elevator wall. "That asshole! Why did he have to be so petty? So vengeful?"

"*Maorach*, we call it," Baltazar says. "Coward. That's what he ultimately is."

"And what about you? Are you just a hired hand, Baltazar Maune?"

The elevator stops and the doors open, but Baltazar hits the "close" button. Turmoil festers in his gaze as he then hits the "stop" button, and he reaches into his pocket and takes out his envelope. The man hesitates a couple of times, but he finally gathers the will to tear it into pieces.

"Jack, you may not remember because you were so young and traumatized, but I'm the one who brought you to Willy the night your family died in that fire."

My breath catches in my throat. "You? Wh-why didn't you say anything?"

He shrugs. "I wasn't sure if it mattered or not, or perhaps I was acting cowardly, thinking I wouldn't mention it if you didn't. But I was on my way home and saw the explosion, knowing that it was a neighborhood where our kind lived, so I thought my fixer services were needed. I didn't imagine I would find dead wizards and a little boy, half-conscious and afraid, trying to grasp hold of what had just happened. So, I took you to the woman who I knew had taken care of many children, who had been a midwife for so many."

"Willy," I say in a low voice.

"I...may not be perfect, Jack, but I still know how to do some good things. If it were up to me, I would've let Hunter go, and let the Council decide her fate."

I release the spell I had been preparing in my mind, but now I have a gnawing sorrow and anger inside that I just can't shake.

Baltazar casts a sympathetic gaze. "It's about time you go talk to your adopted mother about your past, don't you think? And perhaps, some of hers?"

I press my back against the wall, partly because my knees are wobbly, and I barely have any energy left. "I just want to go home right now."

Baltazar hits another button, and the metal doors slide open. "Truly, I am sorry. I'll see you around, Jack."

"Bye."

He steps out and heads for the bar, and I'm still standing there, just feeling numb. I finally force myself to exit and go home, my mind and spirit heavy.

I can't even muster a fake smile for my neighbors, who are crowded in the Blackstone lobby, dressed in costumes and enjoying a community Halloween party. I slip past a cluster of people who greet me, wave to a couple of scantily clad nurses, giving them a double take, then make my way into the elevator and get off on the eighth floor. My feet are heavy, as if iron shackles are locked around my ankles, as I approach my door and take out my key. I unlock the door and go inside, halting when I see Alanna, Sal, and Lucas sitting at my small dining table.

"Happy birthday!" they shout with glee. The looks on their faces stir something in me, and the sadness and fury gripping me lose their hold.

The right corner of my mouth quirks into a slight smile. "Lucas, what did I tell you about letting people into my apartment?"

"We're not just people, brujo!" Sal laughs and offers me a beer.

"Jack," Alanna says, approaching me. "Look what Lucas did for me." She opens her blazer and shows me the pommel of Witchbane hanging at her side, which was perfectly concealed.

The Damascus steel blade, though, can't be seen. I'm curious as to how they pulled that off.

"What did he do?" I ask, gently poking at empty air, thinking the steel blade is cloaked by some spell.

She takes the pommel and holds it upright, and the steel blade shoots up. I always said that type of metal can cut you five times over before you even knew you were struck.

"Nice," I say with a tone of approval. "It's better than walking around with a full-on long blade."

She grins. "And it retracts, too. Any news on Hunter? Is she with the Enforcers?"

I frown, then I gather my friends around to share about what happened. At first, I thought I would get angry all over again and start kicking something, but as I watch my friends experience the same things I felt, it made me feel better knowing that I wasn't alone, and that they're with me on this.

"Man," Sal says, once I'm done speaking, "I'm sorry about that. You did everything you could. This is all on Mishka. He's a cold-hearted criminal."

Lucas's eyes flash with anger. "Everyone deserves a fair trial. He took that away from her. One day, I hope Mishka himself will face justice."

"Agreed," Alanna chimes in. "I understood a little about how she felt, losing her father, wanting to make his murderer pay." She glances down at Witchbane, admiring its beauty and the light hum of magic emanating from it.

"Mishka managed to have her killed by the very people who should've been guarding her," I say. How do we even begin to hold him accountable?"

"We'll find a way," Alanna responds. "Maybe I can talk to Samuel, see if there's something the DMA can do."

My phone rings and I pull it out and answer. It's Willy calling via video chat. "Hey," I say, noticing that the background of the living room she's in is different. "You're not home?"

ALESHA ESCOBAR

"Happy birthday," she says with a wide, red-lipped smile. "I'm here at Zara's place."

She turns the camera toward Charlie who's in her lap, sitting perfectly content. "Hey Charlie," I say to the baby.

"Hi Jack!" Zara's voice calls from somewhere in her apartment. "Sorry we couldn't make it tonight."

"It's okay," I say. "Thanks for the cake, it was good."

Willy's face is back on camera. I chuckle at seeing her maneuver with a baby in her arms. I suspect she misses being a caretaker of children more than she lets on.

"Son, the sadness and darkness surrounding you...it's seeping through. I don't even have to be in the same room with you to feel it."

"It's been a rough day," I tell her.

"I'm not going to give you a lecture about letting it go, because that pain is there to teach you something, and to remind you that you're still a human being with a heart. Learn from this. Grow. That's what I did. Do you understand?"

"Yeah, I do. Thanks, Willy."

"Goodnight, Jack. I need you for an afternoon shift at the shop, if you're available."

I smirk. "Always."

I end the call, my thoughts turning toward Baltazar's revelation about bringing me to Willy the night my family perished. Perhaps when I go into the shop tomorrow, I can have a sit-down with her about it. I put aside my anxiety and questions about the past and focus on the present, finishing off the cake with my friends—well, except Lucas, who doesn't eat. We play a few rounds of poker, where I end up winning sixty dollars cash, a gold ring that Sal swears is a good luck charm, and a pair of enchanted earrings that Alanna apparently bought off that street vendor in Scarletwood.

After a few hours of laughter and comradery, Sal finally takes his leave, reminding me that he'll keep me in the loop on that occult list and the Society of Mystics. Lucas offers to clean up, insisting it's his gift to me, and Alanna returns to handling Witchbane and admiring the magical sword.

"Jack," she says in a quiet voice, "I'm not going to keep the sword locked away in a box. I want to be able to use it."

"I'm sure DMA trained you well with guns and hand-to-hand, but do you wield swords?"

"I took a little bit of fencing when I was young, but I know it's not quite the same. I'll need to train."

She stands and gives herself some room, practicing a few thrusts and strikes. I've got to admit, it's kind of cool. The thought flies out of my head though when the sword lights up with a gentle blue glow, and it vibrates in Alanna's grasp.

Her head snaps toward me with a questioning look, as if telling me, *"You're the magic expert...what's happening?"*

I shrug at first, but then I remember the video footage we watched. Before I can yell out a warning or explanation, a burst of light emits from Witchbane, and when it subsides, the spirit of the sword, Neth, stands before me and Alanna. I'll give her credit for keeping hold of the sword and not dropping it.

"Neth?" Alanna asks in disbelief, observing the faerie spirit. "She's beautiful..."

Neth swivels on her heel then launches herself into the air, clinging to the ceiling. The spirit hisses at me.

"She's also a little wild, Alanna. Put her back into the sword."

Lucas walks in from the kitchen and drops the two mugs of tea he's carrying. "Oh my..."

Neth descends from the ceiling to my sofa. She lunges for me. I send a blast of air toward her and she flies backward, crashing into a book case.

"Jack, don't hurt her!" Alanna pleads.

Neth rushes me again, does a sweeping kick, and knocks me onto the floor. She straddles me and grabs hold of my neck, squeezing. "Not...going...to be a problem!"

Lucas rushes forward, his hands filled with pale-yellow magic, and he sends a blast of energy toward Neth, the magic crashing against her and forcing her to jump away from me and recoil. The little psycho then runs over to Alanna and hides behind her.

"Jack," she says, "I think she's just scared."

Neth crouches behind Alanna then opens her mouth, sending that crazy shockwave of energy toward me and Lucas, the same way she had done to Ora Draper. Me and the automaton go flying into the wall, and at this point, I think I've probably broken something.

I land on the floor with a thud, then rise to my feet, wincing in pain. "*She's* scared? What about us?"

"Neth," Alanna says, "please, don't hurt my friends."

The wild spirit snarls and snaps her teeth at us, but she at least refrains from another attack.

Lucas motions to Alanna. "Use the force of your will. Command her to return to the sword. She is bound to it."

Alanna squeezes her eyes shut, and Neth, still crouched behind her, stares at her with curiosity. Recognition dawns on Neth's face, as she finally identifies Alanna with the auburn-haired girl, she had saved all those years ago. I'll never forget the video footage and how it caught the sadness marring faerie spirit's face when Martin died.

The sword's blade glows a soft blue again, and Neth becomes translucent and is absorbed back into the sword. Alanna opens her eyes and looks around. A satisfied grin creeps up her lips. I suppose she's proud that she had commanded the wild spirit to do something and she listened. For now.

"Did you see that?" she asks, retracting the blade and hanging it back at her side, beneath her jacket.

"Yeah, she's going to kill you in your sleep. Now I'm starting to see why your dad and Samuel had the sword locked up."

She crosses her arms. "I'm not a child, Jack, I know this is magic and it's connected to me..."

"And dangerous," Lucas interjects.

"Yes, but that's all the more reason for me to learn how to use the sword and how to tame Neth."

"Alanna," I say, "there's a lot we don't know about faeries, let alone faerie spirits. We need to be very careful. Don't assume she's going to buddy up with you just because you inherited the sword or because she hasn't tried to claw your eyes out yet."

Lucas gives a thoughtful look. "Also, consider that Ora Draper killed for this sword. She's willing to do it again. I must agree with Jack on this."

She sighs. "My grandfather was able to use it. I remember my dad telling me stories. I may not be an automaton or a badass wizard—"

I raise an eyebrow. "You think I'm badass?"

She waves a hand through the air. "But...*but*, I'm willing to work hard and do what my grandfather did. He used this against Ora Draper. He was able to turn it against her. This is my family's legacy. Please guys, help me on this."

Lucas and I eye each other, and I already see the big softie breaking down inside.

"All right, Alanna," the automaton says. "I will help."

For crying out loud...

I gesture toward the concealed sword. "And who, exactly, is going to train you? In case you haven't noticed, that ain't a normal sword."

Lucas's eyes light up with excitement. "The old man, Xander Pettway! Remember, Alanna, you met him at The Ruined Oak? Not only does he read auras, he's also a skilled sword master."

I throw my hands up in the air. "Thanks a lot, Lucas."

"Why are you standing in my way?" Alanna asks.

"I don't want anything to happen to you, okay?"

She stares me right in the eye. "Then let me train so that nothing does. Will you take me to see Xander tomorrow?"

I already know if I refuse, she'll just go behind my back and do it anyway. She's stubborn. "Fine," I finally say. "This doesn't mean I'm on board with this, but we can go talk with the old man. Maybe he'll agree with me and send you home."

She smiles. "Thank you."

"Don't thank me yet."

"I'm going to my mom's tonight. I'll see you guys in the morning."

"Goodnight, Alanna."

I guess tomorrow we're going to see the sword master.

29

I grab a handful of chocolates left over from last night's Halloween party and slouch on the lobby couch, waiting for Alanna. Lucas is sitting across from me, and I can tell by that gleam in his eyes that he's scanning me for diabetes. I throw a few pieces of candy into my mouth and chew, while wondering which apartment those two "nurses" lived in. Maybe I can get Zara to bake another cake and I'll bring it to them. Part of being a good neighbor and all.

"Are you really going to eat Choco-Treats for breakfast?" Lucas asks.

I hold up an unwrapped candy. "If you could taste these, you would too, buddy."

He shakes his head. "Fine, I'll stop criticizing your food choice."

A smirk crosses my lips. "Did you have fun last night?"

He nods. "I enjoyed the poker game, though I could've easily beaten you all. I thought it would be arrogant of me to do so, though. So, I let you win."

"You're so humble, Tin Man."

The lobby door opens, and Alanna enters, dressed like a fed and with her auburn hair in a tight bun. I can't help but glance at

211

her hip, where I know Witchbane is concealed beneath her jacket. I suppose Neth decided to behave, though I still don't trust the disorderly spirit. I don't know her or her history, or the full extent of her powers. Maybe I'll reach out to Baltazar at some point and ask about it, since he's half-faerie.

"My car or yours?" she asks. "I don't have to go into the office until noon today."

"Yours," I say. "After The Ruined Oak, you can drop me off here and then I have a shift at the shop."

Lucas and I rise from our seats and head outside with her, hopping into her sedan and buckling up. The drive to The Ruined Oak building takes less than twenty minutes, and Alanna pulls into the parking lot and takes a spot close to the entrance. We get out and stroll into the building, greeting Gary in reception. Today, he's wearing a white, long-sleeved shirt and a blue silk waistcoat. He's typing away on a laptop but pauses to gaze up at us.

"Good morning. You're a brave man for returning here. Mr. Tarasov asked if I could place a curse on you, but naturally that goes against my code of ethics."

"Thanks, Gary," I say. "I'm just here to see someone, then I'm out. And I'm *definitely* not going up to the penthouse."

Not unless I'm looking for a death match.

He smiles. "Very well. Good day to you, as well as to you, Lucas and Agent Reid."

Both Lucas and Alanna say goodbye and follow me over to the doorway leading down to the dungeon level. And, of course, my two favorite Enforcers await there.

"Hey Crowley," Darryl says, his tone less jovial than usual. "I heard about your beef with Mishka. Sorry about that."

"Thanks, Darryl. If he tries to get you to kill me, can you give me a heads up?"

The tall, dark man rumbles with laughter. "He may be the owner and manager of this property, but we aren't one of his servants like Eli. Miki and I ultimately answer to the Council."

Miki nods in agreement. "We're here to protect the people inside, and make sure humans don't wander to the Gateway." He glances in Alanna's direction, knowing good and well the Cloaked Council banned her from Grey Haven.

"Good to know," I say, questioning who's really an ally, and who's likely to stab me in the back at Mishka's behest.

They let us through, and we head downstairs, passing along the corridor furnished with black leather chairs and love seats and a red velvet carpet. As luck would have it, Xander Pettway is sitting at the bar with Roy, sipping from a glass of swirling, neon blue scriostóir. Roy gestures for us to come sit at the bar and starts pouring me a whiskey.

"Jack, you didn't get a birthday drink last night," he says, sliding the glass of liquor over to me.

"Sorry about that, Roy. I was tired."

"What can I get for you, agent?" the bald man asks Alanna.

"Just a sparkling water for me. Thanks."

Lucas greets Xander with a warm smile. "It's good to see you, though you usually come in later."

"It is a bit early for me," Xander says, "but Baltazar Maune came around last night asking about Witchbane, and I figured it was finally uncovered. I needed a drink. Maybe I'll have another."

Alanna takes a sip of her water. "It's true, Mr. Pettway. I have it."

The old man's eyes brighten. "Excellent. It's finally where it belongs."

She turns to me and gives me a look, as if saying, *"See? The sword belongs with me."*

Alanna slides into a seat next to him and they start chatting, but I notice Nicolai approaching from the corner of my eye, and he waves to me. I down the rest of my whiskey and head over to speak with him, noting how the dark circles beneath his eyes are gone, and he doesn't look as emaciated or pale. He actually has a smile on his face.

"Jack, I wanted to thank you for rescuing me," he says, offering his hand.

For a moment, I hesitate, bitterly remembering my exchange with Mishka last night. But then I remember that principle about not punishing the son for the sins of the father...or in this case, the nephew for the sins of the uncle. I shake his hand then let mine drop to my side.

"You're welcome. How are you doing?"

"I'm well enough, though my uncle's moved me out of my apartment and into his penthouse. The whole point of me having my own place in Santa Monica was to get away from him, and now I'm stuck with him again."

"Sounds like you don't always get along with him," I say.

He shakes his head. "I heard about Hunter. I'm sorry."

I glance at the stub on his hand that used to have a full pinky finger. "Even despite that?"

His cheeks redden. "I accidentally did that to myself while trying to escape from that sarcophagus. She patched me up, then decided she could use it to goad my uncle on and draw him out into the open."

"It's good to see that you're not exactly like him."

"I just want to live my life, without looking over my shoulder for an enemy or someone with a grudge. I want the cycle of killing and powerplays to end, but Mishka won't let that happen."

"It has to be up to you," I tell him. "You're not so bad...for a crime lord's nephew and all."

He chuckles. "Some family business, eh?"

"I'm curious, there's a spirit, a blonde woman who keeps hanging around Mishka. Who is she?"

Nicolai's smile falters and his expression grows somber. "My mom. She died in a werewolf attack, and Mishka took me in."

"I'm sorry for your loss."

"Thanks." He observes me for a moment, slightly tilting his head. "I've got to say, there's something off about you. I know you're a True Name wizard and have secondary elemental abilities, so where does your spirit magic come from?"

I shrug. "Can you believe, I ate two Names of God?"

I didn't want Marco Welling to invoke those Names, so the quickest and most efficient way to keep them out of his hands was to literally consume them. Now I have spirit magic. I can't wait to see what other ability unfolds with the other Name of God.

A touch of amusement glimmers in his eyes. "Bold move, Crowley. Well, as a thank-you, if you ever need any tips on controlling your spirit magic, hit me up."

I shake his hand again. "I appreciate it. Take care, Nicolai."

He turns and heads back toward the hallway leading to the elevator, and I return to my friends. Alanna's just finished speaking with Xander, and the old man finishes his scriostóir drink and stands. He shakes Alanna's hand then waves goodbye to Roy and Lucas.

He faces me, wearing a wide grin. "I will begin training Ms. Reid tomorrow at your location of choice."

"What's your fee?" Alanna asks, her tone laced with excitement.

"My dear, I wouldn't be alive today if it weren't for your grandfather. I am delighted to train you free of charge."

"Thank you, Mr. Pettway. I'll be ready to train."

I sure hope Neth is in a good mood. My apartment will not be her training ground. Maybe we can use the extra storage room at Willy's shop.

As Xander takes his leave and heads toward the exit, Alanna turns to Lucas, who's still sitting at the bar, facing Roy.

"Lucas, do you want to join me for training tomorrow?"

Roy's wiping down the counter but pauses, giving Lucas a quizzical look. "Guys...is it normal for your automaton friend to do that?"

Both Alanna and I turn him around on his stool, to get a look on his face. His body is completely still, and his eyes are glazed over as if in a trance. The only thing moving are his lips, and he's softly repeating something over and over.

Alanna shakes his shoulder. "Lucas? Lucas? What's going on?"

The automaton ignores her, staring into blank space, still repeating a phrase in a soft voice.

Her forehead creases with worry as her gaze meets mine. "Jack, what's wrong with him? He's never done this before."

I lean in, trying to capture the words coming from his mouth.

Hmph. He's speaking in Latin.

"Roy, give me a pen and slip of paper."

The bartender obliges me, and I start scribbling down Lucas's words. I quickly translate the Latin phrase to English: BRING ME MY AUTOMATON

Lucas's voice crescendos, growing louder and stronger, more robotic and mechanical.

Alanna shakes him again. "Lucas!"

He finally snaps out of it, letting out a pained sigh and his gaze sweeping the area as if expecting an attack. Alanna finally captures his attention, holding his head between her hands and staring him in his eyes.

"Are you okay? Talk to me."

The automaton slowly nods. "My apologies. It appears I malfunctioned."

I hold up the translated note. "No, you didn't. Kenneth Cherish just sent a message through you."

Lucas takes the note and examines it, his hand slightly trembling. He stares at it in disbelief.

"He's not taking you away from us," Alanna assures him.

Roy continues wiping down the bar counter, though he stares at us with wide eyes and a slackened jaw.

"She's right, Tin Man. He's not taking you away from us. Roy, don't give us that look. Listen, Lucas, if we can defy the DMA and keep you out of the Akashic Academy's hands, then we're going to find a way to keep you free of Kenneth."

"What happens if he captures me?" Lucas asks. "What if he reprograms me and makes me forget you all?"

"That's *not* going to happen," Alanna says. "We'll track him down and find him."

"We kind of already have an idea of where he is," I tell her.

Her jaw drops. "Where?"

"The Nowhere Dimension."

I would rather go up to Mishka's penthouse than there.

Lucas's gaze goes between me and Alanna. "If something happens and he regains control of me—"

"Don't even say that," I tell him. "We're in this together. Remember, Tin Man? None of us are alone."

He nods. "I am not alone."

We may know where Kenneth is but confronting him and telling him to piss off isn't going to be an easy task. The technomancer is a brilliant wizard, and we'll be stepping into his territory. But we have no choice. Either we come up with a plan and confront him, or he'll eventually find a way to come after us —and then, all hell will break loose.

DEAR READER

Dear Reader,

Seriously—thank you so much for grabbing a copy of Hexes and Bones and continuing this magical journey with Jack and his friends! If you enjoyed this story and want to find out what happens next, please leave a review at your favorite online retailer and recommend this to your fantasy-loving friends. This lets me know to continue writing these stories and supplying you with more Magic and Mayhem.

There is still a lot to uncover and explore: What will we learn about Willy's and Jack's pasts, and about the night his family died? Is Alanna really cut out for training with Witchbane? Besides speaking to spirits, what other new power will unfold for Jack? What will Lucas do about Kenneth Cherish wanting him to return? And of course, there's the Society of Mystics, Ora Draper and her Dark Coven, and whether or not we'll see more werewolves and faeries.

So many fun questions, and I'm looking forward to the answers!

Make sure to keep in touch:

My Newsletter (twice a month I email you fantasy books that are new or on sale by fantasy author friends, as well as updates and special announcements):

   http://www.aleshaescobar.com/newsletter

My Facebook Readers Lounge (giveaways, Advance Reader Copies, memes):

   https://www.facebook.com/groups/FMMReaders

ABOUT THE AUTHOR

Alesha Escobar writes fantasy to support her chocolate habit. She enjoys reading everything from Tolkien and the Dresden Files, to the Hellblazer comics and classic literature. She's the author of the bestselling Gray Tower Trilogy, an action-packed supernatural thriller set in an alternate World War II.

Besides being a loving warrior mom to her six children, she enjoys crafts, consuming more coffee than is necessary, and spending time with her husband Luis, a 24-year art veteran for The Simpsons television show.

To receive free and discounted book offers from a Alesha, join her Fantasy, Mashups, & Mayhem mailing list today at www.aleshaescobar.com/newsletter

alesha@thecreativealchemy.com

ALSO BY ALESHA ESCOBAR

The Gray Tower Trilogy

British intelligence wants her spying skills. A vampiric warlock wants to steal her powers. The Master Wizards who trained her want her dead... Join Isabella George as she slings magic, slays monsters, and try to save the world in a WWII where the Third Reich has unleashed dark supernatural powers. This bestselling series has been described as "Agent Carter meets Hellboy."

The Immortal Brotherhood

Raina Black steals from corrupt millionaires and warlords to pay for her sister's cancer treatment, and all is going according to plan—until she mysteriously wakes up in an Egyptian pyramid with vampires stalking her. It also doesn't help that Noah, a man she saw die, comes back to life and claims she needs to reunite the Immortal Brotherhood.

The Aria Knight Chronicles

Aria Knight will wipe your slate clean and hold back the gates of Hell... for a price. A Sin Eater has to make a living somehow. But when she's called to assist at the death of a recluse billionaire, turns out he's been murdered—and the evidence points to her.

Made in the USA
Middletown, DE
28 September 2022